She sought revenge but discovered desire.

On a quest to avenge her sister's death, Eleanor Watkins never expected to fall for the man following her through pleasure gardens and into ballrooms. But soon nothing can keep her from the arms of the sinfully attractive scoundrel, not even the dangerous secrets she keeps. Strong, compassionate, and utterly irresistible, James is all she desires. But can she trust him enough to let herself succumb to all the pleasures that midnight allows?

James Swindler has worked hard to atone for his unsavory past. He is now as at home in London's glittering salons as he is in the roughest streets. But when the inspector is tasked with keeping watch on a mysterious lady suspected of nefarious deeds, he is determined to use his skills at seduction to lure Eleanor into revealing her plans. Instead, he is the one seduced, turning away from everything he holds dear in order to protect her—no matter the cost to his heart.

W9-CDE-536

Midnight Pleasures with a Scoundrel

LORRAINE HEATH

AVON

An Imprint of HarperCollinsPublishers

This is a work of fiction. Names, characters, places, and incidents are products of the author's imagination or are used fictitiously and are not to be construed as real. Any resemblance to actual events, locales, organizations, or persons, living or dead, is entirely coincidental.

AVON BOOKS
An Imprint of HarperCollins*Publishers*
10 East 53rd Street
New York, New York 10022-5299

Copyright © 2009 by Jan Nowasky
ISBN 978-0-06-173400-7
www.avonromance.com

First Avon Books paperback printing: November 2009

Avon Trademark Reg. U.S. Pat. Off. and in Other Countries, Marca Registrada, Hecho en U.S.A.
HarperCollins® is a registered trademark of HarperCollins Publishers.

Printed in the U.S.A.

10 9 8 7 6 5 4 3 2 1

For the Foxes
Alice, Franny, Jane, Jo, Julie,
Kay, Sandy, Suzanne, Tracy
Life is much more fun with you ladies
pouring the wine.

Midnight Pleasures with a Scoundrel

Prologue

From the Journal of James Swindler

A darkness hovers inside me. It was born the day I watched my father hanged. A public hanging, with a festive air in the streets, as though I alone understood the loss, as though the object stolen was worth destroying both his life and mine.

I had been born a mere eight years earlier, and with my arrival had come my mother's parting from this world. So it was that with my father's death, I became an orphan with nowhere to go and no one to take me in.

Within the jubilant crowd of curious onlookers were two lads who recognized my plight—the tears streaming down my dirty face while others jeered and laughed, no doubt telling my story. My father had told me to be strong. He'd even winked at me before they placed the black hood over his head. As though his standing on the gallows were a prank, a bit of good fun, something we would laugh about later.

But it wasn't a prank, and if my father is laughing now, it is only the devil who hears.

I was not strong that day. But I have shown strength ever since.

The lads comforted me as boys are wont to do: with a slug on the arm and "stiff upper lip, mate." They invited me to tag along with them. Jack was the older, his swagger one of confidence. Luke was wide-eyed, and I suspected it was the first hanging he'd ever witnessed. As we made our way through the teeming throng, their nimble fingers pilfered many a coin purse and handkerchief.

When darkness descended, they led me through the warren of the rookeries to the door of a kidsman who went by the name of Feagan. He had little use for the likes of me until he'd gathered the precious booty from his workers. Children all. Only one girl among them. A girl with vibrant red hair and gentle green eyes. Her name was Frannie. Once I realized that Jack and Luke had brought me to a den of thievery, I lost all enthusiasm to stay. I had no desire to belong to a place that was certain to lead me straight to the gallows. But I had a stronger desire not to lose sight of the young girl. So I remained.

I became very skilled at ferreting out information, helping to set up swindles. I wasn't as talented when it came to thievery. I was caught on more than one occasion and took my punishment as my father had taught me—with stoicism and a wink.

As a result, I became far too familiar with the fact that the legal system was not fair, and often innocence was the cost. I began to pay close attention when justice was meted out. Why was one boy given ten lashes for snitching a silk handkerchief while another was transported to a prison colony in New Zealand? How was evidence obtained? How did one determine guilt? More importantly, how did one prove innocence?

In time I began to work secretly for the Metropolitan Police. I did not fear the shadows or the darker side of London. Even when I worked openly for Scotland Yard, I traveled where others had no desire to tread.

I drew comfort in knowing I never arrested an innocent. Depending on the severity of the crime, I often sent the culprit on his way with a mere slap on the wrist and a warning that I was watching, always watching. Of what importance is a stolen bit of silk frippery when a man might have lost his

life in the street? I was far more concerned with—
and fascinated by—the grisly crimes.

They appealed to the darkness hovering inside
me, and so it was that they garnered my ardent
attention . . .

And eventually led me to *her*.

Chapter 1

London
1852

Revenge was not for the faint of heart. It might have bothered Eleanor Watkins that she was fairly consumed with the need to achieve it if she took a moment to give it any further consideration. But ever since she'd discovered and read through her sister's journal, learned what horrors had truly befallen her sister when she'd traveled to London last Season, she had little time for anything other than plotting how best to avenge Elisabeth. Eleanor was determined that the man who had escorted her sister from sweet innocence into brutal carnality would pay as dearly for his sins as her sister had for her naivety.

Her quest for vengeance controlled her every action, her every thought, from the moment she awoke to the song of the lark until she laid her head on the pillow to endure another night of fretful sleep and horrendous nightmares fueled by each stroke of her sister's pen as she'd described the shame she'd endured at the hands of the Marquess of Rockberry.

Eleanor's obsessive need for retribution was the reason that she now strolled through Cremorne Gardens long past the hour when any respectable woman would be about. Even decent men had retired for the evening, but then the man she followed could hardly be declared reputable, although he gave a rather good imitation. She'd heard that the fireworks that burst into the air each evening at the gardens were spectacular. But of course, he'd not arrived in time to enjoy so simple a pleasure as watching brilliant flashes of light paint the sky. No, his pleasures leaned toward a darker, more foreboding nature.

And so Lord Rockberry had waited until the good folk had removed themselves from the gardens and the depraved had arrived with mischief on their minds before making his unheralded appearance. His sinister laughter echoed through the pleasure gardens as he periodically stopped to speak with one rogue or another. Tall and slender, he strolled quickly through the throng, his cape billowing out behind him, adding to the sense that among the wicked he considered himself king. But even with his height and top hat, she had to dart around people to keep him within her sights—and she was determined to do it in such a way that he took no notice of her. She'd not fall victim to his persuasive charms as her sister had. If either of them fell, she was determined it would be him.

She had visualized that tonight the dagger would slide into his heart, so all the world would see exactly how putrid and black it was, but she knew the time wasn't right, nor was the place. She had to take care, execute the plan as it had been laid out—lest she find herself hanging from the gallows. As much as she loved her sister, she wasn't quite ready to join her—although if her life was the cost of revenge, she would pay it. From the moment she set foot on this path, she'd been aware that it might eventually lead her to Newgate. She'd not regret it as long as it also led Rockberry into hell.

"Would you care for some company?"

The fair young man who stepped in front of her gave her a charming smile. His clothes were well-tailored and she suspected that if she had someone to properly introduce her into Society, she might dance with him at a ball on another night. "No, thank you. I'm meeting someone."

"Fortunate fellow. If he doesn't show—"

"He will," she lied, cutting him off and skirting around him, hurrying past the splashing fountain, wishing she had a moment to enjoy the beauty of the gardens.

Blast it! Now where had Rockberry gone? She quickened her pace and breathed a sigh of relief when she spied him talking with a buxom woman whose gown was indecently low, giving all in attendance a glimpse of what she had to offer. Apparently she wasn't what Rockberry sought, because he continued on without looking back. No, he preferred ladies of a more innocent bent. For the life of her, she couldn't understand why he'd come here, where naughty behavior was tolerated, expected even. Rockberry had a penchant for the intolerable, forcing her sister to endure depraved acts of sin and debauchery.

For six days now she'd been cataloging his habits and rituals, striving to map out the pattern of his life, working to determine how best to bring that life to an end without sacrificing her own.

Unfortunately, her life in a small village near the sea had hardly provided her with the education or experience to play cat and mouse, and more often than not she feared she was the prey and not the predator in this deadly game. Especially as she had the increasing sense that while she followed Lord Rockberry, someone followed her.

As the lavender bowers scented the air around her, Eleanor fought not to glance back, not to give any indication that she was aware of her pursuer. She'd first become cognizant of a large man trailing in her wake two nights ago, after Rockberry had paid a visit to Scotland Yard. She should have been more discreet in her plans for Rockberry. She might have spooked him with her boldness, making him aware of her presence, hoping he'd begin to question his own sanity. If he went mad and took his own life, so much the better. It would save her from having to take it for him. Instead, it was possible he'd reported her to the police.

She'd yet to catch sight of her pursuer tonight, but she was certain he was there because the hairs on the nape of her neck prickled, sending icy tingles coursing through her.

It didn't help, so near the Thames, that the thick fog was silently rolling in, washing out the color of all that surrounded her. The gaslights became muted hazes, eerily striving to illuminate what many preferred to hide. Behind the elms and poplars, in shadowy recesses, came the murmurs of gentlemen and the seductive laughter of women.

She was no longer certain what she hoped to accomplish by following Rockberry to such a questionable place, but she needed to know what he did, who he met, so she could determine the best moment to strike. Caution over expediency.

He prowled the night as though he were some ravenous beast, but she knew it wasn't food he sought, but rather decadent pleasures—her sister's journal had revealed in intimate and heartrending detail how he had seduced her, not only for his gratification but for the amusement of others. As though her wants had no merit, her dreams were meant to be shattered. Rockberry had destroyed Elisabeth long before she'd flung herself over the cliff into the turbulent sea below.

Fighting back her tears—now was not the time to succumb to her sorrow—she strengthened her resolve to see that Rockberry paid handsomely for his part in her sister's death at the mere age of nineteen.

The loathsome man disappeared around a curve. Drat it! He was too self-absorbed to realize he was being followed, so he must have some rendezvous in mind. She wondered if he'd already singled out his next victim. If that was the case, then she might very well end the game tonight, because she couldn't stand by and let another woman suffer as Elisabeth had.

She swept around the trees and came to a staggering stop, her path blocked by three gentlemen with lascivious grins.

"Hello, sweeting," the one in the middle said,

giving her the impression that he was the one in charge.

The lights in this area were exceedingly dim, and the gray mist didn't help the situation. She could tell little about him save that he was fair, and if not for his wretched smile, she might have even considered him handsome. His friends were dark, one distinguishable by his rather unattractive bulbous nose, and the other by his unfortunate lack of a chin, as though it had somehow fallen into his neck. The way their gazes roamed over her made her skin crawl, and it was all she could do not to shrink before them. They wore the finest of clothes, along with expectations for a grand time, intent upon enjoying their youth while it still belonged to them.

As for herself, with Elisabeth's death, she'd aged well beyond her twenty years.

"Please, excuse me." She made a motion to go around them, but they moved as one to bar her path. Her heart sped up, imitating the rhythm of the train that had brought her to London, clacking and rattling and threatening to jump the tracks at any moment. She took a step back, and No Chin sidestepped over to hinder her escape. Suddenly, she found herself surrounded. It would take very little for the men to drag her into the darkest shadows of the garden where no hope existed for retaining her dignity.

She tried to open her reticule, to find the dagger she kept there as her only source of protection, but No Chin tore it free of her hold, nearly wrenching her arm off in the process. "No!" she cried out.

"Come on, be a good girl," the fair-haired man said as he snaked an arm around her, lifting her to the tips of her toes.

Terror gripped her as she released an ear-splitting scream. But all she heard was laughter as they began carting her toward the dark abyss. She wouldn't succumb easily to what they planned. She would fight, scratch, claw—

"Hold up, gents! The lady is with me."

Apparently, the men forcing her off the main pathway were as surprised by the deep confident voice obviously directed at them as she was. They parted slightly, allowing her to view through a narrow gap the shadowy silhouette of a large man with broad shoulders, taller than any man she'd ever seen.

Abruptly, he shouldered his way in, wound his arm around her waist and untangled her from her captor, using his free arm to shove one of the other men aside.

"I mean you no harm," he murmured quickly in a low, reassuring voice. "If you wish to survive this night with your virtue intact, I suggest you come along with me."

Everything about him was lost to the murky shadows that accompanied the encroaching fog. His hair was dark, but she couldn't tell its exact shade. She could feel the power in his hold, strength as well as confidence. Instinctively, she knew he was not a man who forced women. He had no need. Something about him radiated a protective air, and she realized in all likelihood he was the man who'd been following her, the man from Scotland Yard. She didn't think he was one to fear the devil, and she had an insane thought that perhaps he could help her deal with Rockberry. But even as she thought it, she realized she could no more confide in a stranger than she could a friend. Not about this matter, not when so much—when everything—was at risk.

His gaze shifted away from her, and only then did she remember they had an audience. The three young men were glaring at them.

"Look here, old chap," the leader said. "We claimed her first."

"As I've already stated, she's with me."

"We were told she was available."

"You were told incorrectly." With his arm firmly around her, he began to stride away. She had to move her feet quickly to stay in step. But before they'd neared the main path, the three men moved to thwart their leaving. She heard his weary sigh.

"Do you gents really want to fight tonight, knowing you can't possibly win?"

"There are three of us and only one of you. I like our odds."

"My odds are better. I grew up on the streets, fighting far worse than you."

"You sound like a gent."

"But I fight like the very devil." The underlying threat of his words reverberated through his voice.

It seemed the men who had accosted her were not only mean-spirited, but stupid. Bulbous swung—

She found herself quickly thrust behind her protector—it was how she was quickly beginning to think of him—as he warded off the blow and sent Bulbous to the ground. The other two attacked him. While he used his shoulder to cause No Chin to stagger back, her rescuer plowed his fist into the fair man's stomach. With a gasp, Fair doubled over and dropped to his knees. Then her protector rounded on Bulbous as he regained his footing and stood. The thud of flesh hitting flesh as her protector's knuckles caught the man beneath the chin echoed around them. Bulbous staggered back, arms windmilling. He fell in a graceless sprawl over the ground, unmoving. As his companions tried to get to their feet, her protector made short work of landing two quick punches that returned both to the ground.

"Stay put until we leave," her protector ordered, before holding out his hand to her. "Let's go, shall we?"

If he meant her harm, she thought, he had no reason to take her out of here. While the excuse was flimsy, she found herself nodding. She'd had quite enough of this place, and knew that finding Rockberry now was beyond the scope of her meager skills of detection. She took a step toward her rescuer, then remembered—

"My reticule. One of them took it."

With his foot, he rolled Bulbous over, retrieved her reticule, and halted to stare at the handle of the dagger poking out.

"For protection," she muttered, taking her reticule and closing it over the dagger.

"Little good it did you. Come along. Stay close. I'll hire a hansom, see you safely home."

She had no choice except to let him draw her in and hold her upright, because she realized that she was trembling from the ordeal now that it was over. How could she have been so foolish as to believe she could protect herself in this place by simply not accepting what anyone might offer?

"Have you a name?" he finally asked quietly.

"Eleanor Watkins," she said without thinking, and then wondered if she should have provided a false name. She'd given so much thought to her plans, and here they were becoming unraveled.

"What were you doing wandering the gardens this time of night, Miss Watkins?"

"I fear I got lost." She peered up at him, unable to determine if he believed her. "It seems, sir, that I should know the name of the man who rescued me."

"James Swindler."

On King's Road they found a hansom waiting by the curb. Leaning over, he opened the door and handed her up. "What instructions shall I give the driver?" he asked.

Reluctantly, she gave him the address for her lodgings. He called out the information and handed coins up to the driver.

"Take care in the future, Miss Watkins. London can be a very dangerous place for a woman alone."

Before she could reply, the driver set the vehicle into motion. Glancing back, she saw Mr. Swindler still standing in the street. Large and foreboding, becoming lost to the night, much like the man she'd glimpsed following her.

If he was Rockberry's man, why had he let her go? And if he wasn't, why was he following her?

* * *

"Her name is Eleanor Watkins."

"Elisabeth's sister. I should have guessed. There is an uncanny resemblance."

James Swindler didn't turn to acknowledge the quiet muttering from the shadowed corner following his pronouncement of the name of the woman he'd encountered at Cremorne Gardens—after spying on her for two days now.

Swindler's superior, Sir David Mitchum, sat behind the desk in front of which Swindler stood. As the flame in the lamp was low, failing to cast enough light to reach the corners, Swindler assumed he was to pretend he wasn't aware that another person inhabited the room. That the man smelled of sandalwood, rich tobacco, and nervous sweat made it a bit difficult for him to blend in with the surroundings. The fact that he'd spoken— apparently surprised by the information that Swindler had imparted—added to the ludicrousness of trying to pretend that Swindler and Sir David were alone in the room.

Unlike the man in the corner, Swindler had the uncanny knack of blending in wherever necessary. Still, Swindler gave no indication that he was aware of the other's presence. He could pretend with the best of them. Although he found it inconceivable that the man would believe his identity was a secret, especially as Swindler's investigation of the woman had begun at his lordship's residence. He suspected the Marquess of Rockberry was a conceited buffoon.

"What more have you managed to learn about the woman?" Sir David asked.

After sending the woman on her way, Swindler had taken another hansom, following at a discreet distance and ordering the driver to let him out on a street near Miss Watkins's lodgings. He'd walked briskly the remainder of the way, arriving just as Miss Watkins had entered through the front door. He'd waited until he saw a soft light appear in a corner window—fortunate that her hired room faced the street—to approach. By placing a few coins in the pudgy hand of the landlady who'd opened the door, he'd been able to discern a few more details. "She has a hired room. She has only paid for the month and has been in London for a sennight. She is extremely quiet, never causes a disturbance, does not visit with the other residents, and has no callers. Often takes her meal in her room."

Silence stretched between them before Sir David asked, "Anything else?"

"I fear I have nothing else to add. My instructions were to follow her and not approach her. However, as some young swells were intent upon engaging in a bit of mischief where she was concerned, I thought it prudent to ignore the second part of my orders. They claimed someone informed them that she was 'available.' I don't suppose we have any idea who that *someone* might have been."

"Don't be ridiculous," came from the corner, confirming Swindler's suspicions that Rockberry himself might have advised the young gents to make short work of her. Apparently patience wasn't Rockberry's strong suit.

"A lady wandering through Cremorne Gardens late at night—*alone*—is bound to run into trouble," Sir David said. "She's fortunate you were watching her. I assume she's none the wiser regarding your task." If he harbored Swindler's suspicions regarding Rockberry, he gave no hint of it.

"She knows nothing about my true purpose. I have shared with you all that her landlady was able to reveal. Well, except for the fact that Miss Watkins arrived with one trunk and seems to have a preference for pink. If I might be honest here, from my initial observations, I hardly view Miss Watkins as a threat to anyone."

"His lordship disagrees."

Which was the reason that Swindler had been brought in. To determine what the lady was about. So far she had followed Rockberry through the zoological gardens and Hyde Park. Last night she had followed him to his club—Dodger's Drawing Room, one of London's more exclusive venues for gentlemen of leisure to enjoy the vices. Tonight, Cremorne Gardens. If it were a crime to follow someone, Swindler would be rotting in Pentonville Prison by now.

"With all due respect, sir, I believe I can serve better elsewhere. I heard someone reported a murder in Whitechapel tonight and—"

"I know you prefer solving crimes after they've been committed, Swindler, but our duty first and foremost is to prevent the commission of crimes."

It was the policeman's motto, his creed. Prevention. It was the very reason that so many patrolled the streets. But Swindler believed nothing would prevent someone who was intent on committing transgressions. He was more obsessed with securing justice and ensuring that the correct person paid the price for felonious crimes. He had no desire to deal with a pampered lord who was concerned with a slight of a woman whose head barely reached the center of his chest. God help him, he'd felt like a lumbering giant next to her.

"It would help, sir," Swindler said, "to know what crime we expect her to commit."

"I believe she intends to kill me," came from the corner, the voice a low simmer.

Sir David did little more than arch a dark brow

at Swindler, who fought not to let his impatience with this situation show. He was very close to wanting to strangle the lord himself. "Do we know why his lordship believes Miss Watkins would wish him ill?"

His superior's gaze darted over to the corner. Swindler heard the impatient sigh before the voice rumbled from it. "Elisabeth Watkins had her coming out last Season. We danced on occasion. Nothing more."

There was always more.

"Am I to assume then that it is Lady Elisabeth and Lady Eleanor?" Swindler asked.

"No, her father is merely a viscount. 'Tis *Miss* Eleanor Watkins."

Merely? So the man in the corner with his higher rank possessed a superior attitude.

Weary of this dance, Swindler spun around. He could see one outstretched leg and a well-made boot polished to a shine that barely reached into the light. The remainder of the person was lost in the darkness, but still Swindler knew what the man looked like, as the trail had begun at his lordship's residence. He was not terribly old. He was, however, terribly handsome, with the perfect alignment of features that caused poets to apply ink to paper and wax poetically about the wonders of love. Swindler was damned tempted to address him by name, but for some unknown reason games were being played, and Sir David was tolerating them—which meant that the man either had friends even more superior than Sir David or he'd witnessed Sir David doing something he shouldn't. "If it was Elisabeth who caught your fancy last Season, why would Eleanor now wish you harm?"

Silence greeted his question.

"Your lordship, I cannot be of much assistance if you are anything less than forthright. I am not one to gossip. You could confess to enjoying the most depraved sexual acts—"

Even with the distance separating them, Swindler felt a ripple of tension emanating from the corner.

"—known to man, and I wouldn't tell a soul."

The silence thickened and lengthened. Was that what this was about, then? Some depravity that now haunted his lordship?

Rockberry finally cleared his throat. "Miss Elisabeth Watkins met with an untimely end. It's quite possible her sister holds me responsible, which is ludicrous, as I was nowhere near the silly chit when she encountered her demise. Miss Eleanor Watkins has never confronted me. She doesn't speak to me. She merely watches. Near a lamppost or from beside a tree in the park. I'll be taking a stroll and I'll have a sense of being spied upon. I glance back and there she is, watching . . . always watching. When I try to approach her to determine her purpose, she walks away, disappears in the crowd, and I'm left to wonder if I truly saw her at all. Because of her uncanny resemblance to Elisabeth, I was beginning to think Elisabeth had returned to haunt me. But as I said, we only danced, so I can determine no reason for this annoying game."

With his repeated "we only danced," Swindler wondered who his lordship was seeking to convince: Swindler or himself.

"So you'll continue to follow her, Swindler, see what she's about," Sir David said sharply in a tone that meant he'd brook no further arguments on this matter.

Swindler gave his attention back to his superior. He liked Sir David, admired him, but this matter was beyond the pale. "As I was forced to approach her, I assume you have no objection to my approaching her again."

"Handle this matter however you deem best."

Swindler heard the frustration and annoyance in Sir David's voice. Sir David was no happier about this situation than he was. If Swindler had his way, he'd make the matter go away on the morrow.

Chapter 2

The following afternoon Swindler discreetly followed Miss Watkins from her lodgings to Hyde Park. Holding a pink parasol over her left shoulder, she wore a dress of pale pink and a bonnet with matching ribbons. Her attire possessed a touch of innocence. He couldn't fathom that she had it in for Lord Rockberry—regardless of how annoying he found the man. If the young lady was aware of Swindler's presence, she gave no indication.

As usual, the park was teeming with ladies and gentlemen parading their wares—their fine clothing, their haughtiness, their steadfast belief that they were better than the common man. Swindler had little tolerance for the upper crust—except when it involved his friends who were moving into the ranks of the nobility with alarming regularity. Several years back they had discovered that from birth Lucian Langdon had been destined to become the Earl of Claybourne. Last year Jack Dodger had taken a widowed duchess as his wife. And Frannie Darling, the only woman Swindler ever truly loved, had recently married the Duke of Greystone. Swindler was sincerely happy for her. He'd always been unselfish in regard to Frannie, but unselfishness came with a steep price. His father had taught him that hard lesson, and Swindler had been paying for it ever since.

While his friends didn't lord their stations over him, neither did they move around in the same circles any longer. It was the way of things. He didn't resent their rise from the gutter, but he also recognized that he would always be known as the son of a thief.

He'd loved his father as he'd never since loved any other, save Frannie. Yet his father had left him with an incredible burden to bear. When he was a lad, some nights he'd wept beneath the weight of it. During others the fury had ruled him and he'd destroyed whatever came within his path. He'd lost track of the number of times when Frannie tended his hurts, gently wrapping his bleeding knuckles. His hands constantly ached from the abuse he'd delivered to them. His features had weathered the fights as well, leaving faint scars and a less than perfect profile in their wake. He wasn't what he'd consider handsome, but he hoped there was at least strength in his countenance.

Not that he ever expected to attract a lady with it. Frannie was the only one he'd ever truly wanted. While she'd recently married, it had been a little over a year since she gave her heart to Greystone. Swindler wasn't of a mind to seek another lady. He'd given Frannie his heart, and with her, it would remain. All he required now was an occasional woman to satisfy his baser needs. As he was known for giving women his undivided attention and serving up pleasure—even to those who'd never before experienced it—he had no trouble finding women wishing to spend an evening in his company. Even those accustomed to taking coins seldom took one of his.

Of late, while he satisfied women, none satisfied him, his actions more mechanical, derived from habit. He was always left with an ache in his chest—no doubt the result of his no longer possessing a heart. Although God help him, he couldn't remember the last time he'd taken a woman to bed.

Miss Eleanor Watkins saved him from his own deep thoughts, as she went to stand beside a tree that gave her a clear view of Rotten Row, no doubt awaiting the arrival of her quarry on his fine steed. While Swindler was supposed to be focused on the lady, he'd made a few inquiries regarding Rockberry. He now knew as well as she probably did that Lord Rockberry took a jaunt about the park every afternoon at precisely half past five.

No one seemed to pay any heed to her. The other ladies were occupied seeking to garner the men's attention, and the men were more interested in the ladies who wanted to be seen, rather than the one who didn't. It was all part of the ritual of shopping for a spouse. Approaching her might put her reputation at risk, but he was anxious to get on with this job.

Swindler began to amble toward Miss Watkins. He'd given considerable thought to how he would approach her. He would take on the role of interested gentleman, earn her trust, and then discern the reasons for her fascination with Rockberry— as well as exactly what she intended where the poppycock lord was concerned.

As he came up behind her, Swindler was hit with the fragrance of roses wafting from her. He didn't remember the fragrance from last night. Perhaps it was because it was earlier in the day, the rose water only recently applied. It teased his nostrils as the scent of most women didn't.

"Miss Watkins?"

She spun around. Her eyes—the shade of a cloudless sky—widened and her plump, rosy lips parted slightly. She quickly regained control.

"Why, Mr. Swindler, isn't it? What a surprise. I'd not expected to see you again."

Whatever words he'd planned to deliver to disarm her jumbled in his mind like rattled dice within a cup. By the light of day she was an entirely different creature. So much had been hidden from him in the shadows of the night. Her skin was remarkably flawless, creamy alabaster with a hint of blush curving over her high cheekbones. Her eyes held innocence, softness he'd not noticed before. Her hair peeking out from beneath her bonnet was a pale moonlight, almost white. He was staring at the same woman he'd confronted last night, yet she was more lovely than he recalled. Something about her in the daylight managed to give him a sharp blow to the chest, making it difficult to draw in a breath—which he desperately wanted to do if for no other reason than to enjoy her scent once more.

She bestowed upon him a whimsical smile. "You're not following me about, are you?"

He gave a brisk shake of his head and cleared his throat, giving himself time to regain his wits. Women didn't have this power over him. Ever. Even the most skilled seductress might turn his body to mush, but never his mind.

"No," he finally responded, hoping to charm her with one of his warmest smiles. As a child he'd collected a host of expressions that could be brought forth to help him acquire whatever he needed. Sad eyes when he was hungry and hoping for a scrap of food from a grocer or a cook at the back door of a residence, tears when he needed to draw a lady nearer in order to pilfer her hidden pockets. Cockiness when it was warranted. Humility when it would best serve to garner the prize. There were times when he'd decided he was a vast wasteland absent of emotions, except for those in his arsenal that he could conjure upon command. "Well, yes, I suppose I am in a way. I found something that I thought you might like to have. I was in the process of taking it to your lodgings when I spotted you walking up the street. I decided to present it personally rather than leave it with your landlady."

Reaching into his jacket pocket, he removed a folded map of London and held it out to her. "So you might never again become lost."

Her face lit with surprise and she laughed, a light airy sound that competed with the birds singing in the trees. As she took the map, her gloved fingers grazed his, and his gut tightened with the thought of her grazing something else entirely. He swallowed hard, striving to regain his bearings. She was only a woman, after all. A mark. And his facade had been carefully built just for her—it didn't reflect his true self. That, he showed to only a select few.

"How very thoughtful." Her expression was open when she lifted her gaze to his. How in God's name did anyone think she'd inflict harm on a fly, much less a man? "You must have gone to a great deal of bother to find it."

He'd gone to none at all. He'd bought it last year, when mapmakers had flooded the city with maps in anticipation of the many visitors who would come to London in order to view the Great Exhibition. He gave her a daring combination of humility and confidence. "Going to the bother was part of the gift."

He hated the false words he uttered. It had never bothered him before to fool someone into revealing what he needed revealed. But then he feared he wanted more from her than was practical. He wanted her on his arm. He wanted her rising up on her toes as he lowered his head to meet her lips in a passionate kiss. He wanted her sharing his bed, whispering wicked words in his ear—even as he doubted her vocabulary included the vulgar words about which he was thinking. But he could teach her. He suspected she was a quick study.

But more, he yearned to have her sitting beside him before a fire, listening as he recounted his day, offering words of solace when he bore witness to the brutality and inhumanity of man. It was the last of these that made his desire for her impractical, because the horrors he encountered had no place in her safe world or her innocent mind.

He gave himself a hard mental shake. Whatever was wrong with him to have such fanciful thoughts? It was unlike him to think in such poetic terms. He was a realist. Practical.

"I truly have no idea how I shall ever repay your kindness," she said.

"Perhaps you'd be so kind as to take a turn about the park with me."

She glanced quickly around, and he wondered if she was searching for Rockberry or striving to ensure that no one she knew would see her with Swindler. "I don't suppose it'll do my reputation any harm. After all, you can't take advantage here."

She *was* innocent. Why ever did she think women required chaperones? A man would always take advantage if the opportunity to do so presented itself. Especially when the lady was as enticing as she was.

He gallantly offered his arm. When her small gloved hand lighted upon it, he felt the touch clear to the souls of his feet. As part of his attempt to gain her trust, he'd dressed the part of a gentleman: gloves, hat, a fine jacket, waistcoat, and cravat. He preferred clothes a bit more plain, but he always dressed better when his mark was a woman. Women seemed to appreciate a man who was well turned out. And he needed every advantage he could muster. Next to her, he felt like a clumsy clod, rather than Scotland Yard's most brilliant and accomplished detective.

"You seem to have recovered very well from the ordeal you faced last night," Swindler said, striving to keep his mind on the task at hand rather than his fanciful musings.

"Yes, quite. Thanks entirely to your efforts."

"No lingering ill effects?"

"No, not even a bruise. It was frightfully silly of me to go out so late. I'm not quite sure what I was thinking. I shall certainly take more care in the future."

"I'm relieved to hear that. Have you been in London long?" Swindler asked.

"What gives you the impression I didn't grow up within the city?"

Tilting his head, he gave her a wry smile. "You became lost."

She blushed, her cheeks turning the most becoming shade of rose. "Oh, yes. Quite. I've been in town for only a week."

"Was there something in particular that brought you to London?"

She shook her head. "I wanted to see it." She looked up at the sky as though searching for answers. "My sister visited last year. She was quite enamored with the sights. So I thought I'd come this summer."

"A shame she didn't come with you. Perhaps you'd have not gotten lost."

She brought her gaze back around to him. "She passed recently."

Setting his face to give no clue that the information was not new to him, he placed his hand over hers where it rested on his arm. When he squeezed her hand, he meant to impart comfort, possibly the first honest gesture toward her. "My condolences on your loss."

He noted her hesitation before she revealed, "Our home is near the sea. She wandered . . . wandered too near the cliffs and fell to her death."

An untimely end, indeed. Recalling Rockberry's words, he wondered what role the man had played in the girl's demise. He was tempted to confess everything to Miss Watkins and simply ask her what her true business was, and why she was following Rockberry. Instead, he continued on with the ruse, concerned that she might shy away from him if she suspected he was here because of duty. "Again, my condolences on your loss."

She lifted a delicate shoulder. "My father took ill shortly afterward and passed as well. It's been a very trying few months."

"So you came to London."

She smiled softly. "My sister spoke of all the wonders. She kept a journal. I read it after she died, and became quite envious of all she'd seen, and so here I am."

"A woman traveling alone? You're quite bold."

"You flatter me, sir, but on this matter I have little choice. I have no aunts to accompany me, and no coins with which to hire a companion. And my mother is long gone. Elisabeth came first and I came last. Unfortunately, I believe I was too much for my mother."

"Were you and your sister close in age, then?"

She gave him a warm smile. "Only minutes separated us."

They were twins. No wonder Rockberry had been unsettled by the woman following him and suspected she was a ghost. "I hope you won't consider me too inquisitive, but I wonder why you didn't come to London with your sister last year."

"My father could afford to send only one of us. Elisabeth was the older, if only by a few minutes. She had her coming out. A distant cousin provided her with an introduction to society. It was Father's hope that she'd secure a fine match and then I'd have my turn."

"So you're here for your Season."

"No, I . . . no. I can't afford a Season. I simply came to London in order to see it."

"This cousin won't help you?"

"My family troubled her once"—she shook her head—"things didn't go well for my sister. I'll not take advantage of my cousin again. May we speak of something else?"

The sudden impatience in her voice alerted him that he was dangerously close to interrogating her. Usually he was more subtle, but suddenly with her he wanted to know everything and know it quickly, and not only because of duty. She was courageous, and perhaps a bit reckless, to travel alone. Yet he admired her determination not to require companionship in order to do as she wished. "My apologies for bringing up a sore subject."

The tenseness in her face eased. "You had no way of knowing."

And just as quickly the tension returned, her body stiffening, her steps faltering. He followed the direction of her gaze and watched as Rockberry loped along on his black mount. When Swindler looked back at her, she'd grown pale and all the sparkle had left her eyes, leaving behind deep pain and sorrow.

"Miss Watkins? Are you all right?"

"Yes, I'm sorry . . . I . . . I'm sorry."

He glanced back in the direction Rockberry had gone. "Are you familiar with Lord Rockberry?"

Suspicion quickly lurked in Miss Watkins's eyes.

"How do you know him? Do you consider him a friend?" she asked.

He knew he needed to play the next bit very carefully. "I know him because I have friends who move about in his circles, and on occasion I'm unfortunate enough to be invited to their gatherings. As for his being a friend, no. Quite honestly, between you and me, I don't much like the fellow."

"I don't fancy him either."

"Then perhaps we should walk on, before he notices us and prances over. You're a lovely woman, and from what I understand he can't resist lovely women." And while he knew Rockberry had danced with her sister, knew Miss Watkins was spending her time observing Rockberry, Swindler couldn't let on that he knew any of those specifics. He had to keep his focus on his plan to entice her into revealing all to him, without letting on that he knew even the slightest bit regarding what she was about.

Another tantalizing blush crept up her cheeks before she nodded. Swindler wasn't certain he knew any woman who blushed as easily or as becomingly, but then most of the women of his acquaintance were hardened by life, and had learned long ago not to give away the slightest hint of their feelings. He thought Miss Watkins might be the first genuine person to cross his path. Completely guileless. Whatever mischief possessed her to follow Rockberry could lead to no harm other than annoyance. It wasn't in her nature to be ruthless or calculating.

She was following a lord around, irritating him. Why couldn't Sir David realize that Miss Watkins was harmless? She would soon tire of plaguing Rockberry. No one was in danger here, and Swindler had more important matters to which he should attend. This assignment was petty foolishness.

Still, Swindler turned in a direction that would take him and Miss Watkins away from Rockberry and provide the marquess with only a view of their backs. Swindler didn't trust Rockberry to have the good sense not to approach them and reveal his purpose. While Rockberry's doing so would bring the assignment to a swift end, Swindler wanted its end to come on his terms.

"So how did you come to know Rockberry?" he asked after several moments of silence, when he was certain they were past being noticed by the odious man.

She shook her head. "I don't know him personally. I've never met him."

"But you know of him?"

She nodded, and he could see she was distressed.

"Miss Watkins, if he's harmed you in any way, I shall—"

"No, not me. My sister. He trifled with Elisabeth, so I was curious about him. Shortly after I arrived in London, I asked someone to point him out to me." She paused for a moment, as though wanting to take care with her words, with what she revealed, and it occurred to him that perhaps they were both playacting. Unfortunately for her, he was the master and would eventually discern whatever it was she wished to hide, while she'd learn very little about him.

He was fairly certain he knew the answer already. Rockberry had undoubtedly ruined her sister, and Elisabeth had flung herself from the cliff rather than live with the shame of it. She who was to marry well and help her sister have her own Season had failed miserably. As for Eleanor, perhaps she was striving to discover if Rockberry was worth her sister's affection.

Whatever her reasons, he found himself intrigued by the challenge she presented. He quickly grew bored with women who gave too much, too easily, and while it was her motives, her plans, that he sought, he saw no reason that the quest couldn't be enjoyable for them both.

"I . . . I'm sorry, Mr. Swindler," she finally said. "I've had quite enough of the park. I must return to my lodgings. Thank you ever so much for the map. I shall put it to good use, I assure you."

"Will you do me the honor of allowing me to escort you home? I can see you're upset. I'd like to ensure you arrive safely."

She blinked as though his words were not what she'd expected, or perhaps not what she wanted. At last she nodded.

As they walked on in silence, she was very much aware of Mr. Swindler's gaze riveted on her. She wondered what he was thinking, if he was as unexpectedly drawn to her as she was to him. She'd been surprised by that, by how his presence in the park had affected her. His features were strong, almost craggy, like her beloved jagged coastline, which could appear beautiful one moment and deadly dangerous the next.

She could imagine him standing on the deck of a ship, legs akimbo. His muscles strained the fabric of his jacket. In spite of his largeness, there was a gentleness, about him, almost a playfulness. Yet he also possessed a darker side. Now and then she caught a glimpse of it in his eyes. She thought it should have frightened her. Instead she was intrigued.

If anyone had asked her, even a year ago, what she would do if she ever was granted the opportunity to visit London, she would have innocently—and perhaps all too naively—answered that she intended to attend glorious balls, fabulous dinners, and an occasional opera. She might have even mentioned that she hoped to fall in love. Twelve months earlier—no, as little as nine months earlier—she had believed that London was the place where the daughter of an inconsequential viscount could find happiness, could achieve the realization of her dreams for a loving husband, a good marriage, and contentment. She had thought the nobility was to be admired, had not considered that some among them were hideously dangerous. That some, like the Marquess of Rockberry, would find enjoyment luring young women into the fires of hell.

With the reading of her sister's journal, her life and her reason for coming to London had taken a drastic turn.

The lodging house came into view. It was modest, her two rooms small, but comfortable.

"Thank you for escorting me home," she said.

"It was my pleasure." He gave her a grin that could have been teasing, could have been warning. "I do hope you won't wander the streets alone tonight. I would be sorely aggrieved if anything untoward were to happen to you."

"I plan to retire early," she assured him.

"I'm glad to hear it. I shall look forward to seeing

you at the park tomorrow, perhaps a bit earlier. Say around two?"

His startling green eyes wandered slowly over her as though they provided him with the means to see inside her soul. Their shade reminded her of the verdant grass in the middle of summer, and how often she'd run barefoot across it as a child. But she saw no softness in his gaze, nothing to tickle the souls of her feet. It was imperative that she not become lost in those eyes. She wondered how many women had. They were his most striking feature. Through them, she could almost see the cleverness of his mind. He gave the impression that he was relaxed, at ease, and yet she could fairly see the wheels turning.

With her cheeks growing warm, she wished her purpose in coming to London was different. She tried not to think that if she'd been the first to come to the city, she would not have made Elisabeth's mistakes. She'd even tossed Elisabeth's failings in her face—before discovering the journal and coming to understand all that her sister had endured. She shouldn't enjoy a man's attentions now, but she seemed unable to help herself. "An earlier outing would be most welcome. I shall probably be there, yes."

"Until tomorrow, then." He tipped his hat and began to walk away.

She hurried up the steps and opened the door using the key that Mrs. Potter, her landlady, had given her. She walked into the entryway and was immediately greeted by the fragrance of furniture wax and fresh flowers.

Mrs. Potter bustled out of the parlor, wiping her hands on the hem of her apron. Her black hair had begun to turn into silver, her face had lost the firmness of youth. She had a penchant for gazing out windows, an even greater one for inciting gossip. "That's him, Miss Watkins, the man I told you about, the one who's been making inquiries about you."

"Is he?" She'd suspected as much when Mrs. Potter described him.

"He gave me a crown not to tell you, but my loyalty is to my tenants, especially as you're alone. Is he a suitor?"

"If I'm fortunate, yes. You will let me know if you see him about anymore, won't you?"

"Oh, most assuredly."

"Thank you." She went up the stairs. Inside her corner room, she walked to the window and peered between the draperies. She didn't see Mr. Swindler. She wondered if he'd walked on or circled back to watch her room from some vantage point. She was fairly convinced now that he was Rockberry's man, sent to keep an eye on her. If he meant more harm than that, surely he'd have already seen to it.

She removed from her reticule the map Mr. Swindler had given her. Clever man to devise so sweet an excuse for approaching her. But still, she had no plans to underestimate him.

In the light of day she'd been surprised by his height and the breadth of his shoulders. But it was more than his size that was so dangerous. It was what she'd seen in his face. He looked to be a man who could kill someone simply by wishing him dead. He was not one to be deceived, and yet she planned to do exactly that—deceive him. Deceive him into befriending her, into wanting her, until he would do anything to protect her—even fall on his own sword.

Chapter 3

I hate to be a bother."

"Good Lord, Jim," Lucian Langdon, the Earl of Claybourne, said as he poured whiskey into two tumblers. "I've bothered you often enough."

"You're a lord, it's your right."

Claybourne scowled at him. They'd grown up on the streets together, working for Feagan, until it was discovered that Luke was the lost heir to a title. Swindler had never felt quite comfortable around the aristocracy, but then he felt comfortable around few. He was a skeptic at best when it came to someone else's good intentions. No doubt a result of his father's good intentions leaving him with a wounded soul that still, after all these years, refused to heal.

Claybourne handed a goblet of wine to his wife, Catherine. She was a lovely woman. Her blond hair almost reminded Swindler of Eleanor Watkins's, although Miss Watkins's made him think of moonbeams woven together. He imagined her hair would be soft but catch on his rough fingers. He imagined those same fingers abrading her delicate skin as he brought her pleasure. To spare her any discomfort, on her most sensitive flesh, he would use his mouth, his tongue—

"Jim?"

He snapped himself free of the dreams that had begun to haunt him ever since his encounter with Miss Watkins in the park and took the tumbler Claybourne offered. "Thank you."

Claybourne sat on the sofa beside his wife, stretching his arm across her shoulders, so his fingers could casually stroke her bare arm. Swindler doubted he'd have been as informal were his guest a lord. Or perhaps he would have if their friendship had been woven in the squalor that was the rookeries.

"You had some questions to ask of Catherine," Claybourne prodded.

Swindler took a sip of the whiskey, relishing the taste and the burn. He felt his muscles begin to relax. They'd been tense ever since he'd escorted Miss Watkins to her lodgings. Last night he'd been surprised to discover that she was not staying in one of the better parts of London. As his own lodgings were not that far from hers, he was well aware of what the accommodations offered. They were adequate but nothing fancy.

"Yes. I'm curious about a Miss Elisabeth Watkins. She was the daughter of a viscount."

"Watkins?" Catherine's delicate brow pleated. "I believe I've heard mention of a Viscount Watkins, but I fear I know very little about him. Sterling might, although I suspect it unlikely. Of course, he's not due to return to London for another few days."

Swindler appreciated what she wasn't saying—that the man was in the South of France making love with his new wife, with Frannie. What surprised Swindler was that the thought of her with another man didn't bring with it the usual sense of loss. Since his encounter with Miss Watkins this afternoon, *she* had been the one to occupy his mind, as though no one else mattered.

"I'll be content with anything you know," Swindler assured her, hoping to gather a few more morsels about Miss Watkins in his endeavors to learn about her father.

"If he's the man I'm thinking of, he rarely comes to London. Doesn't even have a residence in town."

Had word not even passed through the ranks that he'd died?

"Elisabeth apparently had her coming out last Season," Swindler told her.

Catherine distractedly patted Claybourne's thigh. "I fear I was far too caught up in my own affairs last Season to give much attention to someone's coming out. I'm sorry."

Claybourne's hand ceased its stroking and closed around her upper arm, offering strength and comfort. It was last Season that their lives had all become irrevocably entwined.

"You might inquire of Jack's wife," Catherine continued. "Before Olivia went into mourning, she may have met Miss Watkins earlier in the Season."

The widowed Duchess of Lovingdon created something of a scandal by marrying before the proper period of mourning had passed—an even greater scandal by her selection of a husband—Jack Dodger. Wealthy though he might be, he owned an exclusive gentlemen's club that was almost as infamous as he.

"Apparently Elisabeth caught Lord Rockberry's fancy," Swindler offered, hoping to prod some memory. Surely they'd not been free of gossip.

Catherine grimaced. "He fancies himself quite the catch, but I've never known him to offer for anyone. Did he take advantage of her?"

"Why would you think that?"

"If her father is as I've heard, without two pennies to rub together, it's unlikely she'd come with a substantial dowry. She could be desperate enough to believe a cad's promises. I fear not all gentlemen are in fact 'gentlemen.'"

Rockberry certainly fell into the category of not a gentleman. "Elisabeth apparently met a tragic end. Her sister, Eleanor, is in London. She's been following Rockberry around town. I suspect she holds him responsible in some manner, and he has the mien of a man harboring dark secrets and guilt."

Since Swindler possessed the same mien, he recognized it when he saw it in others.

"Oh, poor girls," Catherine said. "Elisabeth and Eleanor. Who is acting as Eleanor's benefactor to introduce her to Society?"

"She's not here for Society, but rather to poke sticks at Rockberry."

"That's very dangerous indeed. Rockberry won't tolerate that for long. Perhaps I should speak with her."

Swindler shouldn't have been surprised by her offer. Her nature to help those in trouble had brought her into Claybourne's life. He didn't know quite how to respond. He knew only that whatever Miss Watkins needed, he wished to be the person to provide it. "It's probably too soon to involve you. I've spoken with her. I don't believe she's a true threat. She may irritate Rockberry, but I don't think she's capable of inflicting any lasting harm."

"Don't take offense, Jim, but I suspect you underestimate the determination of aristocratic ladies when they've decided to take matters into their own hands."

"Stubborn more like," Claybourne grumbled, and she jabbed him in the ribs.

Rather than get angry with her, Claybourne gave her a heated look that even Swindler could interpret as meaning she'd pay dearly for it later in their bedchamber. He didn't want to think about the bed he'd sleep in alone tonight. He could seek out company, but he thought anyone other than Miss Watkins would leave him unsatisfied. Not that he had any plans to lure her into his bed. She was, after all, a lady—but that didn't mean he hadn't already given a great deal of thought to the pleasure he'd experience in having her there. He could well imagine her hands skimming over his bare chest, her mouth nibbling—

"Right, then," he said, setting his tumbler aside and coming to his feet while he could still stand without embarrassing himself. "I'll keep your offer in mind should I have any further dealings with Miss Watkins."

Rising, Claybourne assisted Catherine from the sofa. "Please do," she said.

"I'll see you out," Claybourne said as he bussed a quick kiss across Catherine's cheek, giving her more promises for what might transpire later.

Swindler didn't envy what his friend possessed, but for the first time he missed that he wasn't in possession of it as well.

In the hallway, Claybourne said, "If you believe dangers are about, I would appreciate your not getting Catherine involved. My wife has the heart and courage of a lioness. I don't know that my own heart could stand seeing her in harm's way again."

"I suspect Rockberry is more bark than bite. Otherwise, he'd have seen to the matter himself. As for Miss Watkins . . . I think she simply wishes to annoy him for a short time. Then I suppose she'll return home."

He wasn't quite certain why he felt sorrow over that notion. It wasn't as though anything could ever exist between them. She was the daughter of a viscount, for God's sake. He the son of a thief.

"As you're well aware, I've only recently become accepted by my peers," Claybourne said. "I could make some discreet inquiries, see what's what."

"It's probably best if I hold this matter as close to the vest as possible for now. I don't doubt your ability to exhibit discretion, but as I've been assigned the task, I'll handle the inquiries."

"Scotland Yard is having you follow the girl around? You must be chafing at the bit to move on to more important matters."

Strangely, after the encounter in the park, he wasn't nearly as impatient with this duty as he had been the night before. "We are charged with preventing crime. Rockberry believes she aims to kill him."

Remnants of regret washed over Claybourne's face. He'd once killed a man who had hurt Frannie. "Maybe I should speak with the lady. Even when the murder is justified, it's not easy to live with."

"If you hadn't killed him, I would have."

Claybourne shook his head. "Still, your lady should know that vengeance comes at a high price."

"I don't think she has it in her to kill him."

"I hope you're right. If you're not grumbling about the assignment, then the lady must be holding your interest."

"I misjudged her upon first meeting her. It's not a mistake I often make."

"I've *never* known you to misjudge a person."

But he had. Somehow he had.

Claybourne gave Swindler's shoulder a firm, hard clap. "Just know we're here if you need us."

Not two minutes ago Claybourne had been asking him not to involve them, and now it seemed he'd reversed his stance. Swindler knew that if it came to it, they'd help him. Feagan's children always stood together, even when their lives were lived apart.

"Actually, I do have a favor to ask."

"Ask, and if it's within my power it's yours."

"Could I borrow a carriage tomorrow? An open one if the day is sunny. Closed if it's not."

Claybourne grinned. "Putting out a bit of honey?"

Swindler shrugged. "If I must endure this assignment, I see no reason not to experience a bit of enjoyment while seeing to the task."

Swindler was almost to the door of his lodging house when he turned around and started back up the street. He didn't know why he was so restless tonight. Perhaps because even with Eleanor's promise, he didn't quite trust her to stay indoors. He knew he couldn't keep watch over her twenty-four hours a day, but he didn't want her following Rockberry either. Not when he knew he wouldn't be around anyway. He didn't trust the man not to take matters into his own hands and harm her.

It was nearly half past ten. As Swindler neared her lodging house, he saw her silhouette limned by the pale light spilling out through her window. Relief swamped him because she wasn't stirring up trouble with Rockberry. He stopped and leaned against a tree in the shadows.

It appeared she was brushing her hair. Good Lord, how long was it? Based on her movements, it had to reach past her waist. One hand glided the brush through the strands, while the other followed, smoothing them. He imagined the brush in his hand, the silk of her hair pooled in his lap as he sat behind her. Brushing, stroking. Gathering it up and burying his face in its abundant softness. There had been little enough softness in his life, and he'd always refrained from admitting how desperately he wanted it.

The women in his life never stayed for long, because he couldn't give them what they wanted. He cared for them too much to pretend he loved them, but not enough to truly love them.

Miss Watkins wouldn't be in his life for long either. He would slowly earn her trust—slowly because of a sudden he wasn't in any hurry to be rid of her—and when she confided everything, he would convince her to leave Rockberry alone. Or perhaps, depending on the circumstances, he would see to the matter for her. But only after she believed that he cared for her would she open up to him. So convince her that he held a fondness for her, he would. It wouldn't be much of a falsehood. He did feel a stirring of feelings for her, just not the depth of emotion a lady such as she deserved.

She bent her head forward and pulled her hair up and over until it fell like a curtain in front of her face. He rubbed the back of his neck, his attention focused on hers bared. He could almost feel her skin beneath his lips as he skimmed his mouth along her spine, as he pressed a kiss against the soft skin beneath her ear. He would trail his tongue along the shell, nibble on her lobe. Turning her in his arms, he would continue the journey until he had tasted her throat, and then he would settle his mouth over hers for a long, lingering kiss that would have her body softening while his hardened.

She flung her head back and began again the process of smoothing what she'd sent into disarray. The night had grown unseasonably warm. He was of a mind to remove his jacket, but even as he thought it, he realized the air held a chill to it. It wasn't the night, then, that was causing his body to sweat or his breathing to become labored. It was the nymph in the window. He could almost believe that she knew he was watching, that she was putting on a private performance for him.

He glanced up and down the street. It was late. No one was around. His gaze swept the buildings.

If anyone else was awake and watching, he couldn't see them. A good thing, as he suddenly had a savage possessive urge to pound on doors and threaten anyone who so much as glimpsed her.

What the devil was wrong with him? Nothing more than the pest of an idle lord, she would be in and out of Swindler's life in the blink of an eye.

How was it that she managed to bring forth these barbaric thoughts of doing whatever necessary to protect her? His nature was to stand for the innocent, but his feelings where she was concerned scraped the bottom of his soul, didn't allow him to retain his aloof demeanor, which allowed him to act without emotion. He needed to keep a cool head about him so nothing tainted his objectivity.

Swindler turned his attention back to her. Having stopped brushing her hair, she was only partially visible now. He was unable to determine where she looked. What was she thinking about? If he called on her now—

He shook his head at the absurd thought. He certainly couldn't knock on the front door. But ever since he was a lad, he'd developed a skill for climbing. It was quite possible that he could work his way to her window.

And accomplish what?

For God's sake, did he think she was going to pull open the window and allow him entry? Did he think she was going to grant him leave to take the brush from her and glide it through her hair a hundred times?

Reaching up, she pulled the draperies closed. It should have been less torturous with her no longer visible. Instead he imagined her crawling beneath the sheets and settling in to sleep, imagined himself gliding in beside her and folding himself around her.

The light in the window disappeared, and the air seemed to rush out of him. Did she sleep on her stomach, her back, curled in a ball on her side? If he were in the bed with her, would she snuggle against him? Strange to suddenly realize that he'd never slept with a woman in his arms. When business was done—

Business? Was that all it had ever been for him? Had he fooled himself into believing that because he'd taken care with the ladies, it was something more than a bit of fun, a way to while away a few hours on a lonely night?

Christ, where were these thoughts coming from? He'd wanted some evidence that she wasn't out prowling the streets. He had it. She was lost in slumber. It was past time for him to retire as well. But devil take it, he knew it was going to be long hours before his tense body relaxed enough for sleep to claim him.

* * *

Seduce him.

The words were an endless litany whispering through her mind with the constancy of the sea always rushing onto the shore, only to retreat and return again.

Seduce him.

Lying in the bed, she stared at the shadows dancing across the ceiling.

Seduce him.

What did she know of seduction? She'd acknowledged the young gentlemen of the village, but never encouraged their suit because she'd always hoped to come to London, to have a Season, to find a suitable husband. She'd always planned to watch the other ladies in the ballroom and mimic them. She'd always thought that when the time came, her womanly instincts would rise to the fore and she would know exactly what to do to capture a man's attentions.

She'd been restless all evening. She'd read for a while, but couldn't concentrate on the words. She'd spent time on her needlework but hadn't been pleased with the stitches. Finally she'd unfolded the map that Mr. Swindler had given her and spent an hour tracing her finger over all the various streets. It was a souvenir map. It showed where the Crystal Palace had been built in Hyde

Park to display the Great Exhibition. She wondered if he'd walked through it and seen all the marvels. She wondered what he was doing tonight. Was he with friends or alone? Was he in the company of a lady?

She didn't like the unease that stirred within her at the thought of him with another woman. It was silly of her to be so possessive of a man she'd only just met.

Eventually she'd prepared herself for bed and decided to brush her hair by the window in an attempt to relax. At home, she often sat by the window in her bedchamber, brushing her hair and listening as the roaring sea dashed against the cliffs. But tonight she hadn't heard crashing surf. All she'd heard was the echo of Mr. Swindler's promise to meet her tomorrow.

If not for her desire for revenge, she wondered if something more could develop between them. He was handsome in a rough sort of way. Gentle, yet strong. At times she'd thought he was keeping himself tethered, that he wanted to touch her in improper ways. She needed to exploit whatever passions she might stir within him. The thought excited and terrified her.

She wondered if Elisabeth had felt that way about Rockberry. Elisabeth had written about how he'd stirred her passions, and then he'd used those very passions to betray her in the worst way imaginable.

She rolled over in the bed, brought her knees up and slipped her hand beneath her cheek. While brushing her hair, she'd had the sense that she was being watched, and she imagined it was James Swindler, yearning to be with her. Closing her eyes, she knew sleep wouldn't arrive for a while, but she was in no hurry to drift off. If James Swindler occupied her thoughts long enough, perhaps he would inhabit her dreams and ward off the nightmares that frequented her on a regular basis.

Perhaps in her dreams he would even kiss her.

Dangerous, dangerous thoughts. Nothing more could exist between them, even if she wished it, because in the end, no matter what happened between them, he would despise her.

She had a horrible, sinking feeling that she might despise herself as well.

Chapter 4

It was deuced stupid for him to be so blasted nervous, Swindler told himself. He had inspected every inch of the carriage. It sported not a single scratch. The leather seat was thick and comfortable. The driver and groom, splendidly turned out in the noted Claybourne livery, were almost as well matched as the pair of grays.

Standing in front of Miss Watkins's lodgings, he fought not to pace. He checked that his neckcloth was still properly in place and his buttons done up. He wore the same jacket and trousers as the day before, but his waistcoat was dark green brocade, his neckcloth a pale yellow. When he'd gone to Claybourne's to retrieve the carriage, he'd allowed enough time so Claybourne's manservant could trim his hair and nails, as well as shave him. He was not a man accustomed to uncertainty, nor was he generally taken with vanity, but both dogged his heels as the hour of his outing with Miss Watkins approached.

He'd considered waiting in the parlor but didn't think he could manage to sit still. He had sent the groom around to make a discreet inquiry at the servants' door, so he knew the lady had not yet left for the park. He asked the driver for the time for what must have been the tenth time in as many minutes. When had the afternoon begun to creep by?

The lady should be making her appearance at any—

The door echoed a resounding click, and he came to attention as though the queen were passing by.

With a startled gasp, Miss Watkins froze halfway onto the stoop. Then her face blossomed into a beautiful smile that caused Swindler's chest to swell with satisfaction. He'd never in his life courted a woman, not even Frannie, because he'd known she would never return his feelings, that she favored Claybourne and Jack above him. Still, while he was not engaged in courtship at that moment, he thought he could definitely see the appeal in pleasing one woman above all others.

He'd always extended small courtesies to Frannie, and she'd always been appreciative, but he had always known that in spite of his best efforts, he'd never possess her heart. Miss Watkins, on the other hand—he didn't want her heart, but he couldn't explain this unheralded contentment that swept through him with her obvious pleasure. She was once again dressed in pale pink, her parasol in one hand, her reticule dangling from her wrist, her bonnet secured beneath her chin with a perfect pink bow. She was elegance and grace. Her father might have been merely a viscount, but she had undoubtedly been brought up to expect to walk among the aristocracy. He told himself that he needed to focus on his assignment, that she was so far above him as to be unreachable, but it was his own selfish desires that were causing him to want to make his discoveries about her pleasant for them both.

Her blue eyes took in the carriage, driver, groom, and horses before returning to linger on Swindler, as though she were taking in his full measure and discovering that he was not lacking in any regard. Finally closing the door behind her, she descended the steps and came to stand before him, her head tilted back so she could hold his gaze. "What a fine carriage you have, Mr. Swindler."

"I must confess that I've merely borrowed it from a friend. The Earl of Claybourne. You'd mentioned that you wished to see London." He opened the carriage door. "Shall we?"

She glanced in the direction of the park.

"It'll be there tomorrow," he said quietly, disappointed that she hesitated, knowing her thoughts were focused on Rockberry. He couldn't deny the spark of jealousy that threatened to ignite into a full blaze. What if he'd misconstrued her interest in Rockberry? What if she wished to replace her sister's role in his life—whatever that role, however misguided, had been?

She smiled at him, and the warmth and sincerity of it were enough to tamp down his own misguided feelings. For this small moment in time he'd won out over a lord. "Of course it will," she said. "How silly of me to give the park even a second's thought when I have a lovely carriage at my disposal." She placed her hand in his offered one and he assisted her up.

Once he settled in beside her, he urged the driver on.

"I suppose if I knew anyone in London, my reputation would be thoroughly ruined with this little outing," she said demurely.

"I've never quite understood this practice of chaperones. In the rookeries, where I grew up, girls came and went as they pleased."

"And what of their reputations?"

He gave her a wry grin. "They came and went as well." In spite of a thousand little voices in his head urging him against it, he wrapped his gloved hand around hers. "If you were moving about in Society and were known, I would have brought a chaperone. I can still procure one if you wish."

He had little doubt that Catherine would accommodate his request.

The familiar blush that he was coming to adore crept over Miss Watkins's cheeks. "I don't, not really. Besides, it would make things terribly crowded, wouldn't it?"

"It would indeed, so relax and enjoy your tour of London." While he fully intended to enjoy every facet of her.

While he avoided Hyde Park, Swindler ordered the driver to take them through other parks. He found it increasingly difficult to keep his eyes off Miss Watkins as she took in the sights. Her face revealed such exquisite pleasure, her lips continually curling into a smile, her deep blue eyes sparkling with delight.

As a rule, Swindler was not one to talk overmuch, but Miss Watkins was fascinated with everything, and she had the occasional question.

Had he toured Madame Tussaud's?

He hadn't.

Was the inside of Westminster Abbey as impressive as the outside?

It was.

He'd finally ordered the driver to stop at a spot near a river where rowboats were rented. After a couple of false starts—it had taken him a few attempts to get the gist of handling the oars—they were now gliding seamlessly along. A few other couples were in nearby boats. It occurred to Swindler that he'd never taken time to simply enjoy London. In his youth, he'd struggled to survive. As he got older, he'd struggled to learn. As a man, he'd become obsessed with his occupation, with being the very best at what he did. It seemed odd to suddenly find himself doing little more than gazing at the woman in the boat with him. She'd opened her pink parasol so it could provide some shade against the late afternoon sun. She appeared serene, as though she'd left her troubles on the bank of the river.

Yet Swindler couldn't seem to stop himself from imagining Rockberry with her sister, watching her, enjoying her fascination with everything. "Your sister. Did you look exactly alike?" He regretted his words as soon as they left his mouth and she grew somber.

"Exactly. But it was more than our features. Our mannerisms, our interests, were the same. No one could tell us apart, not even our father."

So Rockberry had seen precisely what he

himself saw when he looked at the lady. And Rockberry had taken advantage of the girl. Unfortunately, Swindler could understand that as well, because he was finding it very difficult to be near Miss Watkins and not touch her, not lean over and kiss her.

"It's funny you should ask me about Elisabeth," she said, her attention on the sunlight dappling the leaves above. "I was just sitting here lamenting that a gentleman had never taken Elisabeth rowing. Or at least she didn't write of it in her journal. It's quite pleasant."

"I must agree. I've never before been rowing."

She gave him an impish grin. "I gathered, but you mastered it quickly enough."

"I tend to be a quick study. Growing up on the streets, I learned that the child who survived was the one who adapted swiftly to the unexpected."

Her tongue darted out to touch her upper lip, and his gut clenched. He wondered what those sweet lips tasted of. "You mentioned that you were borrowing Lord Claybourne's carriage and also that you sometimes move about in upper circles. How is it you know the nobility if you grew up on the streets?"

"Are you at all familiar with Lord Claybourne's story?"

"No, my father never felt comfortable around

the aristocracy. I think because his finances were never comparable to most. He always looked exactly as he was: an impoverished lord. He didn't mingle with the other lords. So I fear I don't know Lord Claybourne."

"Just as well. He has—or had—a scandalous reputation. It's settled down a bit since he married Lady Catherine, sister to the Duke of Greystone, but you probably don't know her either." Especially as Catherine had indicated that she didn't know Eleanor. "Be that as it may, Claybourne lived on the streets as I did. His parents were murdered and he was lost for a while."

"How horrible!"

"Yes, it was. Dreadfully so. Although you won't hear him complain about it. Gave him a life unlike that of any other lord. We lived with a kidsman who went by the name of Feagan. Through him we learned to excel at thievery. When Claybourne was fourteen, he ran into a bit of trouble and was arrested." He didn't see the need to reveal that the trouble had involved his murdering a man. "As a result, he came to the attention of the Earl of Claybourne, who declared him his long lost grandson. When he took in his grandson, he took in his friends as well. So for a time I lived in St. James and was taught how to give the appearance of being a gentleman."

"You chose your words so carefully, Mr. Swindler. 'Appearance' of being one? Do you not consider yourself a gentleman?"

He grinned. "Only when it suits my purpose. Often I'm more a scoundrel than gentleman, Miss Watkins."

The heat in his eyes caused her heart to gallop. Oh, she was treading on very dangerous ground here, and well she knew it.

"Is that what you were doing out so late at Cremorne? Scoundreling?"

His rich, dark laughter echoed around them. She thought it was as wondrous a sound as the sea roaring onto shore. If she wasn't careful, she feared she might find herself being even more taken with him.

"Is that even a word?" he asked.

"I'm simply trying to determine if it was providence or simply dumb luck that brought you to my rescue."

"Does it truly matter how our paths crossed?"

She smiled at him. "No, I suppose not. Tell me something else about yourself, Mr. Swindler."

Something else? He was suddenly at a loss for words. He couldn't tell her about the Whitechapel murder.

Because sleep had eluded him last night, he'd gone to the mortuary where they'd taken the woman they'd found in Whitechapel. In spite of Sir David's orders, he'd been unable to let the dead lie without at least trying to determine the story. The woman had been beaten beyond recognition. She'd been discovered sprawled in the alleyway wearing only a silver choker. While Swindler had spent many of the early hours of the morning interviewing those in the area where she was found, striving to at least determine a name for the victim, his thoughts had been elsewhere. It was unlike him not to remain focused on the task at hand.

But this morning every fair-haired woman had caused him to think about Miss Watkins. Every question he asked had prodded him to wonder what questions he should ask of her. Every person peering around a corner trying to discern why he was there reminded him of his responsibility to cease her annoying Rockberry. He was striving to solve a murder that was not his assignment, and he'd been distracted by memories of Miss Watkins: her smiles, her laughter, her innocence.

But he could tell her none of that. Nor could he discuss any other murders that he'd investigated. While they fascinated him, they'd no doubt alarm her. His life suddenly seemed dreadfully dull. The only hope he had of an interesting conversation would come from her.

"Just as you'd never been to London, I've never

been beyond London," he finally told her. "Tell me of your home."

"You've never been outside of London?"

Swindler heard the incredulity in her voice. "No. Would I need a map?"

She laughed, and he wanted to capture the delightful sound and store it in a wooden box, to be heard whenever he lifted the lid. He was not usually so filled with fanciful thoughts, but she charmed him with little more than her presence.

"I daresay, you most certainly would, although the railways make travel a bit easier."

"So tell me about your home."

"It's a small stone cottage built near the cliffs. The music of the sea is a constant refrain, but it's not nearly as noisy as the city. I think that surprised me most—all the different sounds that come together. It's never quiet. Even with the sea at home, I've always found myself able to think without noise intruding. Sometimes I can hardly think here. Well, except for now, of course. It's very pleasant on the river."

"Odd. I don't notice the noises you refer to. I don't know if I would like living by the sea if it gives a man too much time with his thoughts."

"Do you not fancy your thoughts, Mr. Swindler?"

Sometimes they were too disturbing, too menacing, but he wasn't going to share that with her. Instead he sought to put them back on course. "I'm surprised your home is small. I thought all the aristocracy lived in large residences."

"While my father was part of the aristocracy, our beginnings were humble. Although he dreamed of better for his daughters. I suppose that's the way of a father. Is your father still living?"

He should have expected the question, based on his own inquiries. He considered lying. He considered giving only a portion of the truth, but decided that although it pained him to give the answer, he could accomplish more with the truth, build a fragile cornerstone for trust. "No. He died on the gallows when I was eight."

Sorrow reshaped the lines of her face into exquisite beauty, because the emotions were unguarded and true. He'd misjudged the wisest course. He'd thought to disarm her, and instead he was the one taken off guard. She lured from hiding something deep inside him. Emotions he'd locked away long ago wanted to venture forth from the darkness—if for only a moment.

"I'm so sorry," she said, her voice brimming with her need to provide comfort. If she cared this deeply for a man she'd only recently met, what would be the depth of her love for a sister . . . or a husband? "What was his offense?"

He reminded himself he was playing a role, and that whatever developed between them would be frayed with falsehood and weak with deceptions. His words were flat, never allowed to touch his soul. "He was charged with thievery. Left me an orphan. Like yours, my mother died in childbirth. I was apparently an unusually large babe."

"That's how you came to be with that kidsman. Feagan, was it?"

"Yes, I was fortunate he took me in. I had no family. You and I are alike in that regard, I suppose."

He rowed in silence for several minutes, absorbing the quietness that he'd never really noticed before. He watched as she glanced around, wondered if he'd revealed too much, was curious as to what she might be thinking.

She suddenly closed her parasol and set it in the bottom of the boat. Then very slowly, inch by inch, she began to peel off her right glove, revealing skin that up until that moment he'd only been able to imagine. His body tightened as though she'd loosened the buttons on her bodice. She tugged on one finger, then the next, and the next, and with each tug his mouth grew remarkably drier.

At long last the glove was completely removed, exposing a hand as creamy and smooth as her face, her nails clipped short and well manicured. Hers was the hand of a true lady, one who relied on servants to do the hard work. Leaning over slightly, she dipped her hand in the water and her features took on an expression more serene than before, more so than he'd ever seen on anyone.

"I miss the sea," she said quietly. She peered at him through lowered lashes. "Do you swim, Mr. Swindler?"

He started to answer, realized his throat had knotted, and cleared it. "No."

"It's wonderful. You should learn."

"I suppose it's very much like taking a bath."

She laughed. "It's so much more. Elisabeth would only run through the waves, but there is a cove near our home where the water is calm, and I would often swim across it. I have not been there since she died. It was where my father found her." She shook her head. "My apologies. I didn't mean to get maudlin and ruin this lovely afternoon."

"It's quite all right. I know how difficult it is when you lose someone you love. Even now I often think of my father."

"Has there been anyone else whom you've loved in your life?"

"No." He wouldn't tell her about Frannie. His feelings for Frannie, once tender and precious, were for him alone. "Have you ever loved a gent?"

She shook her head. "No." Lifting her hand, she

flicked water at him. "We're getting very personal here, Mr. Swindler."

"It's more interesting than talk of your home. Where is it, by the way?" he prodded, arching his brow, giving her only a glimpse of a teasing smile.

She seemed to give it a moment of thought, as though she couldn't remember. Or perhaps she simply hadn't expected the question. "It's to the north, near the sea, as I mentioned. My father's estate is small, but lovely. I'm comfortable there."

"To whom will it go now that he has died? I hope you don't have a horrid distant male cousin or uncle who will toss you out." Or worse yet, use her for his own gain. Perhaps there was more to her having no one to show her about London than she claimed.

She shook her head. "The land was not entailed. So the cottage is mine. His title was not hereditary. It was given to him for services rendered to the Crown. Unfortunately it came with nothing except the title, but my father was not one to complain."

"You don't strike me as one to complain either."

She gave him another impish smile. "I can be stubborn when I set my mind to it."

He couldn't see her as stubborn either, although he had to admit that her present course contained a bit of recklessness. What did she truly mean to accomplish by following Rockberry around?

"A cottage by the sea seems like a worthy dowry. Have you an interest in marrying a lord?"

"I suspect they'd have no interest in me."

He stopped rowing. He dared to skim his gloved fingers along her cheek, cursing the cloth that prevented his skin from touching hers. Her eyes widened slightly, and then darkened, and he wondered if she was imagining what he was: his hands trailing over more than just her cheek. He quickly grabbed the oar before he lost all sense of propriety. "I believe they'd show a great deal of interest if they were to make your acquaintance."

"But that shall never happen."

"I could make it happen."

She seemed as stunned by his words as he was. Whatever had possessed him to make that declaration? He had no desire to see her within the arms of another man, but neither did he wish for her to waste her time in London seeking some sort of petty revenge against Rockberry. Truly, what could she accomplish other than irritating the man? He wasn't worth her time or attention, and it annoyed Swindler that she was giving Rockberry both.

Seeing her again, he was more convinced that his original assessment of her held true: she was no danger to Rockberry. The man was no doubt reacting to his own guilt over his abhorrent behavior toward her sister. He should be flogged. Swindler was of a mind to flog him. It wouldn't be the first time he'd meted out justice to those who the law considered beyond reach. Was that the reason Sir David had set him this task: not so much to see to the lady, but to the gentleman?

"I didn't . . . come here for a Season," she finally stammered.

"Why did you come here, then?"

"To put a face to a name, to see London, to . . . what time is it?"

"Judging by the sun, nearly five."

She seemed stunned by his words. "Do you not possess a watch?"

"No."

His answer was succinct, to the point, as though he wanted to let the matter drop, and she wondered at the story there. She began to put her glove back on. "Did you bring me on this outing to ensure that I wasn't at the park at half past five?"

"What is to be gained by torturing yourself with the presence of Rockberry in the park?"

"I'm not sure. Every time I see him, it is like a dagger to the heart."

"I fear I've effectively ruined your afternoon."

Her smile was soft but reassuring. "Not at all. Rather, I think you've managed to convince me that I should enjoy London while I'm here. But it is getting late. I should probably return to my lodgings."

He winked at her. "If I can determine how to get us back to shore."

She laughed lightly. "Thank you for the pleasant afternoon, Mr. Swindler. It seems I'm once again in your debt."

"May I call upon you again tomorrow?"

She gave him a demure smile. "I'd like that very much."

Chapter 5

After another day in her company, Swindler still didn't quite trust her not to slip out and follow Rockberry. So after escorting her to her door, he'd ridden the carriage around the corner, hopped out, and ordered the driver to return to Claybourne's. He then took up his post outside Miss Watkins's lodgings.

He didn't know what had possessed him to reveal so much of his past to her. After all these years, the anger over the injustice of his father's punishment still ripped through him. He didn't need the fury now. He needed a clear, cool head to deal with Miss Watkins.

But that was asking almost too much. What was it about her that intrigued him so? She was innocence, but she also possessed determination. Like him, she sought justice. How could he ignore her need to avenge her sister when everything he did was in the name of his father?

If this were a private matter, if he had been personally hired by Rockberry to spy on Miss Watkins, he could handle things very differently. But as he'd been ordered to follow her, his position required a bit more discretion. He couldn't simply go to Rockberry's residence and give him a good flogging.

Swindler waited until darkness descended. He saw the faint light easing between the draperies in her window. He watched her silhouette pass in front of the window and stop. Then it continued on. He wondered if she would comb her hair tonight. If he should stay.

He glanced around. No one was about. He shouldn't be either. He began walking up the street. He would see her again tomorrow. For the first time in a long time, he was anticipating the next day.

Swindler awoke to the pounding on his door. Rolling out of bed, he pulled on his trousers and buttoned them as he crossed into the living area and went to the door. Opening it, he stepped back as Sir David strode by him.

"She followed him to Dodger's. You were supposed to keep an eye on her," Sir David said without preamble.

Swindler fought to suppress his yawn. "I

watched her lodgings until after dark. She was there when I left. She must have gone out later."

"What time did you leave?"

Swindler shrugged. "Perhaps an hour after the gaslights were lit."

"You don't know what time, do you, because you won't carry a damned watch. Blast it, man! If you weren't so good at what you do, I wouldn't tolerate your idiosyncrasies."

"If I'm so good, then why give me this assignment that requires none of my skills?"

"Rockberry asked for you by name. Apparently he saw your name in the *Times* for one crime solved or another."

"But why cater to his whims?"

"Because he is powerful and influential. Now about the girl—"

"I must sleep sometime."

Sir David plowed his hands through his black hair. He wasn't much older than Swindler, but already his hair was graying at the temples. "Quite right."

"Sir David, Rockberry did more than dance with Elisabeth. He trifled with her."

"It's unconscionable, but not a crime. He's certain Miss Eleanor Watkins means him harm."

"She's not a danger to him."

Sir David stilled and scrutinized Swindler. "Are you a hundred percent certain?"

Was he? If he said yes, the assignment might very likely come to an end. And if Rockberry learned that no one was watching her, he might decide to take matters into his own hands. Besides, Swindler suddenly wanted to spend time with her, very much.

"Right then," Sir David said, as though he'd read all the thoughts crossing Swindler's mind. "Keep an eye on her, and for God's sake keep her away from Rockberry."

"Yes, sir."

Late in the afternoon Swindler again borrowed Claybourne's carriage, and the lady was again dressed in pink. He wondered if years from now he would remember her as the lady in pink, for he had no doubt that in his dotage when he reminisced about his most fascinating cases, she would come to mind. Not that he found much to recommend the case itself for further reflection, but the lady was another matter.

She was a bit of freshness in his life, a life that had become stale by all he'd witnessed.

He considered asking her about her late night surveillance of Rockberry, had even considered

driving by Dodger's to gauge her reaction, but he
was so damned tired of Rockberry being even a
hint of a conversation. He selfishly wanted today
for himself, for Eleanor. He wanted to give the impression he was a suitor—and a suitor wouldn't
talk of another man. Even though he knew he
could never be a true suitor to her, he could have
this little bit of time with her.

He loved watching the way she enjoyed the
gardens as the carriage rolled through one after
another. She laughed when he didn't know the
names of the flowers. She pointed out her favor-
ites, but even if she hadn't, he would have known.
Pinks and lavenders. Pale colors. Softness. Nothing
bright. Nothing harsh.

Then she surprised him by asking, "Will you
take me through the part of London where you
grew up?"

She might as well have thrown a bucket of cold
water on him. He'd been considering seducing her,
but the filth that had been his life as a boy would
make any woman squirm with distaste at the
thought of his hands touching her.

"It's not nearly as beautiful as the gardens," he
said, hoping to dissuade her from pursuing that
path.

"But it would tell me a bit more about your
life."

He knew he should have been flattered that she had an interest in his past, might have an interest in him. While he knew he could never leave it behind completely, that it was woven into the fabric of his character, he had no desire for her to actually see the specifics. "Allow me to paint a picture: it was dirty, smelly, and crowded."

"I've noticed that much of London is dirty, smelly, and crowded."

"Not like the rookeries. It is absent of hope. It is not a place that allows in dreams. It's drearily dismal."

She looked at him as though he'd opened up his chest and shown her his heart. "You're ashamed of your past."

"I'm disgusted by it, yes."

Angry at her and his words, he averted his gaze. How had she managed to take control of the conversation and direct it away from where it belonged—with him learning about her?

He was aware of her small hand covering the tight fist balled on his thigh. She squeezed gently. "You rose above your origins, Mr. Swindler. That's to be admired. While I've heard tales of the rookeries, without actually seeing them, I can't fully appreciate them."

He twisted his head around to look at her, knowing his eyes and voice held a hard, implacable determination. "That's my point, Miss Watkins. There is nothing about them to appreciate."

He wondered what she was thinking as she studied his face, wondered exactly what it revealed. The harshness of the life he'd led? How, as he'd grown older, as he became more knowledgeable in the way of things, he came to abhor the life he'd lived? How the first time he'd felt any pride was when he led a constable to a boy who'd pilfered a money purse in order that the innocent boy who'd been arrested for the offense would be set free? How a gang of other boys had beaten him up for squealing on their mate—and so he'd learned to be secretive in his dealings with the police?

Even the rights and wrongs in life weren't crystal clear. Compromises were made for the greater good. The problem there was: who decided the greater good?

He'd had the audacity on more than one occasion to believe it was him. Even now as he sought to gain her trust, to discover her plans, he wasn't certain he'd provide Sir David or Rockberry with any information that could be of any use to them.

"You're a complicated man, Mr. Swindler," she finally said.

"Not complicated at all." He unfurled his fist, turned his hand over, and threaded his fingers through hers. "All I need is a lovely lady to provide me with company."

He watched her delicate throat work as she swallowed. "You claimed to be a scoundrel."

He gave her one of his more charming smiles. "The evening is only just arriving, Miss Watkins."

He'd planned to only be in her company for a couple of hours, but at the end of that time he wasn't yet ready to let her go. Besides, if she was determined to seek Rockberry out at night, then Swindler was obligated to keep her occupied. He'd learned nothing while, if she was a perceptive woman—which he had little doubt she was—she'd learned a great deal. It bothered him that he could so easily reveal part of his soul to her. But it was only parts, bits, and pieces that she'd never be able to fit together properly in order to create the whole. He wasn't even certain he knew the whole fabric of his being any longer.

When he'd become one of Feagan's lads, he'd chosen a new name for himself: Swindler. While it was his nature to swindle others, of late he was beginning to suspect that perhaps he'd even managed to swindle himself into believing that his only interest in the woman stemmed from *her* fascination with Rockberry. Otherwise rather than taking her home, why did he return her to Cremorne Gardens?

"Why ever have you brought me here?" she asked as the driver brought the carriage to a halt on King's Road.

"You've seen the worst of the gardens. I thought you should see the best." He stepped out of the carriage and held out his hand to her. "We'll leave long before the swells begin arriving."

Her sister had written in her journal about the gardens and the spectacular display of bursting lights in the sky. "May we stay until after the fireworks?"

He gave her a generous smile that stole every bit of breath from her body. Oh, he was dangerous to her heart. She'd thought to take advantage, and instead she was finding herself enthralled by him.

"If it pleases you," he fairly purred.

"It would very much."

"Then stay we shall."

After he handed her down from the carriage, he gave orders to the driver to return at nine. At the entrance, he paid a shilling for each of them, tucked her arm around his, and led her through the metal gates into the gardens. The crowd was dense. Ladies and gents strolled along arm in arm. She suspected most were married and those who weren't had chaperones nearby. Even a few children could be seen. It was the time for families, for the proper people to be about.

This was what Elisabeth had seen, what she'd written about in her journal.

"Did your sister visit the gardens?" Mr. Swindler asked.

She jerked her head up and held the familiar green gaze, seeing the compassion and understanding there. How was it that he was able to read her so well? "Yes. She wrote glowingly about the fireworks."

"So although you were lost the other night, you knew where you were?"

"It's possible to be lost, even when you know where you are," she said tartly.

"Are you lost, Miss Watkins?"

His question contained an undercurrent, as though he recognized that of late she barely knew herself, had moments when she felt adrift at sea. Sometimes she thought coming to London was a mistake. She wasn't comfortable here. It hemmed her in. Or maybe it was merely her quest for retribution that made her uncomfortable with her surroundings.

"Since my sister's death and then my father's, yes, I very often feel lost. Untethered." Those words were so true that it frightened her to think she could speak them to him so easily. She wanted to trust him with everything, completely, implicitly, but she knew she couldn't. Too much was at stake. "Do you suppose we could make a pact, at least for tonight, to talk of nothing except the future?"

"How can we speak of what we do not know?"

"The present, then. It seems forever since I've only been concerned with the present."

"Then tonight we shall focus on the here and now. Where shall we begin?"

So much to choose from, she hardly knew where to start. Then her stomach embarrassed her by making a little rumble, taking the choice from her. "I suddenly realized I'm quite famished."

He smiled. "A woman after my own heart. Let's see what we can find."

As he guided her through a throng to the banqueting hall, she thought under different circumstances that she would indeed be a woman after his heart. He was strong, kind, and solicitous. He pleased her in small ways. He brought her smiles when she'd thought to never smile again.

She hadn't come to London to find happiness, and yet it hovered, like a butterfly testing the petal of a wildflower. But no matter how much she wished otherwise, it'd not stay for long.

"Hold me, Mr. Swindler, dear God, please hold me." The words were whispered out of fear, mingled with embarrassment. She seemed to be the only one in a panic as the hot air balloon ascended. The other passengers uttered a few hushed exclamations of awe and wonder.

As Mr. Swindler's arm came around her, she clutched the lapel of his jacket and buried her face in the nook of his shoulder. He was as sturdy as the cliffs, as comforting, as he murmured, "You're perfectly safe, Miss Watkins. We're not going anywhere."

"We're going up." She could hardly believe that she was standing in a basket—in a basket!—floating toward the heavens. She feared that she was going to bring up the warm meat pie he'd purchased her earlier. She'd not considered that watching the earth move away from her would make her head spin.

Hot air balloon rides were a weekly occurrence at the gardens. The balloon was moored so its ascent was controlled. Once the passengers had a good look around, it would be brought down for another group. From the ground it had looked to be so much fun. She didn't know why the thought of going up bothered her. She'd looked out over the cliffs her entire life, but they didn't wobble, they didn't move. Steadfast and strong, they could support her. Could the basket hold the weight of everyone inside it? Or would they find themselves falling through its center to the earth below?

"Listen, Miss Watkins. Is that the quiet you longed for?" he asked softly.

She heard it then. The din of the crowds had retreated. There was no whir of carriage wheels or clatter of horses' hooves. They were above the noise. She almost thought up here that she could hear Elisabeth whispering to her. How close were they to heaven?

The basket gave a little jerk. She released a tiny squeak and tightened her fist on his jacket as though it would hold her up if the balloon started to fall.

"It's quite all right; we've simply met the end of our tether," Mr. Swindler purred near her ear. If she weren't so terrified, she might have swooned from his nearness. "Open your eyes."

"I don't think I can," she whispered, hoping none of the other four passengers were listening to her.

"Don't look down. Simply look across. Trust me, Miss Watkins."

Swallowing hard, she barely opened one eye. She could see treetops. She opened the other and released a startled laugh. She could see rooftops. "Oh, look, there's the Thames."

She didn't know why she was surprised to see it. The gardens were built at its edge. Some people ar-

rived in boats at its waterside entrance. Its nearness
was one of the reasons that the gardens were so
green and vegetation flourished. The sun was beginning to set, creating a spectacular view awash
in orange and lavender. What more was to be seen
beyond this small area? How would her home
appear from on high? She found herself envying
the birds.

"I almost wish it would break free of its tether.
Almost." She brought her gaze to Mr. Swindler's.
He wasn't peering out over the land spread out
below them like some elaborate tapestry. His eyes
were on hers. "You're missing the sights."

His lips slowly shifted up into a sensuous smile.
"I don't believe I'm missing anything."

She wondered at the taste and feel of his mouth.
What a strange thought. To realize how desperately she wanted to experience his kiss, how she
yearned to have him desire her. Even knowing
that his interest in her might be influenced by an
association with Rockberry that he'd not claimed,
she still found herself drawn to him. She'd hoped
to distract him from his purpose in serving Rockberry, and she was the one distracted.

With her tongue, she touched her lips, imagining his causing them to tingle and swell. His gaze
dipped to her mouth, and she wondered if his
thoughts were traveling the same path as hers. His

eyes darkened and narrowed. Beneath her hands resting on his chest, she could feel the stillness in him, the tension building as though he fought some inner battle and was very close to losing whatever control he possessed. He took in a shuddering breath.

He swung his gaze out to the Thames, and she wondered if her small, insignificant actions had stirred his passions. Judging by the deep furrows in his brow and the tightness in his jaw, he was bothered by something. How fascinating, but then she shouldn't be surprised by her interest when everything about him intrigued her.

She turned her attention back to the scenery. She wished they could stay up here forever. What a different world it was, looking down rather than up. She could almost forget her reason for coming to London, the need for retribution that nagged at her. Up here she could imagine that love was attainable.

A pity her heart knew the truth of the matter. In very short order she would sacrifice any chance she might ever have for a happy life.

Eleanor had asked him not to dwell on the past, but for a few hours to simply concentrate on the present. He took her request to heart. He forgot that he was the son of a convicted thief, an orphan raised by a master thief. He forgot that he'd spent his youth arranging swindles designed to line Feagan's pockets with riches. He forgot that she was his mark, his duty. He thought only about the woman who strolled along beside him, taking such delight in the smallest pleasures offered by the gardens. She was as entertained by the acrobats as she was by the puppets. Her smile seldom abandoned her face and her eyes glittered more brightly than the gaslights that were being lit as darkness blanketed the gardens.

An orchestra played lively music. From time to time, as he and Eleanor strolled along, she would sway slightly as though caught up in the rhythm of sound that floated through the gardens. He considered escorting her to the dance platform, but taking her in his arms and gliding her over the wooden flooring was likely to lead to disaster, because he was having a devil of a time keeping his hands from wandering over her now. The balloon ascent had been pure torture with her nestled against him. He'd felt the small tremors cascading through her. If he'd thought he could have successfully carried her down one of the ropes that kept the balloon tethered, he'd have swung her over his shoulder and delivered her safely to the ground. However, all he'd been able to do was offer distractions. While they worked for her, they failed miserably for him. He'd gazed into her blue eyes and all he wanted was to have a private moment with her. No, not *a* private moment—but a thousand of them. The two of them alone where intimacy could flourish, where he could truly forget the past and not consider the future. Where the present could tick along, holding all responsibilities at bay.

Eleanor distracted him from his purpose. He'd brought her back to the scene of their first meeting, because he planned to gently lead her into revealing why she'd truly been in the gardens that night. He needed her to trust him enough to confide in him, so he could get to the bottom of this matter. The policeman inside him knew that.

But the man inside him had other ideas. He'd embraced her notion of enjoying the present, and that meant ensuring that she enjoyed it, that there be no subtle interrogation, no prying.

A boom sounded as the first burst of fireworks filled the sky. With her arm intertwined with his, she used her free hand to squeeze his arm as she exclaimed, "Oh my word."

The fireworks could be seen for miles, and many a night while walking through Chelsea he'd spied them, until he became impervious to their magnificence. But watching Eleanor, he remembered the first time he'd seen them scattered across the velvet blackness and how they'd taken his breath away.

He'd felt then the way he felt watching her—as though nothing would ever compare.

Her head was tilted back slightly, her eyes wide, her lips parted in wonder. Her hair wasn't nearly as tidy as it had been when they'd begun their afternoon outing only a few short hours ago. Wisps had worked their way free of the pins and now framed her face. Even as he wanted to touch them, to tuck them into place, he yearned to remove her hat, release all the pins, and watch her hair tumble down her back. He wanted to pull her farther back into the shadows. He wanted to live up to his reputation as a scoundrel. He wanted to seduce her into revealing her secrets, he wanted to seduce her into revealing her body.

The sky was again lit with a flash of white stars that shot in all directions before fading into the night. Eventually she would fade away as well from his life. But at that particular moment she was still in it, vibrant and lovely, a touch of innocence, a touch of daring.

"My God, but they're so beautiful," she whispered reverently.

"Not nearly as beautiful as you."

Her attention turned from the sky to him. He'd promised her they'd not leave until after the fireworks, but he was of a mind to create his own sparks. There were shadows aplenty, and as the next boom sounded, he snaked his arm around her waist and urged her away from the gathered crowd and the gaslights. She offered up only token resistance, no doubt initially forgetting that they weren't supposed to be influenced by the past this evening. Impatience had him lifting her the last few steps, and then he was ensconced in heaven: her rose scent filling his nostrils, her taste tempting him to seek more as her mouth reshaped itself to fit seamlessly against his. Like some sort of clinging vine her arms wound around his neck, her fingers scraping up his scalp, becoming entangled in his hair. He was taken off guard by how desperately he wanted her.

Nearly a week had passed since he first became aware of her existence, and yet he felt as though he'd known her a lifetime. It was inconceivable that he could harbor such strong feelings for a woman about whom he knew so little.

With a hushed moan, she pressed her body nearer to his, her breasts flattening against his chest. Of their own accord, his hands slid down her sides to her hips, pushing her against his hard, tortuous arousal. He was acutely aware of her slight stiffening, as though taken aback by what he had no ability to hide from her. Of course she'd be disarmed by it. She was a lady in the truest sense of the word.

With a crude curse to emphasize the differences in their stations, he tore his mouth from hers and backed even farther into the shadows.

"Mr. Swind—"

"Christ, Eleanor, I would think after that blistering kiss we could dispense with formalities."

"You're angry."

"Not with you. Finish watching the fireworks. I'll join you momentarily." Once this horrendous ache left him in peace.

"I can see them from here."

"Eleanor," he ground out, hoping the impatience in his voice would be enough to drive her away.

"James."

His name whispered so sensuously and with such longing was nearly his undoing. She was too innocent to understand the torment she could so effortlessly inflict on him. What in God's name was he doing with her?

He felt her tentative touch on his cheek, was aware of the slight trembling in her fingers. Covering her hand with his, he turned his face into her palm and pressed a kiss to its heart. Regret flooded him. Regret over his past. Regret over his true reason for being with her. Regret that he could so easily set his orders aside and seduce her nearer with no thought to how she'd feel afterward when she realized he was there because of duty. Christ! He was no better than Rockberry.

Swindler had no doubt that Rockberry had used her sister to his own ends. He was guilty of the same. Even as he had the thought, he prayed some noble cause guided him. Prevention, protection. He'd gone to work for Scotland Yard because he wanted to save people as he'd never been able to save his father.

The tension left his body, the ache dissipated. He drew her into the circle of his arms, guiding her so she faced away from him. Where moments ago he'd longed to see her hair released from its confines, now he welcomed her bared nape by pressing a light kiss there before whispering near her ear, "You do tempt me, Eleanor."

"I thought you were a scoundrel."

"One with a conscience it seems."

"And if I don't want you to have a conscience?"

"Then we are either headed toward heaven or doomed to hell."

Chapter 6

As the carriage traveled swiftly through the streets, she didn't want this magical night to end. Leaning against James, her head on his shoulder, was scandalous, and yet she seemed unable to help herself. She wanted his arm around her, but she knew that was far too much. It was enough that he held her gloved hand in his.

Whenever she'd imagined a kiss, it had never involved a man boldly sweeping his tongue through her mouth, exploring every inch of it as though he owned it. With James's kiss, the heat had swirled in her belly and rolled outward until even the tips of her fingers and toes burned.

Oh, he was very skilled at seduction—her James Swindler. Yet as he caused pleasure to build within her, it was as though he revealed things about himself as well. He was strong, confident, accustomed to having his way—yet he acquired what he wanted not by force, but by persuasion. She thought she could have easily disappeared into the shadows behind the trees with him, never to return and never to regret it.

The kiss had shaken her to the core. Judging by his reaction, it had done the same to him.

Had Rockberry done this with Elisabeth? Had he charmed her, kissed her, pushed her away, only to lure her back in?

She didn't want Rockberry to intrude on her thoughts tonight, not when they were so filled with James. She wished she'd come to London for another purpose entirely, wished she'd been the first daughter sent, wished she and James had crossed paths a year ago when she wasn't consumed with grief and the need for retribution. It was horrible to hate someone as she did Rockberry. It tainted even the most glorious moments, made her feel as though she didn't deserve them because her sister had never experienced them.

"What are you thinking?" he asked quietly.

Once again she was amazed how he always seemed to know when to speak and when to remain silent.

"How different I was before Elisabeth died. How I wish you'd known me then."

"I like you very much now."

"Tragedy changes us, not always for the better, I think."

"It can give purpose to our life."

She peered up at him. "Is that what it did for you?"

"After my father died, yes."

"You became a thief. Hardly an ambition for which to be commended."

"I sought to survive, any way that I could. We do what we must."

Would he understand if she explained to him what she *must* do? "You must have been very grateful when Lord Claybourne took you into his home."

"Not at first." James gave a low chuckle, a rasp that settled on the night air and lingered to tease her senses, to make her smile. "He insisted we be clean, bathe every week, rather than once a year. I thought for certain that we were done for, that we'd all take ill and die. But we didn't. He bought us clothes that fit. He hired tutors. I was terrified of him, so I didn't dare disobey."

"Did he beat you?"

"No," he said succinctly. "Never raised a hand to any of us except possibly his grandson. I never quite understood why he took in the rest of us. Maybe because of his love for his grandson. We were his friends. Perhaps he didn't want him to be alone in his new surroundings."

"How old were you?"

"Ten. The youngest of the lot."

"Then, earlier, when I said I wanted to see where you grew up, I suppose I misspoke. It wasn't the rookeries. It was Lord Claybourne's."

"No, I grew up far more in the rookeries than I did at Claybourne's. It's a myth that age is determined by years. I didn't stay at Claybourne's all that long. A few years. When Jack Dodger and Frannie left, so did I."

"Who are they?" She enjoyed listening to him talk. Wanted to know every detail of his life, even when she wasn't willing to share hers.

"Jack Dodger, a scoundrel of the highest order. A very wealthy one at that. He owns Dodger's Drawing Room. A very exclusive gentlemen's club."

Where Rockberry was a member. He'd gone there twice now since she'd arrived in London. James paused to study her, and she wondered what he was searching for—if he knew she was well acquainted with Dodger's and what it represented.

"And Frannie . . . she recently became the Duchess of Greystone," James finally continued.

She heard deep abiding affection in his voice when he spoke of Frannie. A spark of jealousy flared, and she fought valiantly to tamp it down. What right did she have to experience such a reaction to a name, to a woman who could be more to him that she ever could? "She's special to you."

She wished she could have taken the words back. What was it about this night that made it perfect for slipping beneath the surface of whatever was developing between them? Why was she even asking all these questions when she knew he would never have a permanent place in her life?

"She was—is—special to all of us. She's always been like a little mother. When we were no longer children, she sought out other orphans, built a children's home for them. Oversees it. Plans to build another."

"And is a duchess. It's almost like a fairy tale isn't it? A daughter of the streets becoming a duchess."

"I suppose your father had hoped that for you and your sister. A titled gentleman."

She imagined she heard more in his words, in his inflection—a reminder that he himself was not titled. And while she knew her father had wanted her to marry a man with a title, she only said, "I think he wanted us to marry well, and for my father, I believe that meant marrying a man who would make us happy."

"What would make you happy, Eleanor?"

Happiness was fleeting, she was discovering. A few hours ago she'd been overflowing with it, and now it was seeping out of her just like the air that had escaped from the balloon so they could return to earth. The nearer they traveled to her lodgings, the more reality began to shove aside dreams and possibilities.

"This evening made me very happy, James."

She was aware of him scrutinizing her as they passed beneath the streetlamps, and she knew that he intuitively understood what she hadn't said. They settled back into silence as though they both knew they were destined to make choices that would leave them each alone.

When the driver pulled the carriage to a stop in front of her lodgings, the groom climbed down and opened the door, handing her down. James joined her and walked her to the front door.

"How long will you be in London?" he asked.

"I'm not certain."

"If I were to bring the carriage back 'round two tomorrow, would you grant me the pleasure of going on a picnic with me?"

She smiled warmly. "I would."

Lifting her hand, he pressed a kiss to her knuckles, and in spite of the gloves, she felt the heat of his mouth through the cloth. "Tomorrow, then."

Taking her key, he unlocked the door and stood on the stoop until she closed the door. As she walked up the stairs, she thought her step should have been light. Instead, it was weighted down with guilt and deception. And she wondered when the time came, how she would ever walk away from him.

* * *

Swindler was not a man who often made mistakes, but when he did they were large and regrettable. During the past week, he'd arranged a series of outings for Eleanor and accompanied her on each one: Madame Tussaud's, an opera, picnic in the gardens, another visit to Cremorne for the fireworks that so delighted her. He began each day with the best of intentions—to deduce her purpose regarding Lord Rockberry—but he became protective of his time with her. He didn't want to discern her purpose where Rockberry was concerned.

Swindler was more interested in learning all he could about the lady herself, and his mind was further occupied in striving to determine how to have private moments alone with her in order to secure another kiss. He'd thought to seduce her, and he was the one being seduced.

But the time had come when he needed to face his responsibilities. Before he did, however, he wanted to give Eleanor one lasting gift, a night she'd long remember, even if she came to despise him afterward.

It was the very reason that he'd come to the home of the Duke and Duchess of Greystone, who he knew had returned from their wedding trip several days prior to his arrival.

"Jim!"

Standing in the elaborate entry hallway, Swindler turned at the calling of his name and looked up the grand sweeping staircase that Frannie was descending. He'd expected this moment of seeing her for the first time after her marriage to Greystone to be awkward, for his heart to give the little pull it always did when his gaze lit upon her, knowing she would never be his.

But his heart didn't begin to ache for wanting, his chest didn't tighten. He had none of the usual reactions that often accompanied him when he was in her presence. He felt gladness at seeing her, but nothing more. No longing, no yearning, no desire for anything beyond friendship.

She looked as she always did: beautifully elegant, with her vibrant red hair pinned up and her face aglow with joy. Her dress, however, was finer than anything she'd worn when she worked as a bookkeeper at Dodger's gentlemen's club. Her green dress was silk and lace, befitting a duchess.

Her husband followed closely behind her. He was fair, well-turned-out. His mantle was his title. He could have been wearing nothing at all and he still would have commanded respect, still would have drawn attention when he strode into a room.

Coming to a stop before Swindler, Frannie took his large hands in her delicate ones and squeezed tightly. Having been brutalized as a child, she'd always been extremely reserved with her hugs, so he hadn't expected one in welcome. What surprised him was that neither did he desire one. It seemed when he thought of a woman holding him, the only image that came to mind was that of Eleanor.

"Your Grace," he said to her, then nodded at Greystone.

"Oh, Jim, please, I'm still Frannie. Don't be formal with me. I'll take it as an insult."

"You're a duchess now."

"I'm your friend, aren't I?"

He could see in the green depths of her eyes how important his answer was. "Yes, of course you are."

She smiled happily at him. "It's so good to see you."

"You're looking well."

He'd have thought it impossible but her smile grew. "The South of France was wonderful. Sterling and I had a marvelous time."

Even knowing that marvelous time would have included lovemaking, Swindler felt no jealousy. He felt nothing except gladness that Frannie was so obviously happy.

"We've been home for a couple of days now," Frannie said. "I was afraid . . . I'm glad you came by to visit. Shall we go into the parlor?"

She didn't wait for an answer but stole her arm around his and led the way.

"What can I offer you to drink, Swindler?" Greystone asked as he walked to a table with decanters.

"Nothing, thank you. I fear this isn't exactly a social call."

"Scotland Yard sent you here?" Frannie asked as she sat on the settee.

Swindler dropped into a chair opposite her while Greystone took his place beside her. "Not intentionally, no. But I'm in need of a bit of assistance with a case I'm working."

"What sort of assistance?" Frannie asked.

"I understand you're having a ball tomorrow night."

"Yes, Sterling thought it essential for the new Duchess of Greystone to host a party as soon as we returned from our wedding trip. Catherine's been handling the particulars."

"I would like you to invite Miss Eleanor Watkins. Her father was a viscount, so it wouldn't be inappropriate for her to attend."

"Good Lord, Jim, she could be a washerwoman, and if you have an interest in her, I would invite her. I suppose I'm to invite you as well."

"Yes, if you don't mind. She may also need a gown."

"She's not here for the Season?"

"No, I believe she's here for revenge."

"Revenge sounds like something that will put my wife in harm's way," Greystone said. "If that's the case, then we can't be of help."

"Sterling—"

"I almost lost you once, Frannie. I'll not risk it again."

With amusement, Swindler watched the silent battle of wills. Apparently the duke had yet to discover that his duchess possessed a very stubborn streak.

She finally turned her attention to Swindler. "Tell me about the lady."

Taking a deep breath, he leaned forward, digging his elbows into his thighs. He explained how she'd come to his attention. "She quite simply fascinates me, but I've never told her my true purpose, what it is I intend to gain from her. Sometimes I feel as though I'm back under Feagan's employ, working so bloody hard to fleece someone without him knowing."

"You're doing your job."

"That's just it, Frannie. I'm not, not really. I'm simply enjoying her company. I'd hoped in time that she'd come to trust me, confide in me, tell me of her plans regarding Rockberry. But she avoids discussing him at every turn. The time has come for me to bring this matter to a close. I must confront her, and when I do, whatever tender regard she might have toward me is certain to sour. I would like to give her this night at your ball, a gift as it were, before she discovers that I've been deceiving her."

Frannie placed her hand over his. "Have you been deceiving her, Jim?"

"I'm no longer sure. I've come to care for her, but I must tell her the truth about what I know and what I need to know. I fear she won't be pleased to learn the truth."

Rockberry had taken advantage of her sister. She was likely to think Swindler had done the same. He was dreading the confrontation and was hoping one final night of happiness would soften the blow he would deliver.

"Miss Watkins! Miss Watkins!"

The resounding knock nearly rattled the door to her rooms off its hinges. Eleanor crossed over as quickly as possible and flung it open. "Yes, Mrs. Potter?"

The woman was breathing heavily, her face flushed with excitement. "You have a caller. The Duchess of Greystone herself. My word." She pressed her hand to her heaving bosom. "Nobility in my parlor. I never imagined . . . What tea should I prepare, do you think? Oh, it doesn't matter. I shall prepare every flavor I have. I do wish I had cake. Biscuits seem so trite. Hurry. You mustn't keep Her Grace waiting."

As her landlady scurried down the hallway toward the stairs, Eleanor followed at a more sedate pace, her stomach quivering with nervousness. Why ever had the duchess come to call?

By the time she reached the bottom of the stairs, she'd regained control of her breathing and calmed the tremors that had been dancing through her. She entered the parlor and the duchess rose gracefully from the chair. A young lady, obviously a servant, also came to her feet.

The duchess smiled softly. "Miss Watkins."

Eleanor curtsied. "Your Grace."

She didn't know what to say beyond that. Should she be forthright and ask why she'd come to call or should she simply wait? Had Elisabeth suffered through these moments of insecurity, of not knowing the exact behavior that was expected? Was that how Rockberry had managed to lure her into hell? Eleanor fought not to show the anger she felt with her father at the thought. If only he'd brought them to London on occasion, if only he'd exposed them to more of the world, Elisabeth might still be alive, they might all be happier. She herself might have had an opportunity to be properly courted as well.

"I must apologize for arriving at an inappropriate hour, but I feared if I waited until afternoon, I wouldn't have enough time to accomplish all I wish to. I've come to beg a favor of you," the duchess said.

"I'm not certain how I could be of service."

Unexpectedly, the duchess stepped forward and took Eleanor's hands. "I'm a dear friend of James Swindler. I believe he's mentioned me. We grew up on the streets together. I know he's been calling on you. I'm holding a ball this evening. I've invited Mr. Swindler. I was hoping you'd do me the honor of attending as well."

To attend a ball, a duchess's ball at that. Eleanor hardly knew what to say, other than the truth. "I fear I have nothing to wear."

"I thought that might be the case. Jim mentioned that you had no sponsor and weren't making the rounds. He also described you to me—quite accurately, if I may say—so I took the liberty of selecting one of my gowns that I think would look lovely with your complexion. You're a bit smaller than I am, but Agnes here, my lady's maid, is quite skilled with a needle. She could make alterations."

"Oh." Once again she hardly knew what to say.

It was only then that she noticed the large long box resting on the sofa.

The duchess squeezed Eleanor's hands, which she'd yet to relinquish. "I hope you'll forgive me. I may be playing a bit of matchmaker. Jim has never spoken to me about another lady, so I know you must be very special indeed."

Eleanor's stomach tightened into a painful knot. This was what she'd wanted, but now that the moment was here . . .

The duchess seemed to sense her hesitation. "Why don't we have a look at this gown, shall we? If it doesn't please you, we can select another."

How could it not please her? Eleanor thought as Agnes pulled it out of the box and held up the white gown edged in pink satin with tiny satin flowers adorning the skirt. "It takes my breath it's so lovely."

"I thought you might like it," the duchess said.

"I hardly know what to say."

"Say you'll attend."

Eleanor couldn't stop her triumphant smile. "I'll attend."

Mrs. Potter joined them several minutes later with tea—and cakes. While it was not her usual habit to impose when her tenants had guests, she seemed unable to get beyond the notion that she had a duchess sitting in her parlor, sipping tea, nibbling on a cake, and chatting as though they were all familiar friends. The duchess had such an unassuming manner that Eleanor had little doubt she charmed anyone she encountered. For someone not born into the aristocracy, the duchess had adapted very well to her elevated position in society. Eleanor was left to wonder if she might have adapted as well if she, instead of Elisabeth, had been the one her father had chosen to send to London first. Or would she have been as naive as Elisabeth and followed her footsteps toward disaster?

"I've enjoyed the visit so much," the duchess finally said, "but I fear I must be off. I'll leave Agnes with you, so she can alter the gown as needed." She rose and everyone came to their feet as well. "I'm leaving a carriage for Agnes and shall send one 'round for you at half past eight, if that pleases you."

"It pleases me very much," Eleanor said.

Once again the duchess took her hands. "I think it shall please Jim as well."

After the duchess left, Eleanor and Agnes retired to Eleanor's rooms. The gown required very few alterations, but the duchess had been correct. Agnes was deft with the needle. A couple of hours later, when the work was finished, Eleanor stood in front of the cheval glass, admiring her reflection. The sleeveless gown's low cut revealed an enticing bit of cleavage. The duchess had provided long gloves that went past Eleanor's elbows, and pearled pink slippers.

"I could prepare your hair before I leave," Agnes offered.

Eleanor shook her head. "No, thank you. I shall probably take a short nap before I begin final preparations. These affairs usually go late into the night, don't they?"

"I know the ones Lady Catherine gave lasted well past midnight. She's been helping Her Grace with the arrangements so I suspect this one shall as well."

Eleanor smiled at herself in the mirror. She wondered if Lord Rockberry had been invited. If she had her way, tonight would be the night that he got his comeuppance.

Chapter 7

*Eleanor has accepted my invitation. I've prom-
ised to send a carriage 'round for her at half past
eight. Send word if you'd rather do the honors.*

—F

Swindler had known Frannie would win Eleanor over. To the lad who'd delivered the message, he simply said, "Tell her I'll see to it."

He then sent word to Claybourne that he needed
to borrow his carriage for the night, knowing full
well that Claybourne would use his coach to arrive
at the ball. He always escorted his wife around in
the coach, because it was grander and worthy of
the lady he loved.

Swindler then took great care in preparing
himself for the evening. While he'd have preferred
that his friends leave him behind, he'd known

they wouldn't and that sooner or later he would be invited to one of their grand social events. So, months ago, he'd visited one of the better tailors in London.

Now he stood before the mirror admiring the cut of the black swallow-tailed jacket, hunter green silk brocade waistcoat, pleated white shirt, and white cravat. He wasn't quite as rough-looking as usual. If he was honest with himself, he'd have to admit he looked quite elegant. He'd fit in nicely with the lords who'd be strutting about. He didn't want to admit that he cared how Eleanor viewed him, that he didn't want to be seen as lacking in her eyes. He had little doubt that her dance card would fill up within minutes of her walking into the ballroom. Frannie was providing her with an opportunity to be seen, to be informally introduced into society. If she caught some young man's fancy, it might be enough to turn her attention away from Rockberry.

It was only as Swindler's hands began to ache that he looked down and realized that he'd balled them up into tight, punishing fists. He didn't want to think about her in the arms of another man, waltzing with him, smiling up at him, bestowing her smiles upon him, charming him with her laughter. While her father's title hadn't been hereditary, she was still part of the aristocracy. She had every right to expect some lord's son to favor her—a second son, a third son, even a tenth son of a second son would be more worthy of her than Swindler.

But the reality regarding his lack of a position didn't stop him from wanting her.

He'd sought to gain her trust in order to learn why she was obsessed with Rockberry and what she hoped to accomplish by shadowing him, and all he had managed to do was come to desire Eleanor as he'd never desired any woman—not even Frannie. He wanted Eleanor in his bed, his body pounding into hers, her cries echoing around him. He wanted the woman who smelled of roses and wasn't afraid to shower him with seductive smiles.

He jerked on his white gloves, understanding the wisdom in wearing them. If his bare skin were to touch hers, he wasn't certain he'd be able to control himself. He was growing damned tired of his duty, of this assignment. He'd learned nothing of any value to Scotland Yard. He knew only that each moment spent in Eleanor's presence was both heaven and hell.

Perhaps tonight he'd put duty aside, put his own needs, wants, and desires first. In so doing, perhaps he'd discover if the young lady was as aware of him as a man as he was of her as a woman. And finally gain what he'd been searching for all along: the reason behind her interest in Rockberry.

Once he had that, perhaps he could give her another reason to stay in London.

It was the most exquisite gown to ever touch her skin. Even the two gowns her father had paid handsomely to have made for Elisabeth paled in comparison. As she stared at her reflection in the cheval glass, with her hair pinned up and adorned with a diamond tipped hairpin her father had given her, she thought she'd never looked more beautiful.

Vanity was a tool of the devil, she knew that well enough, but she seemed unable to help herself. If it wasn't for the fact that tears would ruin the entire affect, she would have wept. She'd wanted desperately to have a Season, to attend a ball. She wasn't deserving of this night and yet she couldn't turn away from it.

She picked up the small matching purse that she'd found in the box. It seemed the duchess had thought of everything. Little wonder James thought so highly of her, referred to her as a little mother.

James. She never should have begun to think of him as anything other than Mr. Swindler.

James created a sense of intimacy that should have been forbidden between them, and yet it seemed so right. She couldn't explain what she was feeling where he was concerned. Intrigued, charmed, infatuated. She longed for his kisses and his touch. Elisabeth had written about wantonness that had led to her downfall.

And now she feared she was traveling the same path.

Before she could convince herself that she should stay in tonight, she hurried out of her rooms. At the top of the stairs she heard a deep masculine voice floating up. She would have recognized it anywhere, from a thousand miles away. Her body went languid, because she knew he'd come for her.

When she reached the bottom of the stairs, his gaze shot past Mrs. Potter to settle on her. His eyes darkened and his nostrils flared. She could see the deep satisfaction reflected in his eyes, along with a bit of possessiveness. Any other woman might have taken offense, might have resented the implication that she belonged to him—but how could she resent what she knew was true, at least for tonight?

He was so remarkably handsome in his black swallowtail jacket. Looking at him dressed as he was, no one would question his origins, no one would even consider for a single moment that he wasn't a gentleman of the highest order. He possessed such confidence. He might have been disgusted by his origins, but tonight they were no-where to be seen. Standing before her was a man who'd risen from the gutter, and nothing on earth would ever send him back to the filth.

And judging by the heat smoldering in his beautiful green eyes, he wanted her desperately. She couldn't deny that she wanted him in equal measure.

"Oh, I say, you look lovely," Mrs. Potter said, breaking the spell.

She felt the heat creep along her cheeks, but her eyes never left him. "Thank you."

"I have something for you," he rasped, his voice husky, the way she imagined a man who'd only just awakened from a night of passionate love-making might sound. He extended a velvet box toward her.

Without even opening it, she said, "Oh, I can't accept something like that."

"You don't even know what it is yet."

"It looks to be jewelry. It would be improper."

"It's not for you to keep, only for you to borrow."

"Is it from the Duchess of Greystone?"

His mouth curled up into a teasing smile. "It can be if it'll make it easier for you to open."

Laughter almost erupted from her, because she could tell that he thought she was being silly. What did it matter who it came from? Only it did. Especially if it came from him, if it was his thoughtfulness. Her hand was trembling as she took the box, opened the lid, and stared at the beautiful string of pearls.

"I thought it possible that you might not have jewelry to wear tonight," he said quietly.

"I can't accept this," she repeated.

"As I said, it's only a loan. A lady shouldn't attend a ball without her pearls, should she, Mrs. Potter?"

"I daresay she should not." Her landlady stepped forward and smiled kindly. "It's a special night, Miss Watkins. I can see no harm in it."

Before she'd even agreed, James was taking the necklace from the box. His hands were bare, no doubt so his fingers could better control the clasp. His warm flesh brushed along her sensitive neck, causing heated desire to pool throughout her. She thought if she were a candle, she'd most assuredly melt into a molten pool of wax.

He withdrew his hands and said, "Just as I thought. They're as perfect as you are."

Sidestepping around him, she went to the mirror in the entryway. They *were* perfect, resting just above the hollow at her throat. She had this absurd need to weep. "I feel like a princess."

"Perhaps you are."

"I never pictured you as the fanciful sort, Mr. Swindler. I hardly know what to say for so precious a gift, even if it will only be mine for a few hours."

Suddenly, without making a sound, he was standing behind her, locking his gaze with hers in the mirror. "Reserve a dance for me."

"You may have them all."

"That, sweetheart, would create a scandal."

An emotion flickered over his face too quickly for her to accurately read it, but if she had to guess, it seemed something about his words bothered him, and she wondered if it was the endearment, if it had slipped out with his giving it no thought, and he wasn't entirely comfortable with it.

"We should be off," he said, as though he'd decided he needed to put distance between them.

"Enjoy yourself, Miss Watkins," Mrs. Potter said. "And Mr. Swindler, tell your sister that next time she simply must come in as well."

As he ushered her through the door, he said, "Thank you, Mrs. Potter, I will. As I said, she's a bit shy."

Once they were outside, she said, "I didn't realize you had a sister."

"I don't. But neither did I want Mrs. Potter to think you were traveling in the carriage without a chaperone."

"What will you tell people at the ball?"

"I don't think anyone will ask. Frannie is taking you under her wing, and she's married to one of the most powerful lords in Great Britain. You could walk in wearing not a stitch of clothing and they'd all compliment you on your gown."

The laughter bubbling up from her throat served to calm her nerves. She was scared to death of making a fool of herself tonight. But it occurred to her that with James by her side, she could get through anything.

As the carriage rattled to a stop, a footman standing in the drive opened the door and assisted her out. James quickly followed, put his hand beneath her elbow and escorted her toward the grand residence. Carriages were dropping off other couples and they were strolling more quickly toward the open doors.

But she wanted to take her time, to absorb every facet of the night.

"It's almost like a palace, isn't it?" she whispered.

"A little too large for my tastes," James said.

She peered up at him. "I quite agree, but still I don't mind visiting."

He led her through the double open doors into the entry hallway where the massive chandelier glittered. A footman took her pelisse and James's hat, then directed them toward the parlor.

"But everyone else is going up the stairs," she said quietly to James.

"It's all right. We're special."

In the parlor, a dark-haired gentleman and lovely blond-haired lady stepped forward. "Ah, you must be Eleanor," the lady said. "I'm Lady Catherine and this is my husband, Lord Claybourne."

The gentleman pressed a kiss to the back of her gloved hand. "A pleasure."

"James has told me about you," she said to Lord Claybourne.

"Not too much I hope."

She couldn't imagine that this man had grown up on the streets. Nobility was evident in his bearing.

"I didn't tell her anything to make her think less of you," James said.

"Then the conversation about me must have been rather short," Claybourne said with a grin.

"Frannie told us you were coming," Lady Catherine said. "We didn't think Jim would provide you with a chaperone so we shall serve in that role, if you've no objections. No sense in starting gossip straightaway."

"I would be honored."

"Let's go, then, shall we?"

Nodding, she thought of the distant cousin with no real connections who'd brought Elisabeth to London. How different things might have been had a countess stood at her sister's side.

"I daresay, you and Jim make a lovely couple," the countess said quietly as she led the way up the sweeping stairs, with the gentlemen following.

Heat warmed her cheeks, and she could think of no adequate reply.

"I'm sorry if I've embarrassed you," the countess said. "Jim is a dear friend. I'm most pleased to see him happy."

"He's unlike anyone I've ever met."

"Most of these scoundrels are."

"Scoundrels?"

She laughed lightly. "It's how I think of my husband and his friends. They've become respectable, but a small bit of being a scoundrel remains to them. Don't let it alarm you. It can come in quite handy at times."

Halfway up, they turned onto a landing that ended at the large ballroom. People were waiting in line to be introduced.

Her heart pounded as she looked over the elegant ladies and handsome gentlemen. They all seemed so confident, so comfortable—smiling, talking, and laughing. Anticipating the night.

"You're as good as any of them," James murmured near her ear.

Turning to smile up at him, she nodded. "I can't imagine an entire Season of this."

"I think it would grow tedious rather quickly."

She shook her head. "No, I think each night would be wonderful."

As they approached the door, Catherine spoke to a man there. He nodded. Then his voice boomed out, "Lord and Lady Claybourne, Miss Eleanor Watkins, Mr. James Swindler!"

She looked out over the grand ballroom and thought she'd never seen anything so magnificent in her life. Coming from a small village, she thought it was almost like stepping into a dream. Little wonder Elisabeth had fallen for Rockberry's charms.

As she glided down the steps, she was grateful to have a woman of experience beside her. At the bottom of the stairs, Catherine greeted their host and hostess.

"Frannie, Sterling, I hope you're pleased with everything."

"Dear sister," the duke said, "I never had any doubts you would provide us with a night to remember. And this must be Miss Watkins. My wife enjoyed visiting with you this afternoon. It's a pleasure to have you in our home."

She curtsied. "It's a pleasure to be here, Your Grace." She turned to the duchess. "Your Grace, thank you so much for the loan of the gown."

"You're welcome to keep it. I have far too many. And who knows? After tonight you might have need of it again."

"You're most generous."

"Enjoy yourself."

"Oh, I will."

Looking back, she met James's gaze and saw in his green eyes that this night was hers, all hers. As Catherine escorted her away, she suddenly found herself being introduced to one gentleman after another.

Unlike Elisabeth, she would not be a wallflower. In spite of the marvels and excitement that surrounded her, she felt a moment of sadness that her sister had not experienced anything near this much attention. Then all her sorrow floated away as the first gentleman escorted her to the dance area.

Swindler had yet to dance with Eleanor. From the moment she'd walked down the stairs into the grand salon, she'd captured everyone's imagination and attention. Not that he could blame them for being fascinated by her. The gown she wore accentuated every curve. He desperately desired the opportunity to put his hands on her waist, draw her near.

He snatched a flute of champagne from one of the passing footmen and downed it in one swallow.

"Preparing to go into battle?"

Giving Claybourne a sharp glare, he gratefully accepted the tumbler of scotch he offered and tossed it back as easily as he had the champagne.

"Easy there, Jim, you look as though you're on the verge of killing someone. You'd best slow down. You know the liquor only serves to make you angrier."

Swindler had always admired Claybourne the most of all of Feagan's lads. Perhaps because his origins had been the upper crust of society, he'd never appeared to really belong with Feagan's motley gang of thieves. "I'm not angry."

"You're giving a good imitation."

Claybourne was almost as tall as Swindler, but he had a slender, aristocratic build. He was also the only person, other than Frannie, who Swindler truly trusted. "I didn't expect all the gents to be fawning over her."

"Why not? She's a beautiful woman."

Truer words were never spoken.

"Your anger is preventing you from seeing the

situation clearly," Claybourne said somberly, handing Swindler his own tumbler of scotch.

Swindler hurled the liquid to the back of his throat, relishing the slow burn that spread through his chest. "I said I'm not angry."

"Jealous, then."

Bloody hell. Swindler nodded. "Mayhaps."

"She has no interest in any of the other gents."

Swindler released a scornful scoff. "How can she not? She may be at the lower end of it, but this is her world. She's danced with a duke, two marquesses, four earls, and so damned many second sons that I've lost count."

"I didn't think you knew that many in the nobility."

"I was standing near when they were lining up like paupers hoping for a bowl of gruel. Worst of all, she danced with Dodger, no doubt the wealthiest man in all of London."

"He's also very happily married."

"God, those are words I never thought I'd hear strung together when talking about him." He wanted another gulp of scotch, whiskey, rum, gin. It didn't matter as long as it had the ability to burn away this powerful torment that had wrapped itself around him.

"And why hasn't she danced with you?"

Swindler held his tongue. Claybourne elbowed

him in the ribs. "Because you haven't asked?"

"I wanted tonight to be special for her. Her sister had the opportunity to come to London and Eleanor didn't. I wanted to give this to her."

"She's not enjoying dancing with the other men, you know. Have you not noticed the way her gaze never stays on them long? Or how it darts around the room as though she's searching for someone? Her smile is so frozen that her jaws must be aching. Ask her for a dance."

"Her dance card is probably filled."

"Wouldn't stop me if I wanted to dance with Catherine."

Normally it wouldn't have stopped Swindler either. What the devil was wrong with him? he wondered. Guilt over his deception. He should tell her the truth, but even as he thought the words, he knew everything between them would change as soon as they were uttered. Her affection for him would turn to loathing. Her interest in him would wither away like a rose plucked from the vine and left too long without water.

The final strains of a violin echoed into silence. Eleanor didn't even have to leave the dance floor as her next eager partner replaced the previous one.

Swindler handed the tumbler back to Claybourne and, without another word, strode through the crowd to the area where the dancers were just beginning to step in time to the music. He patted Lord Milner on the shoulder. The man looked as startled as he did when he was playing cards at Dodger's and was dealt a good hand. "Sorry, m'lord, but this one's mine."

If he'd been a larger man, Lord Milner might have challenged Swindler. Instead, he excused himself. Before the next beat of music sounded, Swindler had Eleanor in his arms and was sweeping her across the dance floor.

She'd waited the whole night for this moment. "What took you so long?"

He gave her a wry grin. "I wasn't certain you'd want to give up a dance with a lord for a man who has little to offer except two clumsy feet."

"You sell yourself short, James. You are quite the accomplished dancer."

"As are you, Eleanor."

They circled the dance floor as though no one else was upon it. It occurred to her that they were closer than was proper, but she didn't care.

Earlier one of her partners had mentioned that she reminded him of a lady he'd danced with last Season. He couldn't remember her name. Was it her? he'd asked. Sadness had swamped her because her sister had been in London and no one remembered her clearly. Just as she was certain no one would remember her tonight.

She was part of these people's lives for only a fleeting moment in time. Tomorrow night there would be other dance partners for them, while she would hold close the precious memories. And the one that was being created now with James would be the most precious of all—or at least of all the ones from the ball.

They hardly spoke. It was as though no words were needed between them. They conversed with a look, a squeeze of a hand, the brush of a thigh.

When the dance ended, he removed her dance card from her wrist, slipped it into his pocket, and claimed the next dance as his own. She didn't protest. It was what she wanted more than she wanted to breathe.

During their third dance he asked, "Will you save the last dance for me?"

"I'm perfectly fine with this being the last dance of the night."

"Are you ready to go home?" he asked.

"No," she said, wondering where the sultriness in her voice had come from. "But I am ready to leave with you."

When the music ended, they said good-night to their host and hostess. Outside the air was cool. While he draped her pelisse over her shoulders, it was his nearness more than the cloth that warmed her.

As they settled into the carriage, he said, feigning surprise, "Well I wonder where my sister has gone off to. Whatever will happen between us without a chaperone?"

She cradled his face with her gloved hands. "It is my hope, James, that we'll kiss."

As the carriage rolled away, she found her hope being realized as he crushed his mouth against hers, and she parted her lips to receive what he offered. Once again she was amazed by his taste, but tonight it was different. No meat pie. Rather, it was rich and smooth and decidedly dark. Not champagne. He'd had something else to drink, something strong, something that would appeal to a man. Whatever it was, she liked it—enjoyed the flavor on his tongue as it stroked hers.

His arms stole around her back and hips, and she found herself being pulled onto his lap. Almost immediately the angle of the kiss shifted and deepened, as though he was intent on touching her heart. How was she to tell him that he already had, in so many small ways, like a ball made up of scraps of yarn that came together to create an intriguing whole? The loan of the pearls, the fireworks, the drives through London. Conversations and waltzes. An invitation to a ball. She'd come to London with a goal, and he'd slowly worked his way into her life until she had a difficult time remembering what her plans had been.

Selfishly, to her everlasting guilt, Rockberry seemed insignificant when compared with what she might have if she turned her focus away from the vile man.

James's heated mouth trailed along the curve of her jaw, then journeyed over her throat, leaving a damp mist in its wake. Her pelisse fell away from her shoulders, baring them to him. Without hesitation, he began to nibble on the exposed skin. His teeth gently nipped her collarbone, before his tongue tenderly apologized.

Squirming on his lap, she pressed her legs together, relishing the tiny tremors of pleasure that seemed to originate there and spread outward. She'd never experienced anything like this. It was as though by touching her in one place, he had the ability to create that touch over her entire body. Everything wanted to curl into itself, tighten and expand.

His harsh breathing echoed through the confines of the carriage as his large hands traveled over her. She felt the hardness of him bulging against her hip. His raspy groans filled her ears before he returned his mouth to hers with a hunger that exceeded her own.

She had no doubt that he desired her, that he was hers to command, that she was his to treasure.

The carriage came to a halt, and he released a low groan as he tore his mouth from hers and pressed his forehead against hers. She knew she should have moved off him, was certain he knew he should have pushed her away.

But instead they clung to each other, as though they were both drowning in a tumultuous sea. Even when the footman opened the door, James didn't loosen his hold.

"Give us a moment," he ground out hoarsely.

The door immediately closed, blocking out the world that required chaperones and propriety, enclosing them in their own world where behavior was dictated by them.

"It's been the most magical night of my life," she whispered, her heart pounding so hard that she was certain he could hear it. "I don't want it to end, not here, not like this."

He drew back, and in the shadowy confines of the carriage, she felt more than saw his gaze wandering over her face as though he was searching for an explanation of her words. "What are you saying, Eleanor?"

"I want to stay the night with you."

Chapter 8

He knew it was a terribly bad idea, even as
he ushered her into his lodging house and
up the stairs to his rooms. But he wanted her too
desperately, and even if he was compromising his
integrity, he didn't give a damn. He'd have a talk
with Sir David and make everything right in the
morning, work things out to the satisfaction of
Scotland Yard and Lord Rockberry.

The hood of Eleanor's pelisse hid her face. Swindler was not in the habit of bringing young misses
to his lodgings, although his landlady was accustomed to him keeping late hours. She seldom
stirred from her bed when he arrived home. Tonight, thank God, was no exception.

With his key, he quickly unlocked the door to
his apartment and ushered Eleanor into the room.
Barely taking the time to close and lock the door
behind him, he pulled her into his arms. God help
him, he'd never wanted a woman so desperately,

had never wanted to feel her body pressed against his, had never wanted to drink so passionately from her mouth. She'd only just entered the room, and already her rose scent was taking up residence, mingling with the more earthly scented cologne he used so sparingly.

Her mouth eagerly opening to his, she intertwined her arms around him like a rose seeking out its place on a trellis. No coyness, no doubts, simply need and desire spurring her on. He banished his own doubts that he was ruining her. If she was so willing to give him tonight, she could quite possibly give him more. Where they would take this was a discussion for another time. For now, all that mattered was that everything that had been building inside him since he first kissed her in Cremorne Gardens was about to be brought to fruition.

If he could just hold on, just hold his own needs in check. He wouldn't allow her first time to be tainted by his inability—

His mind came to a staggering stop, as did the kiss. He always gave ladies his attention, but tonight he wanted to give her more than he'd ever given to anyone, because she meant more to him than anyone else ever had. With nimble fingers that had never served him well as a pickpocket, he quickly loosened the fastenings on her pelisse.

In the darkness, he heard the whisper of it pooling at her feet.

Tearing off his gloves, he tossed them toward a nearby chair, but based on the thud, they'd landed on the parquet. The faintest light from the street eased shyly into the room, silhouetting them, providing no details. Now, he thought, now with the darkness providing its own haven, he should explain to her how he'd come to be in her life. He should tell her that he'd see to Rockberry, that he would ensure the man paid for whatever he'd done to Elisabeth. He would be her champion. Even as he considered that now was the time to reveal all, he wanted nothing to detract from this moment. Later he would tell her everything, after he'd spoken with Sir David, once he'd set things into motion.

But tonight was just for them. He didn't want Elisabeth or Rockberry or Sir David invading this moment, becoming part of this memory. Just as that night at Cremorne Gardens when she'd not wanted to discuss the past, so now he selfishly and greedily wanted this moment to focus on the present, on them, on what they could share with each other. Gently, he cradled her cheek. "It's not too late if you've changed your mind."

He'd very likely expire on the spot, but he had never forced a woman, and he wasn't about to start now, especially with her.

He could see her sweet smile. "I haven't. Have you?"

Laughing, he swept her into his arms and strode into his bedchamber. "Never. I've wanted you since that first afternoon in the park."

"You've shown remarkable restraint."

"You've no idea."

He set her down beside the bed, before turning to the bedside table and striking a match. The wick of the lamp flared to life.

"Wouldn't darkness serve better?" she asked.

"No." But he turned down the flame until it allowed in enough shadows to provide the intimacy he thought she required.

"Your bed is so large. I've never seen one like it." He heard the nervousness in her voice.

"I had it made especially for me to accommodate my height. But it's only a bed, Eleanor, and nothing will happen within it that you don't desire."

He detected the tiniest of flinches. With both hands, he cupped her face to draw her attention back to him. "I won't hurt you."

"I know. I trust you implicitly, James. More than I've ever trusted anyone."

He brought his mouth back to hers and kissed her deeply. Tasting the lingering flavor of champagne, he prayed the heady drink wasn't affecting her decision. But she wasn't swaying, not yet anyway. If he had his way, she would before long. She'd become drunk on his kisses, on his touches.

He dragged his mouth along her throat, feeling her pulse quickening against his lips. With a sigh and her hands clutching the sleeves of his jacket, she dropped her head back, giving him easier access to whatever he might wish to plunder. Her hair first, he thought, as he straightened. He skimmed his knuckles down the column of her throat. "You have the most enticing neck."

"Is it my best feature, do you think?"

"A little vain, Eleanor?"

Her brow pleated. "No, I just . . . I'm nervous, I suppose. I don't want you to be disappointed."

"There is absolutely nothing about you that could disappoint me."

He saw in her eyes the pleasure that his words brought. It was only the first bit of pleasure he intended to bring her. After deftly removing her pins, he watched her hair cascade around her shoulders and tumble down her back. It was more glorious than it had appeared at a distance. He almost confessed about the night he'd watched her brushing it in the window, but then he'd have to explain why he'd been outside her lodgings. He didn't want anything to distract her from his attentions.

He took her hand and began to peel her glove down her arm until it was bunched at her wrist.

His thumb grazed her pulse there and he felt it jumping beneath his touch. She watched him, and he wondered what she was searching for, hoped she could see how very much he treasured these moments with her.

"I could do that," she whispered, her voice a rough rasp.

"It's my pleasure to do it." He tugged on each finger until they were all free enough that he could finish removing her glove. Tossing it away haphazardly, he skimmed his fingers over her hand.

"The glove belongs to the Duchess of Greystone. I should take more care with it," she said.

"She won't mind. I'll purchase her new ones if need be."

He began working to remove the other glove. With the bared hand, she touched his cheek, skimmed her fingers up into his hair. It was the first time she'd stroked him with a bare hand. Although it was only his face, his hair, his scalp, a shudder of pleasure coursed through him. He wanted her touch so badly. Everywhere. He discarded the second glove with equal abandon.

Very slowly he turned her around.

She'd not expected him to take his time, but then where he was concerned, she had quickly learned that he was a constant surprise. He made her feel lovely, desired. She saw in his eyes that even something as simple as letting her hair down pleased him.

Now he moved it so it all draped over one shoulder. Then he began to work on her gown. She felt the first button set free, then the second. She tried to remember how many buttons there were, how long it might take before the gown was removed completely. Before she'd finished the thought, he was easing it off her shoulders.

He touched his mouth to her neck, and it was as though he'd poured hot wax into her veins. Warmth swirled through her.

She knew she was wrong to be here, to take matters this far, but Elisabeth's death had taught her that one never knew when everything of value could be stolen. James was hers for tonight. She had no promises that he'd be hers tomorrow.

Happiness was fleeting. Love an illusion.

She would make the most of what time she had with him, cherish it, pray that she never came to regret it.

She pushed back thoughts of Elisabeth and Rockberry. For this small space of time, she wanted no sorrow to intrude, no quest for retribution. Selfishly, she was going to take all that James offered her and hoard it away for the lonely nights that would no doubt await her.

Leisurely, so leisurely that her skin grew more

sensitive, he removed cotton, silk, lace. He untied ribbons, loosened buttons, eased aside cloth. Each piece was discarded without care, until nothing remained except for the pearls, while his fingers gave the greatest care and attention to her skin. His mouth followed his fingers, touching and tasting, stirring passions until she thought she'd go mad with wanting more.

Pivoting around to face him, she judged his reaction, hoping he wasn't disappointed that she wasn't acting demure. She wanted this night with him, wanted it so badly she would trade her soul for it. No doubt she already had.

His breathing became short and shallow as his gaze took a leisurely sojourn from the top of her head to her wiggling toes.

"You're so beautiful." His voice was scratchy and rough, his eyes heated, his craggy features now so familiar and yet tonight so different, as though each part of her somehow managed to re-shape him.

"We should put away the pearls lest they break," she told him.

"No, leave them. They somehow suit this moment."

She was surprised that he ceased to touch her. "I won't break," she assured him as she tugged on his neckcloth.

"My hands are callused."

"I like the way they feel," she said, taking one and bringing it to her lips. She circled her tongue around its center and he released a low strangled groan.

"You torment me," he rasped.

To her surprise, she released a short burst of laughter. "Me? I'm not the one still wearing clothes."

He rewarded her with one of his rare, sensual smiles as his jacket was added to her pile of clothes. His waistcoat and shirt followed, then everything else, until all that remained were his trousers. He was magnificent. Sculpted stone could not have contained or revealed more perfection.

Running her hands up his chest, she felt his muscles bunch and relax as she journeyed over them. For his size, he was all lean muscle and flesh. Stepping closer to him, she brushed her breasts against his chest.

"Christ!" he growled as he took her mouth with an urgency that surprised her.

Swindler had waited as long as possible to actually touch her, knowing that once he did so, this slow waltz would end. He would no longer be able to restrain himself. He wanted her too badly.

Her arms came around his sides, caressed his back, the touch so light, but fleeting. He would feel her touch and then he wouldn't. It was a strange sensation of touch, then absence. He'd never let any other woman glide her hands over his back. He always distracted them one way or another, often simply holding their hands away from his body. But with her, he wanted to experience everything, was willing to risk losing it all, because he didn't want her in half measures. He couldn't explain it, but he wanted to know everything about her, down to her tiniest secret and her smallest imperfection. For some reason, it was important that she know his.

Stiffening, she broke away from the kiss, her face set into a frown. "What's happened here?"

"It's nothing."

He didn't stop her when she peered around him.

"Oh, dear God." Looking at the crisscross of scars on his back, she felt the tears well in her eyes. "Who did this to you?"

"The law."

Straightening back up, she studied him, truly looked at him, past the handsome exterior to the wounded man.

"I wasn't very skilled at thievery," he explained. "Usually I got the whip rather than time in prison."

"How old were you?" she whispered, not certain

why that particular fact was important. What he'd endured shouldn't have been inflicted on anyone.

"Eight the first time, nine the second. Feagan warned me that if I got caught once more, I'd see myself on a ship bound for New Zealand."

"Transported." She'd never before given any thought to the punishment criminals received. Oh, she'd heard about it, but it was like listening to someone explaining the plot in a story that she had no interest in reading. It was simply words, without soul, without heart. "I'm so sorry."

"Don't be. They don't hurt. The thickest of them don't feel anything anymore." He touched her cheek. "I've never shared them with anyone else. I've never let any woman touch them. You're different. What I feel for you is different. I don't want any secrets between us."

She almost wept from the sincerity in his voice. If he hadn't pulled her into his arms and kissed her, she might have told him everything about Elisabeth, but she knew if she did that, the kiss would cease, and she wanted it more than she wanted to draw in breath, more than she wanted revenge.

They tumbled onto the bed, a tangle of arms and legs, the action breaking them apart, ending the kiss.

"You still have your trousers on," she told him, as though he wasn't aware of the fact that she was completely unclothed and bared to him while he still retained a modicum of modesty.

"I fear if I remove my trousers that any control I'm presently exhibiting will go with them."

She pressed her hands to either side of his face, her thumbs against his lips. "Remove them."

"Eleanor . . . " He gave her a sardonic twist of his lips. "I'm not sure you know exactly what it is I'm controlling."

"You want to make love to me desperately, and without your trousers there's nothing to stop you."

"Exactly."

"I want to make love to you desperately as well. Remove them."

Before she'd finished taking her next breath they were gone, leaving her to worry if she'd ever be able to breathe again. He was large in all things, her James.

His bare body covered hers as he slid between her thighs, and she thought she'd never felt anything as wonderful. His skin was slick and velvety in places, coarse and hairy in others, but she adored every inch, every texture.

Once more he joined his mouth to hers. She thought she'd never tire of his kisses. Each one was different, yet the same. Each one caused desire to build inside her.

His weight bore down on her, but there was no discomfort. In spite of their sizes, her delicacy and his large muscled body, it was as though they fit together perfectly.

With his touches, he was much more daring than she. He trailed his mouth down her body until he reached her breast. He kissed the inside of one and then the other. Her body reacted strongly, straining for more. He lathed his tongue around her nipple, teasing, teasing, teasing . . .

She scraped her nails over his shoulders while her body curled into itself.

"What do you want, Eleanor?" he rasped.

"Don't talk, please don't talk."

"What do you want?" he persisted.

She wanted to weep, as his breath wafted over her nipple until it tightened into a pebble. "I don't know. Something."

"This," he growled, before his mouth closed over her breast and he began to suckle.

She thought she was going to come off the bed, like a hot air balloon breaking free of its moorings. She twisted into him, bucked against him.

His hand skimmed along her stomach until it reached her nest of curls. She felt his finger slip inside her, deep inside her.

"You're so wet, so hot, so ready," he whispered.

And she was. Almost as ready as he. Every

muscle in his body was tense and vibrating. His heart pounded so hard that he thought it might actually burst. He loved having her beneath him, the silkiness of her skin, the velvetiness of her womanhood. He wanted her so badly that it was a testament to his control that he'd not yet taken possession. As his finger glided into her, he felt the tightness.

"I may hurt you after all," he murmured with regret.

"I don't care." She skimmed her hands over his chest and back, as though she couldn't get enough of touching him.

Every place she touched mourned when she moved on to give her attentions elsewhere. His body was screaming at him, screaming for him to have her now. To take her.

She was wet, so very wet. Hot, so very hot.

He wished he'd considered this moment, but he'd never before taken a virgin. He should have plied her with whiskey.

Too late now. He shifted up so he was hovering above her.

She thought she should have been afraid, but she wasn't. Whatever discomfort she felt, she knew it was nature's doing, not his. He'd prepared her with his hands and his mouth, his fingers and his tongue.

She felt him probing gently. Fighting not to tense, she concentrated on the feel of his shoulders beneath her hands, the dew that had gathered as he denied his satisfaction, the bunching of his muscles as he prepared to join them together.

As he entered her, there was pain. She couldn't deny it, and she could tell by the sorrow that touched his eyes that she'd done a poor job of masking it. His arms trembling, he stilled when she knew he wanted to break free of the moorings and fly.

"I'm all right," she assured him.

"I'm in no rush." He lowered his head and kissed one corner of her mouth—

"Liar."

—and then the other.

"We have time," he assured her.

Not as much as he might think.

She wiggled beneath him. Kissing her chin, he slowly began rocking against her. The pain began to ease as though her body, after stretching to accommodate him, was adjusting to his welcomed arrival. Other sensations began to replace the ache. She began to concentrate on those as they began to drown out all others.

He was like the sea, so strong as it crashed against the shore, so calm as it retreated with a promise to return. A promise he kept, returning over and over, slamming forcefully into her, carrying her up toward the highest crest of the waves. It was glorious, riding out the storm of pleasures with him. Sensations swirled and spiraled.

When they crested, she dug her fingers into his buttocks and arched her back to meet him. She'd never known anything so powerful, so arousing, so incredibly wonderful. Until he began to move faster, jerkily, his groans echoing around her. She hung onto him, watching the muscles in his face contort.

"Eleanor!" he ground out through clenched teeth as his body spasmed and one last thrust, if at all possible, struck more deeply than any of the others.

Collapsing on top of her, his breathing harsh, he pressed a kiss to her shoulder before rolling over and drawing her against his side.

It had been the most meaningful experience of her life, yet all she wanted to do was weep.

Chapter 9

Absently, Swindler glided his hand up and down Eleanor's arm. Never in his life had he experienced anything as intensely satisfying. Eleanor had touched him more intimately than any other woman. Pleasure had rocked her with a force that astounded him—and if he were honest, stroked his masculine pride.

She was so easily aroused and not at all afraid to share what she was feeling, experiencing, thinking. While he'd enjoyed the company of many ladies, with Eleanor he sensed there was no guile between them. Her reactions were all honest, her cries all heartfelt. She was unlike any woman he'd ever known. He didn't want her to leave his bed.

She would have to in a few more hours, before the sun rose, before anyone was up to see her leave his lodgings and arrive at her own. They'd had an illicit night, but nothing about it had seemed forbidden. If anything, it felt like the most natural thing in the world. They belonged together, she and he. After what they'd shared, he no longer had any doubts.

For several minutes now she'd been slowly skimming her finger down the center of his chest and back up again. Occasionally she would trace a figure eight around his nipples. She might be recovering, not truly trying to arouse him, but his body was reacting just the same.

"What are you thinking?" he finally asked.

"About Elisabeth. I'm wondering if this was what Rockberry had promised her, or at the very least what she'd expected."

"Did he get her with babe?"

"No, I don't think so. If he did, it wasn't obvious from looking at her. She arrived home in July and fell from the cliffs in September. Surely she would have shown by then."

He didn't want to talk of her sister, as it would dampen the mood or her memories of this night. Once he talked with Sir David and confirmed a plan of action, he'd pay her a visit and explain not only what he'd been doing the night he met her but how he planned to take the situation in hand to gain satisfaction for her regarding Rockberry. But until then he wanted nothing to sour what they'd shared, and had little doubt that her initial reaction to the fact that he'd been following her was not going to be well received.

He didn't want her to throw what he was certain would be a horrendous tantrum in his lodgings. Nor in hers. Finding an appropriate place was going to be a bit of a bother. And he was certain a tantrum would be forthcoming. Ladies tended to look unfavorably on gentlemen who'd not been honest in their dealings with them—even when the dishonesty wasn't their choice.

"Do you remember Cremorne Gardens when you confessed that you didn't want the night ruined by—"

"By talk of the past?"

"Yes."

"I shouldn't let it ruin this night either." She pressed a kiss to his chest, and he immediately hardened.

They lay in silence for several moments, simply absorbing the nearness of each other. He wondered how he was going to manage without her in his bed—in his life, for that matter. She was still aristocratic by birth. Surely she'd realized at the ball that she could find a good match in London. He'd been selfish to so willingly pounce on her words when she indicated that she wanted to spend the night in his arms.

"I hate the scars on your back," she said softly.

His gut clenched and tightened. He'd kept them from everyone except her—and Frannie, who'd tended them. "I know they're hideous."

"No. No, they're not." She rose up on her elbows and held his gaze. "They're a testament to your . . . ability to survive. You could have ended up like your father—hanged."

He didn't think his gut could clench any tighter. He was wrong. "If we're not going to talk about your past, I'd rather not talk about mine."

With a nod of acquiescence, she laid her head in the center of his chest. "I can hear your heart beat. I like the sound of it."

"It always beats faster when you're near."

She dug her chin into his breastbone.

"Ouch!"

"Don't feed me false flattery, Mr. Swindler."

"I never would, Miss Watkins."

She reached up and nipped his chin. He liked this playful side of her. Her character possessed so many different facets that he thought he needed a lifetime to study them all.

"Your rooms surprised me," she said. "Especially your bedchamber. I was expecting something a bit more . . . decadent from a self-professed scoundrel."

"What did you have in mind? Perhaps I can accommodate."

She wrinkled her nose. "I don't know. Something a bit more . . . red."

"Brown suits me."

"It doesn't stand out."

"I'm not one for wanting to stand out. Besides, I have the one thing in my bedchamber that every disreputable scoundrel must have."

Her brow furrowed in concentration, she glanced around the room: at the bureau, at the chair, at the pile of clothes. "I can't imagine what it might be."

He gave her a teasing grin. "A lovely woman he can't keep his hands off of."

She released a tiny screech as he rolled her over until she was beneath him.

"Besides, Miss Watkins, what I have in my bedchamber isn't nearly as important as what I *do* in it."

Then he proceeded to take them both to paradise.

The sun was only just beginning to chase away the fog when he slipped her out of his lodgings. Thankfully, the carriage was still waiting for them. How wonderful it was that he had friends with the means to demand of their servants inconvenience.

As he assisted her inside and she settled on the bench, she fought not to have regrets. When his arm came around her, she buried her face in the nook of his shoulder, inhaling the wondrous fragrance that was him. And then she remembered his gift.

"Oh, I forgot the necklace. Will you help me remove it?"

"Take it. It's yours."

She jerked around to face him. "But you said it was on loan."

"I lied. I didn't think you would accept it otherwise."

"It's too grand a gift. It would be improper."

"Eleanor, we've just spent the entire night being improper. Don't be a hypocrite."

She fought not to show how the harshness in his voice had hurt her, but he must have guessed because his face gentled and he tucked his finger beneath her chin, forcing her to look at him. "I have no one in my life for whom I can purchase gifts, and money means nothing to me. Please accept them as a token of my esteem."

She shouldn't, she knew she shouldn't, but the truth was that she loved them. Touching her fingers to them, she said as graciously as possible, "Thank you."

"My pleasure."

They said not another word, but then the journey was short. A few streets over. It wasn't until he was standing before her at the door, his ungloved hand cradling her cheek, that he spoke again. "I want to call on you this evening."

She smiled at him and nodded.

"I know you have concerns," he said quietly, "because your sister came to London and fell into disgrace, but that will not be the way of it between us. I promise you that, Eleanor. We have known each other only a short while, but what I feel for you cannot be measured."

The hot tears burned her eyes.

He leaned down and kissed the corner of each eye. "Until tonight."

Taking her key, he opened the door and ushered her inside. He didn't follow her in. Simply closed the door. She leaned against it, listening to the clatter of hooves and the whirring of wheels taking him farther and farther away from her.

Swindler decided to take advantage of having Claybourne's carriage. He'd send it back later. For now he had matters that needed his attention. He returned to his lodgings, where he took care in preparing himself to meet with Sir David. He didn't want to give any evidence of what his night had entailed. However, in the early hours of the morning while Eleanor had lain in his arms, he'd decided it was time to put this nonsense to rest.

When he walked into Sir David's office, he didn't give the man the opportunity to say anything other than "Swindler" before he began explaining where he thought matters needed to go.

"I'm quite convinced that Miss Eleanor Watkins is no threat to Rockberry. If anything, the man, himself, is the culprit. I intend to confront him this morning and ask him exactly why he believes Miss Watkins would want him dead, I intend to interrogate him thoroughly in order to determine precisely what he did to Miss Watkins's sister. There, sir, is where I believe the crime resides, and I intend to get to the bottom of it."

Sir David leaned back in his chair, his face an uncompromising mask. "That might be a bit difficult, Swindler, since Rockberry was murdered last night."

Chapter 10

Staring at his superior, Swindler felt as though Sir David had delivered a blow to his midsection. Swindler had been charged with protecting the lord, and he'd apparently failed miserably. "Murdered? Are you sure?"

"I'm quite familiar with what a dead man looks like."

"No, sir, I wasn't questioning that he was dead, but perhaps his heart simply gave out."

"It did. After the dagger sliced into it. Your Miss Watkins has just been brought in."

"It can't have been her."

"I'm afraid it was. Rockberry's brother had apparently returned to the residence after a late night at the pleasure gardens, and he spied Miss Watkins going into the library. Sometime later, when he was in want of some brandy, he went to the library and found his brother soaking in his own blood, Miss Watkins nowhere to be seen."

The anger surged through Swindler. His father had been hanged for a crime he didn't commit. He would be damned before he allowed the same to happen to Eleanor. "He's lying. Miss Watkins was with me—until dawn."

Sir David's dark eyebrows shot up.

"I have little doubt Rockberry's brother killed him in order to inherit and is trying to place the blame on Miss Watkins," Swindler said. "He no doubt knew she'd been following Lord Rockberry, was probably aware that we'd been so informed. He sought to use the knowledge to his advantage."

"God, I do hope you're wrong about that. Her majesty is not going to be pleased to learn that her nobles are behaving badly."

"It's quite possible there is another explanation, but I assure you, Miss Watkins is not involved. From the moment I arrived at her lodgings to escort her to the Duchess of Greystone's ball, she never left my sight."

"You'll stake your reputation on that?"

"My life, sir."

As she sat at a table in the dismal room, she'd never been so terrified in her entire life. Two men had been waiting in the parlor for her. They'd emerged mere seconds after she heard the carriage depart. They'd had a warrant for her arrest, accusing her of murdering Rockberry.

While she'd proclaimed her innocence, they revealed not even a hint of believing her. Of course, she hadn't provided them with an alibi either, had refused to reveal where she'd been all night and why she was arriving with the dawn. She wasn't certain it was her place to do so, and considering the harsh glares they'd given her, she wasn't convinced they would have believed her anyway. They were stern-faced and harsh. They'd not even allowed her an opportunity to change out of her gown before whisking her away.

As soon as the opportunity arose, she'd send word to James. Surely he would speak for her.

The door suddenly opened and a familiar outline filled the doorway. With a gasp of recognition, she burst out of the chair, rushed across the room and flung herself against the man. His arms came around her, offering comfort and strength.

"Oh, my God, James. They think I killed Lord Rockberry."

"I know," he said quietly, in that deep, raspy voice that possessed such confidence. The man never doubted, never questioned his ability to handle any situation. "I've explained to Sir David that you can't have killed him, because you were with me . . . until dawn."

With a sense of dread shimmering through her, she jerked her head back and looked up into his eyes. She'd expected to see disgust or shame. Instead she saw concern, compassion, and caring. So much caring, as though he were revealing his heart.

"I know your reputation is now in tatters, but I decided better your reputation than your neck." As though to emphasize his point, he trailed his finger along the column of her throat, at the bottom of which rested the pearls he'd given her. In spite of her terror, she shivered in response.

She felt the tears well in her eyes. With his large hand, he cradled the back of her head and pressed her face against his sturdy chest, where she could hear the slow, steady pounding of his heart. Hers was fluttering like a bird fighting not to fall from the sky, and he remained so calm, so confident.

"Not to worry, Eleanor. I'll see that your reputation is not ruined for long."

The gentleness of his promise caused more tears to surface. She was going to be like an overturned bucket of water before long if he continued on with his understanding and kindness.

Tucking her against his side, beneath his arm, he said, "Let's get you home."

She reared back to stare at him. "Just like that? They're going to let me go?"

"You have one of the most respected inspectors of Scotland Yard vouching for you, Miss Watkins," she heard coming from the side, and turned to see one of the men who'd interrogated her earlier standing there. Sir David. He'd not been the one to come to her lodgings, but the one who marched into this room with such determination that her mouth had gone dry.

"Be quick about getting her settled, Swindler," Sir David said. "If she didn't kill Rockberry, we need to determine who did, and swiftly. After all, he is a lord of the realm. The queen will not be pleased with his demise."

"Yes, sir. I shall meet you at his residence as soon as I've seen Miss Watkins home."

The carriage they'd used last evening was waiting for them at the curb. She supposed he'd not had a chance to return it to his friend before he received word about Rockberry. James climbed into the coach after her and held her near.

"I've never been so terrified in my life," she said, her voice quaking. Even with him holding her, she seemed unable to stop shaking. "Why do you suppose they suspected me?"

"His brother was apparently in residence and claims he saw you arrive around midnight. Says

Rockberry joined you in the library. The brother went to bed, then decided he was in need of a drink. He claims he found Rockberry sprawled on the floor, a dagger to the heart. I suspect the brother is the culprit, lying through his teeth. He's not the first to kill in order to gain a title. He was aware that you were following Rockberry. Knew Scotland Yard knew. So he thought to use the knowledge to his advantage. Now I just need to prove it."

"Can you do that, do you think? Prove it was Rockberry's brother?"

"I have a reputation for solving murders. Once I've taken a look 'round Rockberry's, I should have a better sense of exactly what happened. Right now my assumptions are premature. I shouldn't have even revealed them to you. But I wanted you to know that you have no cause for worry." He brushed his lips over her temple. "Everything will be all right, Eleanor."

Her heart clenched and her chest tightened painfully. There was so much she wanted to tell this man, and so much she couldn't.

They traveled the remainder of the journey in silence, with her wrapped in the cocoon of his comforting embrace.

When they arrived at her lodgings, he handed her down. As they stood on the walk, he slipped his finger beneath her chin and tilted her head up. Then he gave her the gentlest of kisses, which made her want to begin weeping all over again.

When he drew back, he held her gaze. "I want you to rest for a bit, put all this behind you. I must see to Rockberry's murder. When I'm done there, I'll return to you." He gave her a tender smile. "Then we shall see to your reputation."

"James—"

"Shh, Eleanor." He touched his thumb to her lips. "I shall do right by you, my darling."

He ushered her inside, and although Mrs. Potter appeared to see to her needs, she felt instantly bereft when he departed. She slowly made her way to her room. Once there, all she wanted to do was curl up into a ball on the bed and weep.

Chapter 11

Swindler couldn't deny that relief swamped him when he stepped into Rockberry's library with Sir David and didn't smell Eleanor's familiar rose scent. While he knew it was impossible for her to have been there, to have committed the crime, something nagged at him. She'd been in his arms from the moment they departed Frannie's ball.

He wished he'd been here before the body was removed. It could have told him so much. But apparently when Sir David had come searching for him, he was still traveling through London with Eleanor, kissing her in the carriage before they'd decided to return to his lodgings.

Blood marred the carpet. Two wineglasses sat upon the side table. That bothered him.

"What time did you say you saw the lady

enter?" Swindler asked the new Lord Rockberry. Swindler had been surprised to discover that he was the blond-haired man who'd accosted Eleanor at Cremorne Gardens.

"A few minutes after midnight."

"And you're certain it was Miss Watkins?"

"Yes."

"The same Miss Watkins that you attacked at Cremorne?"

"I didn't attack her," he said impatiently. "My friends and I were going to have a bit of fun with her. I knew she was following my brother. He was none too pleased with the police not taking more effective action. Thought to scare her off."

"We have a witness who says Miss Watkins was with him last night," Sir David said.

"Then your witness is lying," the new Rockberry said with confidence.

Swindler and Sir David exchanged glances. He saw no doubt in Sir David's eyes. He'd not considered when he placed Eleanor's reputation at risk that he was also placing his own.

"I believe you have the right of it," Swindler said. "Someone is lying, but I suspect it's you."

"For what purpose?" the young Rockberry asked.

"To gain the title."

"Don't be daft, man. I didn't want this. It comes

with responsibilities, duties. My brother gave me a generous allowance, and I was a true gentleman of leisure. I cared nothing for the title."

"Why do you suppose Miss Watkins wanted to kill him?" Swindler asked.

"Something to do with her sister. My brother . . . as much as it pains me to say it—and I don't wish to speak ill of the dead—was not always kind to women."

"He took advantage of Elisabeth Watkins?"

"In all likelihood, yes."

"Thank you, my lord," Swindler said. "I have no further questions at this time."

After the marquess left, Sir David asked, "So what are you thinking, Swindler?"

"His brother had the most to gain, although I suppose it's possible there is another woman who was wronged and sought revenge. The new Lord Rockberry simply misidentified her."

"You're quite certain it wasn't Miss Watkins?"

"From the moment I first danced with her, near ten o'clock, she never left my arms."

"Before that?"

"Never left my sight."

"What time did you leave the ball?"

"Half past eleven."

"I do hope this nasty matter doesn't come down to your word against the new Rockberry's."

"I shall do all in my power to ensure that it doesn't."

Nodding, Sir David sighed. "Right. So what is your plan?"

"Make inquiries, see if I can find this mysterious woman. If nothing comes of that, then I suspect we'll find ourselves arresting the new Lord Rockberry."

"Before we do that, just make bloody sure we've got the right of it."

"Yes, sir. I always do."

"I know, but I thought it bears repeating. This situation needs to be handled very delicately, Swindler."

Swindler spent two more hours at Rockberry's, making sketches of the room, trying to notice anything that appeared out of place. He questioned the servants. No one saw a lady arrive, so the only way she could have entered was if one of the Lords Rockberry had admitted her.

His next step would be to see if he could find another lady who'd been taken advantage of. It was always possible that she wasn't of the nobility. He would have to give more scrutiny to Rockberry's papers and documents. Some clue might be hidden within them. He would also talk with Catherine. She'd been of little help when it came to Elisabeth Watkins, but she might know of another lady.

But before he moved forward with the investigation, he wanted to see Eleanor again. He wanted to comfort and reassure her. He also intended to ask for her hand in marriage. He couldn't deny that it was a hasty proposal, delivered in part to spare her reputation, but he also had to admit that he'd never been as drawn to a woman as he was to her. The hours she spent in his bed had seemed far too short. He thought it very likely that they could have a good life together.

Still in possession of Luke's carriage, he made his way to Eleanor's lodging house and knocked briskly on the door.

When Mrs. Potter opened it, he didn't wait for an invitation, but simply brushed past her. "Will you please inform Miss Watkins that I have come to call?"

Mrs. Potter closed the door. "I'm afraid she's gone, sir."

He could well imagine Eleanor needing to walk, needing to brush off the scare she'd had that morning when she was arrested. She'd find comfort in the park, no doubt. Or perhaps she'd walked elsewhere. He could go in search of her or simply wait. He had no doubt she wouldn't be gone long. He faced Mrs. Potter. "If you've no objection, I'll wait in the parlor for her return."

"I fear you'll be waiting a dreadfully long time.

I don't think she's planning to return, sir. She packed her bags. Told me not to worry about the days remaining to her, that I was welcome to hire the room out to someone else. That she'd no longer need it. She left two packages."

Stunned beyond measure, feeling as though his body had turned to stone, Swindler watched her go into the parlor. He looked at the stairs. That was where he needed to go. He needed—

"Here, sir!"

As though someone else controlled his legs, he walked into the parlor.

"The large box there is addressed to the Duchess of Greystone. I suspect it's the lovely gown she brought over for Miss Watkins. Then she left this for you. I suspect I know what it is as well."

Swindler opened the velvet box and stared at the pearls that only that morning had adorned Eleanor's lovely throat. He felt as though one of the bullies from the rookeries had plowed his fist into his gut. "Are you quite certain she's left for good?"

"Yes, sir. Bit hard to miss when she hired a couple of lads to carry out her trunk."

She was gone? After everything they'd shared, she was gone?

The words kept echoing through his head, blocking out all other thoughts.

She was gone.

*   *   *

As the train rumbled over the tracks, Eleanor stared at her reflection in the window. The deed was done. She should have seen satisfaction on her countenance, staring back at her. Instead, in spite of her best efforts, she saw a touch of regret. She shifted her gaze over to another reflection, one re-markably similar to hers.

"Why the long face, Emma?" she asked.

"I began to fall in love with him, Eleanor."

"Well, that was a rather silly thing to do, now wasn't it?"

Emma blushed, but then she tended to do so quite easily. It was the one area in which they differed, but no one in London would know that since neither of them had visited the town before a month ago. They'd known no one in London when they arrived. The advantage to having a reclusive father who'd never felt deserving of his title.

"What would have been the harm in me stay-ing?" Emma asked.

"A careless word, Emma, a misstep, and we'd both find ourselves hanging from the gallows. Once we realized Mr. Swindler was following us, and you encountered him at the park, the natural course was to use him. You should be grateful for the short time you had."

Silently Emma nodded before dropping her eyes

to her gloved hands balled in her lap. He'd seemed like the answer to their prayers.

She followed the man who was following Eleanor through Cremorne Gardens. Like Eleanor, she believed he was Rockberry's man. For good or ill, though, she couldn't say. She'd first spotted him the night Rockberry had gone to Scotland Yard. She and Eleanor always kept an eye on each other, taking extreme care in never being seen together, but always trying to keep the other within her sight.

As she rounded the curve, she caught a glimpse of Eleanor surrounded by three men who suddenly began pulling her into the shadows. Her heart leapt into her throat. She started to rush forward, to scream when she saw the pursuer quicken his pace. By the time she was in a position to better see what was happening, he had his arm protectively around Eleanor and was obviously trying to leave the area.

Then one of the blokes took a swing—

She'd never seen a fight before, had never witnessed anyone coming to blows. The large, powerful man made short work of the bullies, and then his arm was again around Eleanor, leading her away from the men who writhed on the ground.

Her heart was pounding for a different reason now—no longer because of fear over Eleanor's safety, but because she'd never seen anyone as magnificent as the man who'd come to her sister's rescue.

Following them out of the gardens, always keeping to the shadows, always watchful, she arrived at the entrance just as he was helping Eleanor into a hansom cab. She saw Eleanor leave. Then the man climbed into another hansom.

"Follow her at a discreet pace."

As the driver sent the vehicle into motion, she scurried from her hiding place and gave similar words to the driver of the hansom she entered. "Follow him."

Just as he had, she disembarked on another street. She carefully made her way to the lodging house, again keeping to the shadows, until she spotted him observing the building. Eventually he went to the door.

After he left, she remained as she was for another hour before she saw the signal in the window—the draperies drawn closed—to indicate that Mrs. Potter had retired for the evening. It was safe to come in.

Once inside her room, she hugged Eleanor tightly. "You were accosted. I saw."

"And I was rescued. Did you see him?" Eleanor asked, working herself free of Emma's clinging embrace.

"Yes, of course."

"His name is James Swindler."

"You went with him! Do you know how dangerous that was when we know nothing about him?"

Eleanor sat in a nearby rocker, staring at the empty hearth. "Was he the man who's been following me?"

"Yes. But it doesn't matter. We must stop this mad-

*ness of trying to avenge Elisabeth on our own. We
should go to the police."*

*"He may very well be the police. Do you not see how
this works to our advantage? If he's following you while
I do the deed, we have our alibi. I can't possibly be at
two places at once. It's what we planned all along, only
better. The word of a policeman will be above reproach.
The perfect crime."*

So they had decided to try to seduce him, to
bring him even closer. But it was Emma who had
been seduced. As the train took her farther from
London, she wondered how she could have not
known how much she would come to care for
James in such a short time.

She tried to imagine his reaction when he arrived at Mrs. Potter's, and discovered that Emma—
or Eleanor as he knew her—was gone. Even Mrs.
Potter had been unaware there were two sisters
sharing the same living accommodations. They'd
timed their comings and goings so no one was the
wiser. They would have taken rooms in different
lodgings but money was scarce and it seemed silly
to spend money that didn't need to be spent.

Along with Elisabeth, they'd had a lifetime of
fooling people, of arranging pranks where they
pretended to be each other or caused others to
question who they'd really seen.

It had been so incredibly easy in London because

their father had never taken all three daughters there, and apparently had never even announced that he'd been graced with three daughters. As they weren't sons, he'd deemed them insignificant.

Until it came time to send one to the city for a Season. Then suddenly he'd had hopes of a good marriage and money being available for his other daughters. Emma had loved her father dearly, but his head had always been in the clouds. She didn't even know exactly what he'd done for the Crown to be honored with a title.

Now, watching the passing rolling hills, she wondered what James would think of them. It had been so difficult to say good-bye to him, knowing it was forever, knowing she would never again taste his kiss or feel his touch. Knowing she'd never again hear his voice or look into his eyes.

"What if he tries to find us, Eleanor? That man at Scotland Yard said he was the best."

"You told him we live to the north, didn't you?" Her sister shrugged. "He'll give up long before he thinks to look to the south."

Would he give up? Would he even begin to search for her? Or would he simply accept that she'd left?

Emma had become so good at living a life of deception. She'd even lied to Eleanor with such ease that it had been almost frightening. As far as

Eleanor knew, she and James had simply ridden around London in the carriage until dawn. Her sister had no idea that she'd sacrificed her virginity or spent the night in James's bed.

She pressed her hand to her stomach, wondering if she might be carrying James's child, surprised to discover that the thought brought her a great deal of joy. She didn't think she'd ever feel for another man the way she felt about him.

He was so generous, so giving. She was grateful for every second she'd spent in the company of James Swindler.

Still, just once Emma would have liked to have heard him whisper her name.

Chapter 12

S he's gone."

It was the first time Swindler had voiced the words aloud since they'd begun echoing through his mind two days ago. Spoken aloud, they sounded incredulous.

"I beg your pardon?" Sir David asked, leaning back in his chair.

"Miss Watkins. She packed up her things and left her lodgings."

"What do you make of that?"

Swindler sighed, the truth of the situation difficult to admit. "I may have been duped, sir."

Sir David arched a brow. "The lady wasn't with you that night?"

"She was."

"Then maybe she was simply unsettled about the murder of Rockberry and being arrested."

"There may be more to it than that, sir."

"Explain."

"In Rockberry's library there were two glasses of unfinished wine, which leads me to believe Rockberry may have known his murderer."

Sir David nodded. "Go on."

"I went to the morgue to study the body. The dagger that killed Rockberry—I've seen it before. That night at Cremorne Gardens."

"Did it belong to one of the swells who attacked Miss Watkins?"

"No, sir. It belonged to Miss Watkins herself. I'm afraid, sir, that she may have had an accomplice."

"Damn it, man! How did you miss that?"

"I was focused on the lady. I believed as long as she was within my sight, Rockberry was safe. I believe it's imperative that I find her, and my search may take me outside of London."

Sir David stroked his thumb and forefinger over his mustache. "Could still be the brother. He could be the accomplice."

"Possibly, but I know I must find the lady." If not for the crime, then for himself. It made no sense to him that she'd leave unless she was trying to hide something.

"You have leave to do what you must, Swindler. Report to me when you have something."

"Yes, sir." He turned to go.

"Swindler?"

He glanced back.

"You don't look yourself. Do whatever you need to do so you're back to snuff. I need my best man at his sharpest."

His best man. If Sir David knew how easily his best man had been duped, he'd have demanded that he leave Scotland Yard.

As though following his thoughts, Sir David added, "You're not the first to be fooled by a pretty face."

Swindler took no consolation from the words. It was more than her pretty face. It was everything about her that had fooled him.

"Viscount Watkins's estate, you say?"

Swindler watched as Greystone's brow furrowed. It didn't sit well with Swindler that he'd needed to come to Frannie's husband for assistance, even though he respected the lord more than he did most. Greystone had proved his worth by putting his life at risk for Frannie last year.

"Unfortunately, until recently I was so absorbed by my own wants, I paid very little attention to anyone outside my father's sphere of influence. I can make some inquiries. Someone is bound to know where his estate lies."

"The land wasn't entailed, so that might make it more difficult."

"Still, someone must know him."

"Eleanor told me they lived to the north, by the sea. I suspect all or part of it is a lie." What other lies had she told? Had her feelings for him been false as well? If not, then how could she have left?

"I could always ask the queen," Greystone said.

"I'd rather not involve her majesty."

Greystone gave a little shrug. "I can be most discreet."

"You should have him ask, Jim," Frannie said. "Now is not the time to be stubborn. If she were in London, you'd have already found her by now. No one can follow a scent like you can."

"Where she's concerned, I'm all turned about, Frannie. I can think of no logical reason for her to have left as abruptly as she did."

"It can be quite unsettling to be arrested. Perhaps she was simply frightened."

He shook his head. "She was with me. She had no reason to fear being arrested again."

"Perhaps she simply wanted to go home."

Swindler shoved himself out of the chair. "Without even leaving me a note?" He strode toward the window, stopped, plowed his hands through his hair. "My apologies."

"It's all right." Frannie came up behind him and placed her hand on his back. "You grew to care for her. Even I could see how much during the ball. Come back and sit down. Tell us how we can help."

He glanced back at her. "I'd rather pace."

She smiled. "All right. So where do things stand?"

"I've had no luck finding the lads she hired to carry her trunk. I suspect she took the train. I tried to draw a portrait of her, to ask at the ticket window if anyone had seen her, but I've never been skilled at drawing people. I can sketch a room to the smallest detail to help me solve a crime, but Eleanor . . . I can't draw her likeness to save my life."

"Sterling can. He's an artist. Do you remember her well enough, Sterling?"

"Yes, I believe so." Her husband got up, went around to the desk, and opened a drawer. After pulling out some paper, he sat down and immediately began to sketch.

Swindler thought it might be the first break he'd had in two days. He gave his attention to Frannie. "Did you notice anything that might be helpful while you were visiting with her?"

"I'm afraid not. I only spoke with her in the parlor." Her face suddenly brightened. "Oh."

"What?"

"Agnes went to her rooms to alter the gown."

Five minutes later a very nervous Agnes was standing in front of Swindler and wringing her hands.

"Did you notice anything?" Swindler asked.

"Like wot?"

"Anything unusual."

The young lady shook her head, then scrunched up her face. "Well there was one thing I thought odd. She changed into the gown in her sitting room. The door to her bedchamber was closed. We didn't go in there. But then, when I was finished with my sewing, she opened the door and went to look at herself in the mirror."

"Did you see anyone else in there?"

"No, but . . . I could see a dress draped over a chair in the corner. The thing is, it looked exactly like the dress on the sofa in the sitting room—the dress she'd taken off to put on the gown. I thought maybe it was her favorite dress, so she wanted two of them."

"You probably have the right of it. Thank you, Agnes. That's all I need," Swindler said. He walked to the window and gazed out on the night.

"What are you thinking?" Frannie asked.

"I don't know what to think. Do you have dresses made that look the same?"

"Before I was married, when I spent my night at Dodger's, my dresses were very similar."

He remembered. Drab and blue.

"Jim, what if Elisabeth didn't die as Eleanor claimed?" Frannie asked quietly.

He shook his head. "No, the grief over the loss of her sister was not false. I know true grief when I see it." He'd seen it in his eyes often enough as a lad.

"Here you are," Greystone said, holding out a sketch.

The likeness was uncanny. Swindler felt as though someone had reached into his chest and torn out the heart that had started to grow there. "Perfect," he said, and he could have sworn the temperature in the room dropped several degrees.

"What are you going to do, Jim?" Frannie asked.

"I'm going to find her, if it takes me the remainder of my life."

Chapter 13

Standing near the edge of the cliffs, Emma Watkins watched the whitecapped swells from the sea and the darkening sky herald the approaching storm. With the strengthening wind surrounding her, she breathed in and absorbed the fury of the tempest. She almost wanted to fling herself into the turbulent water just to be surrounded by something other than the dull, somber nothingness that had become her life since she returned from London.

It was as though she and Eleanor had left behind their laughter, their joy, their very essence, as though they were little more than empty shells going about their daily rituals only because failure to do so would bring them a slow agonizing death.

Food contained no flavor, greeting the day no joy. Sleep came in fits and starts. In the two weeks since they arrived at their small home, she'd lost track of the number of nights she heard Eleanor cry out when her sister eventually found sleep.

Fear of discovery didn't hammer at them. Emma thought it might even be a relief to face up to what they'd done. No, to their everlasting surprise, remorse was making a banquet of them. Where once they'd laughed and shared silly secrets, their shared dark secret weighed them down.

Every morning, Emma began her day by writing a letter to James, explaining why she'd left. A letter she never sent. She fought not to envision the expression on his face when he returned to her lodgings to discover she was no longer there. She tried to convince herself that he deserved that betrayal. From the beginning she'd known his attentions were an attempt to seduce her into confiding in him. A thousand times she wished she had.

Following the ball, during the hours she spent in his arms, she'd decided she could trust him with anything. She'd prayed that Eleanor had not possessed the strength to carry through with her part of the plan. She was going to convince her sister that they needed to tell James everything, that he would help them see justice done.

But when she'd been arrested, she knew it was too late. The deed was done, their course was set.

James would despise her for her role in Rockberry's demise. How could he not?

So she and Eleanor had packed their trunk.

Emma had gone to the street and hired two boys to carry it out. Then she asked Mrs. Potter to make her a meal for the journey, and while Mrs. Potter was in the kitchen preparing it, Eleanor had sneaked out.

Simple. The three sisters had always found it simple to switch roles, to pretend to be each other.

But never had Emma regretted their skill more.

With a sigh snatched by the wind, she turned and began walking back to the cottage. A few sheep, cows, and chickens grazed about. They had long ago sold the horses. The only place they needed to go was to the village, and it was reached with an hour of walking. They'd had a light buggy for traveling when their father and Elisabeth were alive. But now it sat unused—the same as their laughter.

Opening the door into the front room, she felt the loneliness of the house even more. Perhaps tonight she would write a letter to James and thank him for the wonderful time he'd shown her in London—even if his ultimate goal hadn't been to impress and charm her, he'd given her precious memories she'd never forget. Perhaps this time she would send it.

Remorse and guilt gnawed at her, and she wondered if James had deduced everything. How long would it take him to realize he'd been duped? And when he did—dear God, she didn't share

Eleanor's conviction that they were both safe.

She walked through the dining room and into the kitchen. "Well, I do believe we have a storm coming up."

She came to an abrupt halt at the sight of Eleanor pumping water into the sink, then scraping a rough brush over her hands with a vengeance.

"Oh, Eleanor," Emma said as she hurried over and wrenched the now red-stained brush free of her sister's hold.

"I can't get his blood off, Emma. No matter how hard I scrub. My skin feels so slick and dirty."

"It's not his blood, sweeting. It's yours." Gingerly, she guided Eleanor to a chair at the table. "Sit down while I fetch things."

After gathering up the cloths and salve, she joined her sister and very carefully took her hand. Then, as gently as possible, she cleaned the raw, oozing flesh.

"It's not my blood, it's his," Eleanor insisted.

"I'm going to clean it off, put salve on your hands, and wrap them up. His blood won't come back after that."

"You said the same thing yesterday."

Emma lifted her eyes to Eleanor's. "I'll do it properly this time, but you mustn't remove the bandages until the wounds heal."

"They start to itch and burn. They hurt."

"When that happens, come to me and I'll take care of them."

Nodding, Eleanor turned her head to look out the window. "Oh, my God, Emma, he's here."

Emma didn't have to ask who. She heard the despair in Eleanor's voice. And when she dared to peer out the window, her heart leapt at the sight of James riding astride a large brown horse. How often had she imagined him arriving to sweep her away and into his arms? Just as quickly, her heart crashed into the pit of her stomach. If he swept her away at all, it would be toward gaol.

Swindler owed Greystone another debt. The sketch Greystone provided had allowed Swindler to much more easily follow Eleanor's trail from the train station to this nice stone cottage near the cliffs. It also helped that Greystone had made some inquiries of his peers and managed to discover the location of Viscount Watkins's residence.

Swindler had ridden the train as far as it would take him, and then hired a horse for the remainder of the journey. At a nearby village he'd managed to garner precise directions to his destination.

He wanted to remain level-headed until he questioned Eleanor. Presently, he only had suspicions regarding her duplicity. He held out hope that another explanation existed—that she'd not in fact arranged Rockberry's murder and then used Swindler as her alibi. But if she hadn't, why had she left him? Had she been overcome with shame for coming to his bed? Was it her reputation she was striving to protect?

His head and his pride were in a continual argument. He was not a man prone to emotions, but he wavered between boiling rage and crushing disappointment. Then he'd remember the wonder of her in his arms, before remembering that she had shattered the fragile trust developing between them.

Then there was the matter of the dagger. He'd only caught of a glimpse of it in the shadows. Perhaps his memory of it wasn't clear. But he'd taught himself over the years to pay attention to details. It was unlikely now that he'd become careless.

He'd barely brought the horse to a halt when she opened the door. She wore a simple dress of pink, her hair held in place with a pink ribbon.

As he dismounted, the emotions roiled through him like some sort of tempest. He was angry, yet still he desired her. He wanted the taste of her, the scent of her, the feel of her. He wanted her naked beneath him. He wanted her asking for his forgiveness, wanted her sharing her secrets. He wanted her arms wound around his shoulders, her fingers in his hair, her legs wrapped around his hips, her eyes holding his.

He barely remembered striding to the door, but suddenly she was in his arms, her mouth greedily greeting his. He'd been searching a fortnight, and every minute of every day had been hell, knowing what his duty would require of him when he found her, selfishly fearing he might never again set eyes on her. Desperation clung to him now, to yearn to have this forever and to know that he couldn't.

She still smelled of roses. That much was real. She still moaned softly as he deepened the kiss. No deception there. Her body molded against his as though it belonged, and damned if he didn't want it to.

But she'd betrayed him, betrayed his trust.

Breathing harshly, he tore his mouth from hers and cradled her face between his hands. "Why in God's name did you leave?"

She merely shook her head.

"You did it, didn't you?" he demanded. "Arranged for his murder. You had an accomplice. You used me to establish your innocence."

She shook her head only slightly this time.

"Don't lie to me, Eleanor. For God's sake, tell—" Catching movement out of the corner of his eye, he jerked his head up and saw a woman standing just beyond the doorway. The resemblance between the two women was uncanny. Frannie had the right of it. "Elisabeth," he whispered.

"No," the woman in his arms said quietly. "Eleanor."

He studied more intensely the woman he held. Everything about her was familiar. The taste, the fragrance, the feel of her in his arms, the way she molded against him. He shook his head. "No, you're Eleanor."

"No, I'm Emma. I've always been Emma."

He remembered that first meeting in Cremorne Gardens—how he'd rescued the woman, yet been anxious to bring the assignment to an end. How during the light of day the following afternoon she'd taken his breath, how he'd been struck that something about her was different. "So you deceived me from the beginning?"

"You deceived me," she said tartly. "You claimed to be a scoundrel. You didn't reveal you worked for Scotland Yard."

"I am a scoundrel. But I never once lied to you. Not about anything."

Three sisters. There had been three identical sisters!

Swindler wasn't certain he'd ever heard of such a thing.

The fury had shot through him as the depth of their deception became clearer. He'd hardly been able to stand to look at either woman, so he decided to see to the horse, to give himself some time to calm down. He couldn't recall ever being as furious, to know that the sisters had planned to use him, to wonder how much of Elean—no, Emma's action had been devised to lure him into her carefully devised trap. The deceitful wench!

The irony did not escape him. He—who was so very skilled at planning and executing the swindle—he'd been effectively swindled.

Removing the saddle from his horse, he draped it over one side of the stall, near where he'd earlier hung the bridle and bit. Having rarely ridden a horse, he wasn't a skilled horseman. Nor did he have any experience in actually caring for the creatures. He'd expected to at least find a groom here who could see to the matter for him. He patted the horse's neck. It shied away from him. The closer they'd come to the sea, the more skittish it had become. Damned big brute, but then Swindler needed it to accommodate his size.

He went in search of oats. The barn was small, in need of repair. There didn't appear to be any servants about anywhere. Perhaps Emma hadn't lied about her circumstances. She'd not had the means to have a proper Season.

Where once he'd felt sympathy with her plight, he was no longer certain what he was now experiencing. He cursed Rockberry for bringing Scotland

Yard into his personal mess. He cursed Sir David for deciding Swindler was the best man for the job. And he cursed himself for failing miserably at ensuring that a lord was not killed.

He'd given no credence to Rockberry's claims or fears. Eventually his duty had become secondary to his desire to be with the lady. He'd put his own wants and needs first.

He finally located a nearly empty bin of oats. After scooping some into a feed sack, he walked back toward the stall where he'd left the horse. He was in the process of slipping the sack over the horse's head when he heard a large clap of thunder. The horse whinnied and reared up. He had been so distracted with thoughts of the woman he now knew as Emma that he was slow to react. He twisted—

His head exploded into sharp, blinding pain.

Blackness.

"What do you suppose his intentions are?" Eleanor asked as she and Emma closed and secured an outside shutter on the house. They'd begun the task after James had ground out, "I need to see to my horse" and had led the large beast toward the small barn.

For the briefest of moments, when he took her in his arms and slashed his mouth over hers, Emma had dared believe he was here for another reason. But his kiss had been punishing, his arms like iron bands around her. He was furious. Not that she blamed him. But she also knew he possessed a kindness, a gentleness. But more, he understood justice. She'd seen, touched, the scars on his back. If anyone knew the unfairness of the criminal justice system, it would be him.

"I suspect he intends to return us to London where we can pay for our sins."

"If that's the case, then he only needs to take me," Eleanor said stubbornly. "After all, I'm the one who actually did the deed."

She loved her sister dearly for striving to spare her. "We're in this together."

With a sigh, Eleanor marched around the corner to close up the next window. Emma began to follow, then changed her mind. She needed to speak with James—alone. She was halfway to the barn when she saw his horse grazing nearby. She wondered if James had no luck finding grain for beast. Quickening her pace, she entered the barn.

Her heart pounded in her chest at the sight of him sprawled near a straw-filled stall. "Oh, my God."

Rushing over, she knelt beside him. She could see blood matting his hair. Very gently, she moved the strands aside. He had a nasty gash on the side of his head. The horse must have—

James's eyes flew open. She released a startled gasp. The walls spun dizzily around as he grabbed her and flipped her onto her back on the straw before pouncing on her like some wild beast. She started to pound her fists into him, but he grabbed her wrists and pinned her hands above her head. His face was pained, but she thought it was more an emotional pain than a physical one. His harsh breathing echoed around her.

Then his face gentled, almost as though against his will. He held her wrists with one meaty paw while he used his other hand to stroke her cheek. "Eleanor," he rasped, a wealth of emotion wrapped in the single word. She could hardly stand to hear her sister's name uttered between his lips.

"Emma," she corrected softly.

"Emma." He lowered his head until his breath was wafting over her cheek like the first breeze of spring, gentle but determined to herald in the change of seasons. "Emma."

She didn't protest when his mouth covered hers, but the kiss was very much like the one he'd delivered at the door, harder, almost desperate, as though he wanted to recapture what they'd had in London but knew as well as she did that it was lost to them. He was correct. Whatever they'd been building was erected on the faulty foundation of lies and deception. It couldn't withstand the storm of betrayal. It would crumble, and if he possessed even a shred of mercy, he'd allow it to be swept out to sea.

But at that moment she sensed there was no mercy in him. His hand tightened around her wrists until her fingers began to numb. Yet she didn't tell him to stop, because to do so would mean moving her mouth away from his, and she wasn't yet ready to give that up. How was she to know which stroke of his tongue would be the last? When would his lips stop molding themselves against hers?

His large hand cradled her side, slid down it, and tucked her up more firmly beneath him. The weight of him felt so very good. He was sturdy like a rock along the shoreline, which the wave— no matter how mighty it might be—could not move. He smelled slightly different than he had in London. Now she inhaled the scent of horse, leather, and salt from the sea air that had blown through his hair as he'd traveled to find her. Yet beneath it all, she detected the essence that was him. Everything about him was wonderful. Everything about him would soon be stripped away from her and reduced to memories that would haunt the remainder of her life.

"Well, what have we here?"

Emma startled at Eleanor's voice echoing through the barn. James lifted his head, then went very still.

She could see the confusion in the green eyes she adored, and she was left to wonder if the blow to the head had disoriented him. Anger and disappointment clouded his gaze just before he rolled off her. With a low groan, he sat back against the side of the stall and put his hand to the back of his head.

"I think his horse must have kicked him," Emma said, her face growing warm with embarrassment. Scrambling to her feet, she nearly lost her balance. She'd forgotten how weak her legs became whenever he kissed her. They were like jam trying to support her. "He has a nasty gash."

"Yes, I saw his horse out there," Eleanor said. "That's the reason I thought I should investigate."

"You should come to the house so I can stitch you up," Emma offered him quietly.

"I'll finish seeing to your horse," Eleanor said.

"Don't even think about running," James commanded in a stern voice. "There is nowhere on this earth that you can go that I will not find you."

Eleanor threw back her shoulders and lifted her chin. "In case it's failed your notice, Mr. Swindler, there's a storm coming. Only a fool would run in the storm."

Judging by the harsh, uncompromising look James gave Eleanor, Emma was of a mind that only a fool *wouldn't* run when the predator was near.

Chapter 14

Swindler sat in a chair near a window in an upstairs bedchamber so Eleanor—no, Emma—would have better light by which to work, because they'd closed up the windows downstairs. He couldn't deny that her sister had the right of it. He could see heavy dark clouds rolling forward in the distance, dimming the sunlight. He tried to focus on the weather but seemed unable to concentrate on anything other than Emma's slender fingers gently parting his hair. He felt the fool for allowing her to entice him into wanting her. The hell of it was that she didn't even need to try.

"This is likely to hurt," she said softly.

"As you're well aware, I've suffered worse. Just get on with it."

As she worked the needle through his flesh, he clenched his jaw, but everything else remained as still as stone. Well, not quite everything. His heart pounded erratically with her nearness. Emma. Strange, but the name suited.

"Tell me about your sister," he commanded.

"Eleanor can be quite stubborn when—"

"Not Eleanor. Elisabeth. Three of you were born on the same day."

"Yes. I told you the truth there. Elisabeth was the first, I was the last, and Eleanor came between us. Our mother did die in childbirth. We were too much for her. Her death nearly broke my father's heart, I think. He hired a lady from the village to watch over us, but he gave us little time. It's the way of it, I suppose. What do men know of children? Did your father ignore you?"

He didn't want to think of his father, didn't want to talk about his past, but still he answered. "No. He and I were very close. We had only each other to get us through. Oh, sometimes he would spend the night in a woman's bed, and I would sleep nearby, wondering if she was how my mother smelled, hoping he might stay with this one—a night, maybe two, and then he moved on. I take after him in that regard. I never stay long with a woman I've bedded. *Damnation!*"

"My apologies. The needle slipped."

No, it hadn't. He was fairly certain that she'd lost her concentration with his words and dug it in farther than she'd intended. He didn't know why he'd said what he did. He only knew that he didn't want her to realize how very important she had become to him, how devastated he'd been by her betrayal, her leaving. Because he had been interested in staying with her for more than a few nights. He'd stupidly begun planning to stay with her forever. The thought of always having her in his arms at night and waking up to find her in his bed had brought him almost as much pleasure as the act of making love to her. Now he realized that all he'd known of her was what she'd wished him to know. Without moving his head, he glanced around the bedchamber as much as he was able.

Pale green wallpaper dotted with tiny pink roses decorated the walls. A pink counterpane draped the bed. Pink curtains adorned the windows that looked out on the cliffs. "Are those the cliffs—"

"Yes," she answered before he could finish the question. Although he couldn't see her face, he could feel the tension radiating from her.

"Is this your bedchamber?" he asked.

"Yes." He felt the tension drain from her.

"You like pink."

"I adore pink."

The room was a study in femininity. Even the white furniture had a delicate air about it. Everything in his rooms was dark, like his soul. But she was light and airy. She was joy and dreams.

"It was Eleanor that night at Cremorne Gardens, the one I rescued."

"Yes, but I was there in the shadows. We never went out alone, always stayed within sight of each other. I saw how you protected her."

"Which is how you recognized me the following afternoon at Hyde Park."

"Yes." He heard the snip of scissors, felt the tug as she tied off her handwork. She began wrapping a bandage around his head. "How do you know for certain that it was me at Hyde Park?"

"Something about you was different. I thought it was a reflection of the sunlight." He felt like a romantic fool telling her. He should have simply kept his thoughts to himself.

"The only time both of us didn't go out was when you began taking me around London. Eleanor was afraid you might catch us and the jig would be up."

Unlikely that he'd have noticed her, he hated to admit to himself. All of his attention, all of his focus, had been on the lovely lady in his company.

"There, all done," she said with a featherlike touch to his head. "You should probably try to sleep until the headache goes away."

Because his head was pounding unmercifully and he was feeling disoriented, he brought himself to his feet, walked over to the bed and leaned against the post at its foot. "She killed Rockberry."

Emma gave one quick nod, averting her eyes as she did so.

"You stayed with me that night deliberately to provide her with an alibi. You knew what she was about."

She stared at the floor as though she hoped it might open up and provide her with the means for an escape. "Yes," she whispered before lifting her gaze to his and saying more forcefully, "and no. Eleanor had gone downstairs to greet the duchess when she came to issue her invitation. I was abed with a headache. When Eleanor realized I had the opportunity to attend a ball, she decided it was the perfect night to finish what we'd begun. She assumed sooner or later Rockberry would return home, and when he did . . . she would see to him. My part was to stay with you until dawn. But I wanted to be with you. I came—" She licked her lips. "—to care for you."

"You'll forgive me if I don't believe that part, since you ran away."

"I didn't see that I had a choice. You're very clever. Sooner or later I might have said something to give us away."

"You thought I would simply let everything go if you left?"

"I hoped . . . you would. I wasn't as confident

as Eleanor that you would simply shrug off my leaving."

"Why me?"

With a sigh, she moved nearer to the window and looked out.

He could hear the wind picking up. A storm was indeed brewing, but it could never compete with the one stirring inside him. "Why me?" he repeated more harshly.

"Eleanor and I kept a constant watch on Rockberry, always taking care that he only saw one of us at a time. We nearly expired on the spot when he went to Scotland Yard. Shortly thereafter, we became aware of you following us, and we assumed you were the result of his visit with the police. Eleanor thought we could take advantage of the situation."

"And take advantage of me." He couldn't contain the seething anger that escaped.

She spun around. "You don't know what he did to our sister. We were determined to avenge her. You can't possibly imagine what it is to lose someone unjustly."

Oh, he could. He thought of his father.

"That day in Hyde Park, when I first approached you, why had you decided it would be you who sought to . . . entice me into your web?"

He heard her swallow. "That was simply coincidence. Had you arrived twenty minutes later, it would have been Eleanor whom you followed. But after you made my acquaintance, we took care to make certain that it was always me who was with you. You and I talked about so much . . . Eleanor was afraid she might inadvertently say something to cause you to question who you were with."

They *had* talked, about so many things. The ease with which he spoke to her had surprised him. He'd never been verbose around the ladies. He communicated in other ways. But everything with her had been unlike anything he'd ever experienced with anyone else. That she could betray him so easily—

"I've brought you some of my father's whiskey," Eleanor announced as she glided into the room. Her dress was a pale blue adorned in darker blue. It didn't seem to suit her, but he supposed he was viewing her through a kaleidoscope of murder. Strange how he saw her as the more cunning of the two sisters, how she stirred nothing within him except disgust.

If his head weren't threatening to explode, if he were better able to think, he might not have taken the glass, but as it was, he thought whiskey could dull the pain, sharpen his thinking. He downed it, relishing the bite and the warmth that burst through his chest.

"Shall I bring you some more?" Eleanor asked.

"No, that'll do for now."

Eleanor watched him with obvious avid curiosity. He wondered how much Emma had shared with her. He remembered that when he first began to follow her, he'd thought her nothing special. Even the first night at Cremorne, he'd come to her defense because it was in his nature to protect the innocent. But the following afternoon, everything changed, something had been different about her. He hadn't been able to determine exactly what it was. He'd only known that when her fingers touched his when he handed her the map, he wanted her to touch all of him.

From a great distance he heard himself say, "Explain the circumstances that led to Elisabeth's death."

"To discuss our sister's poor choices with you seems a sort of betrayal," Eleanor said.

"I might be able to help you if I understand everything." His words sounded slurred and he suddenly staggered.

"Lie down, Mr. Swindler," Eleanor said, taking his arm and guiding him to the bed.

"Eleanor, what did you do?" Emma asked as she rushed over.

"Given him something to make him sleep while we decide how best to handle this."

As though his mind had left his body, he was aware of them arranging him on the bed. His eyelids grew heavy. He couldn't keep them open. He wanted to explain that nothing would deter him from his purpose save death, but his mouth seemed unwilling to accommodate his need to speak.

Giving in to the comforting lure of sleep, he closed his eyes. A blanket was brought over his body, and the sweet fragrance of roses surrounded him. He wanted to pull Emma in but his arms didn't respond to his commands. All he did was drift back into the blackness.

"How could you do that to him?" Emma snapped.

"How could I not? We have to think very carefully about what we wish him to know."

"We should tell him everything."

"Absolutely not. He'll use it against us."

"Eleanor, it's too late to deny what we did. If we explain to him the why of it, he might be able to help us."

"And what if we have to explain the why of it at our trial? I'd rather hang than disgrace Elisabeth before all of London." Eleanor strode from the room.

Emma bent down and pressed a kiss to James's forehead. "I'm so sorry."

Then, because he was asleep and Eleanor wasn't about, she touched his hair where it poked up over the bandage. It had been windblown when he arrived, giving him an almost barbaric appearance. She trailed her fingers around his face, relaxed now, but the cragginess that she so loved gave a hardness to his familiar features. When he'd leaped from his horse, his fury matched the worst storm to ever sweep over the land. She wasn't sure what she'd expected of him. That he'd taken her in his arms had both terrified and thrilled her.

Resting her hand against his throat, she felt the thready pulsing of his blood. She wanted to smack Eleanor for giving him a draught. Hadn't they done enough to him?

Charm him, seduce him, distract him, Eleanor had urged. Emma found the task to be heaven and hell. She'd enjoyed every moment in his company, even as each one was tainted with guilt.

She'd known every time he began to ask her questions that he was striving to determine her purpose. How often she'd wanted to confess all, to seek his opinion, to share her doubts. Eleanor had been convinced that a lord of the realm would go unpunished in spite of his abhorrent behavior. They'd had to take matters into their own hands, had to make him pay for what he'd done to Elisabeth—and perhaps others.

Emma had agreed that Rockberry needed to be dealt with. But she'd never wanted to hurt James. That last night in his arms, she'd known that no matter how desperately she wished otherwise, she would bring him pain.

Taking his hand, she brought it to her lips and pressed a kiss to his knuckles.

Revenge was not for the faint of heart, but she'd discovered too late that neither was it for her.

When Swindler awoke, darkness had descended and the wind shrieked, a forlorn sound that echoed the cries of his own heart. Knowing everything he knew about Emma's conniving, how was it that once again he'd allowed her to bewitch him? How could she still look so innocent? In her eyes, he could have sworn he saw regret, but also tenderness and a powerful yearning that matched his.

He rolled over, swinging his legs off the bed, and sat up. Dizziness assailed him, and he gave it a moment to pass. His head throbbed dully—he suspected more from whatever Eleanor had put in his whiskey than from the horse's kick. He wished he could take only her back to London and leave Emma here, but how would he explain his providing the alibi? Either way he would look the fool, but at least the truth wouldn't destroy his reputation, only sully it. Without Emma he would be viewed as a liar, his days working with Scotland Yard behind him.

He'd worked so damned hard to rise out of the gutter, to no longer be thought of as the son of a thief. He refused to let all his struggles go for naught. Although he was dead, his father deserved a son more worthy. Swindler had always been determined not to disappoint him.

Rising to his feet, he walked to the window and peered out on the darkness. Rain lashed at the windowpanes. With the flashing of lightning, he saw the white crests of the distant turbulent sea and trees bending from the force of the wind. Deafening thunder cracked. Living so near the sea was not for those easily frightened by strength and power. Little wonder Emma was as courageous as she was. She'd no doubt been shaped by these storms, knew the force of nature, knew how to withstand its onslaught.

Emma. Just the thought of her filled him with mixed reactions: wanting and aversion. She and her sister had taken justice in their own hands. Damn it all, it made him a hypocrite not to admit that he'd done the same on occasion. He'd always justified his actions, believing he knew what constituted justice because he'd seen so much injustice in his youth. Arrogant bastard. Emma was making him face his own shortcomings and he didn't much like it.

Turning from the window, he strode to the door, turned the knob, and discovered it was locked. Pressing his forehead to the wood, he laughed darkly. Apparently, even after everything they'd shared during their brief time together, Emma had absolutely no clue with whom she dealt.

In the kitchen, Emma carefully folded the cloth napkin that she would place on the tray she was preparing for James. It was silly, really, that she wanted everything to be perfect, especially as he'd no doubt wake up in a foul mood from Eleanor's tampering with his whiskey.

"I know you're angry because I gave him the sleeping draught," Eleanor began as she sliced the mutton. It had been almost an hour since they'd spoken. While Eleanor had begun preparations for dinner, Emma saw to the animals, herding them into the barn before the storm broke.

"I'm more than angry. He's done nothing to deserve such distrust," Emma replied, beginning to lose patience with her sister and her inability to understand that they'd crossed a fine line once. It wasn't going to become their habit.

"He's come to arrest us and I've been thinking long and hard about it. Our best course is to convince him that he should leave you here. Truly, what good can come from both of us being hanged? It was my idea, after all. You only went along because it's your nature to go along."

"My recollection of our conversation is something along the lines of your suggesting that we should kill him and then our arguing about which one of us should have the honor of doing him in."

Eleanor's lips twitched. "I suppose you didn't take any convincing that he needed to be done in."

"None at all. I'd read Elisabeth's journal as well."

"Then perhaps I should read it." The deep voice echoed through the room.

With tiny screeches, Emma and Eleanor both spun around. They stood close enough that they managed to come together, holding each other as though the devil had risen from hell in order to claim them. But it was only James, filling the doorway, appearing incredibly handsome despite his somewhat disheveled state. He'd removed the bandage from around his head, but hadn't bothered to put on his waistcoat and jacket—or rebutton his shirt, for that matter. His throat and a narrow V of his chest were visible, but it was enough to make Emma's hands itch to touch him. If Eleanor hadn't been squeezing them so tightly, Emma might have crossed over to James and done just that: touched him, stroked him, held him.

A corner of his mouth hitched up into that cocky smile that she so loved. "You didn't honestly believe a locked door was going to keep me in that room, did you?" He held up a small diamond hairpin, and Emma recognized it as the one she'd worn in her hair the night of the ball, the one she'd forgotten and left in his bedchamber. "I was raised among thieves and pickpockets. A lock is child's play."

Emma broke free of her sister's hold and glared at her. "You locked the door?"

Eleanor gave her a mulish look. "While you were out tending the animals. I wanted to be certain we weren't disturbed while we worked out our plans if he awoke quickly."

"Eleanor—" Before she could go on, Eleanor glared at James.

"It was rude of you to startle us so," her sister said, her voice sharp enough to slice the mutton. Emma knew her tartness harbored her fears that she was no longer in control of the situation. Eleanor was the plotter, the planner, the one with grand schemes and designs. Once, they had focused on how to acquire the best husband; lately, they were centered on how best to avoid the noose.

"Your hospitality is rather lacking," James said.

"I suppose you expect me to apologize for the sleeping draught."

He shook his head. "No, I don't expect anything of you."

His words contained a wealth of meaning, as

though Emma and Eleanor were the lowest of the low, snakes—like the ones they'd seen at the zoological gardens—to crawl on their bellies because they were too vile to be given the means to stand.

"I was preparing a tray . . . your dinner," Emma said, her voice unsteady. She was anxious to change the subject, to make some sort of peace offering.

"I'm able to eat at the table. I don't need to be waited on."

Emma nodded jerkily. "Well, then, we shall serve dinner in half an hour."

His eyes slowly roamed over her, before his gaze settled on Eleanor. "Put anything in my food or drink again and you'd best hope it kills me, because when I awaken you'll suffer my wrath, and trust me on this—it's not at all pleasant."

He strode from the room without another word.

"I won't be able to eat a bite with him sitting at the table," Eleanor said.

Emma wouldn't either, but she suspected her reasons were very different from Eleanor's. In spite of everything, she wanted nothing more than to once again lie in his arms.

Chapter 15

The wind continued to howl outside, locking them all within the cocoon of the dining room. With the storm, the darkness was arriving earlier. Candles flickered on the table. Dishes were passed around, mutton, potatoes, and beans heaped on plates, and silence reigned, except for the occasional scraping of silver over china.

What surprised Emma was that James had come to the table cleanly shaven, once again wearing his waistcoat, neckcloth, and jacket. No matter how he appeared—like a ruffian or a gentleman—the sight of him did strange things to her stomach, made it flip over again and again.

He sat at the head of the table while she and Eleanor were on either side of him. Her father had never commanded that seat as James did—as naturally as though he were a king. She fought not to imagine how satisfying it would be to see James in that spot every night. He was not made for the quiet life here near the coast. Although at that moment, the night was anything but quiet as the windows rattled.

"Is there the slightest chance this house will be blown into the sea?" he asked calmly.

"No," Emma assured him. "As the wind is coming from the sea, I suspect if it were to be blown anywhere, it would be blown into the village."

His eyes glinted with amusement. She could almost forget that he was here for a reason that was anything except humorous.

She fought not to wonder—if she'd been the daughter chosen to go to London last Season, if she might have met him at any balls. Would he have looked across the room and noticed her? Would he have asked her to dance? Would the attraction between them have sparked as quickly when mystery surrounded them?

He studied her now over his wineglass. Earlier he'd brought an unopened bottle up from the cellar, opened it, poured it himself, and not allowed it to leave his sight. Slowly, almost suspiciously, he shifted his attention to Eleanor, then returned it to Emma. "When I questioned your landlady, she was aware of only one lady staying in the hired rooms."

"Don't say anything, Emma," Eleanor ordered

sternly. "Presently he comes to us with little more than speculation and conjecture. He can prove nothing. There is no evidence that *you* were ever in London."

His uncompromising gaze settled more firmly on Emma. "Because wherever you went, whatever you did, you claimed to be Eleanor. I believe you always planned to be somewhere, with someone, while Eleanor saw to the deed. I fit rather nicely into your little scheme."

"Yes." She forced the word up from a pit of regret. She'd hoped to use someone of Rockberry's ilk, not quite as dastardly as he but a man who deserved to be used. She'd never expected someone like James, with a moral compass that always pointed to decency, honor, and principles.

With his finger, he slowly tapped his wineglass, *tap, tap, tap,* as though he was locking pieces of a puzzle together. His finger stilled, extended as though he needed to make a point.

"It might have worked . . . if you hadn't left incredibly quickly—without so much as a good-bye." The heat in his eyes almost matched that of the small fire in the hearth. "Especially after . . . the intimacy we'd shared."

He wanted to hurt her, wanted to throw back in her face what she'd given him. She could see that also in his gaze, and she supposed she deserved it.

"What trouble could you get into in a carriage?" Eleanor asked.

Dear Lord, but she had no idea. Emma wasn't about to provide particulars, especially as most of the intimacy had not taken place in the carriage. "I wanted to wait, I wanted to see you again, but I was afraid you'd see the truth of it in my eyes."

He didn't ask which truth: the truth that she'd helped take a man's life, the truth that she'd fallen in love with him, the truth that her last night with him had been the most glorious of her life. Perhaps he realized the enormity of her reasons for leaving, because he returned his attention to his food. For several minutes the silence and awkwardness returned. She suspected they were all pondering the gravity of their intertwined lives. Deception didn't provide a sturdy foundation on which to build anything that would last. Even her relationship with Eleanor had become strained since they'd returned from London.

"So you grew up in this area."

His sudden voice in the silence was like a crack of thunder. Emma startled and Eleanor went so far as to drop her fork on her plate. He'd not worded his statement as a question, yet Emma thought it required some response. She peered over at Eleanor, who'd retrieved her fork and was occupied moving her food from one side of her plate to the other.

"Yes," Emma said. "We were born in this house. It's been in the family for two generations, hardly any time at all when you consider how long England has existed."

"Have you no servants?"

"We did before Father passed. We had a cook, a maid of all work, and a male servant who served as butler and footman." She knew she was rambling. What did he care about the particulars regarding their servants? But she could hardly tolerate the tension and the awkwardness emanating from her and Eleanor. James, on the other hand, was distant yet still appeared comfortable with his surroundings. "Are you attempting to tell us that the food is awful?"

"I've had much worse."

Wiping her damp hands on the napkin in her lap, she remembered that he'd never been outside of London before now. She would have dearly loved to be beside him as he took in the countryside. "Did you enjoy the sights as you journeyed from London?"

"I hardly noticed them."

"A pity. There is some lovely country. Perhaps I can share a bit of it with you before you—we—return to London."

"For pity's sake!" Eleanor burst out, coming to her feet. "Can we stop with the politeness? He means to see us hanged, Emma. I for one have no desire to show him anything."

Tossing her napkin on the table, she strode from the room, very much mimicking the storm thrashing about outside. Watching her leave, Emma couldn't help but feel a bit of gladness to have some more time alone with James.

She cleared her throat. "You must forgive her. She's not been herself lately."

"How is it that you're so calm? Do you think to use your wiles to convince me to overlook your transgressions?"

"No, I'm done lying to you. Quite honestly, facing up to what we did will be a bit of a relief. I've not slept at all since we left London. Barely eaten. I don't regret that he's dead. But there are moments when I regret that we're the ones who did him in. Do you have any regrets, James?"

He rose from his chair and came to kneel beside her. His lovely green eyes held compassion as he cradled her face and touched his thumbs to the tears on her cheeks, which she had not even realized she'd begun to shed. "They have guided my life, Emma."

His lips touched hers, so gently, so sweetly. The passion had always seemed to roar through them as though they'd both known their time together was short, and once passed would be gone forever. Now it was banked, but she could still feel the embers of desire fighting not to die, striving to flame as hot and as high as they'd once burned.

When he pulled away, he said, "I want to read Elisabeth's journal."

For a wonderful moment she'd thought—hoped—that he'd forgotten he was a policeman with a duty. But she suspected his duties were never far from his mind, just as her sins were never far from hers. Wiping away her remaining tears, she nodded. "I'll fetch it for you."

She couldn't have been more surprised when he helped her clear away the table. As she washed the dishes, he dried them.

"I'm not accustomed to a gentleman in the kitchen," she said. "My father always left the table and went to his study to enjoy a bit of brandy with his pipe."

"I don't trust that your sister didn't pour laudanum into all the liquor. As for the pipe, there's enough bad air in London. Don't need more in my lungs. I like the smell of the air here."

She smiled. "Wait until the storm passes. It's really quite lovely then."

As though he didn't want to contemplate what would happen when the storm passed, he said,

"When I lived with Feagan, we all had our chores. Mine was to wash the dishes. Most of the lads didn't care one way or another, but I can't stand the smell of rancid food."

"Can hardly blame you there."

"It reminded me too much of the smell of Newgate when I went to visit my father before they hanged him." His voice was somber, and she heard in it the stirring of unpleasant memories.

"You sound as though you still miss him."

"Every day. A little over twenty years now."

She handed him the last dish. "It's good, really, not to forget. Sometimes it's as though Elisabeth is still with me. I'll get the journal for you now. Meet me in the parlor."

Eleanor refused to leave her bedchamber. Emma didn't mind. It left her alone in the parlor with James. She had brought him the journal, explaining that the pertinent parts began last June when Elisabeth arrived in London. In a fashion typical of his thoroughness, which she was only beginning to recognize, he opened the journal to the first page and began there.

Strangely, she wasn't impatient with his reading. Judging by how long it was before he turned the page, he wasn't a fast reader. If he intended to read the entire journal before leaving, then she and Eleanor would have a few additional days of freedom to put matters to right. They had to make arrangements for someone to take the few animals they had. There was also the matter of the house. They could lock it up, but eventually it would need to go to someone. Or perhaps they should sell it. They would need money for a solicitor, and those with money also fared better in gaol.

While he read, Emma saw to her needlework. James had lit the fire in the hearth before she arrived, so the room was nice and warm. Apparently deciding that Eleanor hadn't tampered with all the liquor in the house, he had helped himself to her father's brandy. A half-filled glass rested on the table beside the chair in which he sat. Emma sat in a chair on the other side of the small table so they shared a lamp. She was near enough to catch his fragrance, to hear the crackle of the paper as he turned the page.

These moments were like the ones she'd dreamed about when she imagined her life in later years, when she thought of herself married and with children. But the years that awaited her would have no moments like this in them. Her mouth grew dry and her tongue seemed unwilling to cooperate. "Do you suppose there is any chance they'll transport us rather than hang us?"

He looked up from the journal, his face unreadable. "Is that what you'd prefer?"

She wanted to swallow but the dryness continued. "I don't know. I should think any life at all is preferable over death, even a harsh life."

"It's more than harsh. It's brutal."

She nodded. She'd never known anyone who'd been transported. In truth, the only person she knew who'd ever been to gaol or prison was James—and she'd seen what they had done to his back when he was a child. She couldn't imagine how much harsher the punishment would be for an adult.

As though aware of the distressing thoughts plowing through her mind, he said, "I shouldn't worry about it overmuch, if I were you."

"You're absolutely right. I should make the most of the time I have here while I'm here." She studied the clumsily done needlework in her lap. "I don't even know why I'm bothering with this. I can't possibly finish it before we leave. I doubt—"

"Emma."

His voice was firm, yet gentle, and it drew her in the same manner that everything about him did. She found comfort from his nearness even as she knew that he'd be the death of her. "Say my name again."

She didn't understand the struggle she saw

in his features. Was he repulsed by her, by the thought of her name rolling off his tongue?

"Emma," he finally murmured.

"You can't imagine how many times I longed to hear you say my name rather than Eleanor's." She looked down because she didn't want him to see the damnable tears that had surfaced yet again. "How much do you despise me for my deception?"

It seemed that minutes ticked by before he finally said, "Probably not nearly as much as you despise yourself."

She peered over at him, surprised by his candor, yet relieved by his words. Although judging by how much she loathed herself, perhaps his dislike for her was greater than she wanted. "You are oh so very wise, James Swindler."

"My life has brought all sorts through it. Some guilty. Some innocent. Some deserving of what fate brought their way. Some not. There was one lad I knew, long ago, cocky bastard. Greedy, too. Wanted everything he set his eyes on, he did. One day he saw a gent take a gold watch from his pocket. It was so shiny. The boy thought, 'Oh, I'd like to have that, I would.' So he pinched it. But he wasn't very good, you see.

"The gent missed his watch straightaway, started yelling for a constable. The boy got scared.

His father was standing nearby, so into his father's pocket he dropped it. I suppose it was the surprised look on his father's face that caused the constable to search him. And the gent, well, he was a lord. Didn't appreciate having his watch pilfered. He saw to it that the man was hanged for his offense within the fortnight. Not once did the man ever declare his innocence. Not once did he ever point the blame at his son. He walked up the steps to the gallows as though he had no regrets. The regrets were left to his son."

Her chest ached as though it had grown too small to contain her heart. "You were the son."

She saw the answer reflected in his eyes. Twenty years to live with regret.

"My father told me we were playing a prank, we were swindling justice. When Feagan took me in, when he took anyone in, he made the boy change his name. Swindler seemed to suit a lad who'd managed to have his father hanged in his place."

Although all these years had passed, her heart still went out to the boy who was now sitting before her as a man. "Oh, James, he wouldn't have wanted you to live with the regrets. He knew what he was doing. Parents sacrifice for their children all the time."

"It doesn't make it any easier to live with, Emma."

"That's the reason you don't carry a watch."

"Can't bring myself to purchase one—even though I can now well afford it."

As though they'd only been talking about the weather, he returned to reading the journal. Because she could think of nothing significant to say to comfort him, she left him to it.

Chapter 16

Because he'd taken an overly long sleep that afternoon, due to the unfortunate draught that Eleanor—strange how the name he'd once adored suddenly grated on him—had slipped him, Swindler was far from tired when the clock on the mantel chimed ten. Emma, on the other hand, was wilted. She told him to sleep in her bedchamber. She had plans to sleep with Eleanor. If sleep came at all.

Although aware that he appeared a buffoon without manners, he didn't stand when Emma rose from her chair. He knew if he got to his feet, nothing on earth would stop him from approaching her, taking her in his arms and carrying her to bed. If he could last that long. His body was wound so tightly from being alone in her presence that it was quite possible he'd try to have her before they ever left the room. So he'd stayed where he was, given her a distracted good-night without ever looking up from the journal. It was bloody hell to sit so near her without touching her.

To make matters worse, he'd revealed his deepest, darkest secret as though it were a fairy tale. Whatever had possessed him to confess his sins regarding his father? Now she knew he, too, was responsible for a man's death. He may as well have murdered his father, dropped the noose around his neck. The guilt had gnawed at him for twenty years now, leaving behind raw wounds that would never heal. No one knew about them, not even Frannie, but where Emma was concerned, he seemed unable to keep any secrets.

It was long past midnight when Swindler set the journal aside. He wanted to come to know the girl so he could better understand how whatever had happened might have affected her. Perhaps a bit of him was also searching for hints regarding Emma. He didn't want to believe that she'd been completely duplicitous while in London. She had to have shared her true self with him, even if her name and her reasons hadn't been honest. Damn it, he didn't want to lose her, lose the woman he'd met in London, the one who intrigued him, made him laugh, made him glad to get up in the morning, gave him reason to anticipate the day.

He thought the woman he'd known in London was more Emma than the woman who watched

him here, the one with worry in her eyes and suspicions. He didn't blame her for whatever doubts
she might be harboring. He wasn't even certain that
he could explain all the reasons that had brought
him here. Pride, because he'd allowed a murderer to
escape his clutches. Honor, because his word could
so easily be brought into question. But it was more
than work. It was so much that he couldn't explain.

The storm still raged outside. Swindler wasn't
certain he'd be able to sleep with all its howling
and shrieking. Even the rain was louder than anything he'd ever heard in London. Rubbing his stiff
neck, he decided that with both ladies in bed, what
he really wanted was a hot bath.

Just off the kitchen he found a bathing room. No
doubt a recent addition. While he was able to pump
water to fill the tub, because he preferred it near to
boiling and because he liked it full and was in the
mood for a bit of indulgence, it took him a while to
get the water to his satisfaction. He'd just pulled his
shirt over his head when the door opened.

His heart galloped as he turned around, and just
as quickly it slowed to a canter. "Eleanor."

Releasing a soft laugh and drawing her shawl
more tightly over her night rail, she took two steps
toward him. "Oh, James, I can't tell you how it hurts
me that you fail to recognize me. It's me. Emma."

"The bloody hell you are." Dismissing her, careful

to keep his back from her view, he dipped his hand in the water. Still hot enough, but not for long.

"I can't believe after all we shared—"

Spinning around, he grabbed her wrist before she could touch his bare shoulder. He wasn't certain what his face revealed, but judging by the widening of her eyes, it was exactly what he was thinking. "Leave me be. I want nothing to do with you."

She sagged as though all remaining life had been drained from her. "You really can tell us apart. No one else has ever been able to do that. Not even Father. How can you be sure I'm not Emma?"

Releasing his hold on her, he stepped away. "Your eyes."

"They're the same shade of blue."

"The same shade, perhaps, but the souls they reveal are very different."

She released a harsh scoff. "Mine is harder, I suppose. He deserved it, you know. You'll see. Once you've finished reading the journal. Emma said you want to read all of it. There's little point. It was last summer that destroyed her."

"I'll handle this matter as I think best." Dipping his fingers in the water again, he nodded toward her bandaged hands. "What happened?"

She rubbed them together. "I can't get his blood off. I keep trying, but there's always a little bit that I seem to miss."

"Soak them in vinegar. It dissolves the blood."

"Truly?"

No, but the remedy had worked after his father's hanging, when Feagan took him in. Swindler had scrubbed his hands raw trying to get off the blood that only he could see—he and Feagan. It had been years before he realized that Feagan had tricked him into believing what he needed to hear so he'd stop scraping the imaginary blood off his hands. But the nightmares were something Swindler had been forced to come to terms with on his own. They still visited on occasion, usually on the anniversary of his father's death.

"I've seen it work," was all he said now.

"I shall try it in the morning and leave you to your bath now." She turned to go, then looked back. "She wanted to stay in London, to be with you. I convinced her we were only safe if we stayed together. It should be enough that only one of us hangs. See to it that she doesn't. I shan't be able to live with myself otherwise."

He watched her walk away. He still didn't trust her, but he was fairly certain she loved her sister—both of them. It didn't excuse what she'd done, but it made it a bit more understandable.

With a shake of his head, and no resolution to his dilemma, he turned his attention back to his bath. His water was too tepid now, so he set about heating another pot. Once he had the water again to his liking, he removed the remainder of his clothes and climbed into the tub. The hot water swirled around him as he sat in the cramped confines. He missed the large copper tub he'd had specially made to accommodate the length of his body. But at least the hot water in which he soaked eased away some of his tension.

He wasn't certain what he'd expected to find when he began his journey here. The woman he'd known in London, to be sure. But he hadn't known if he wanted her to be the same or different from the lady he'd taken to his bed. If she were different, he could rely on his anger to get him through bringing her to justice. If she were the same, each step of the journey would be hell.

He dropped his head back. It was hell.

He wanted to saddle up the horse he'd hired and leave her here. Return to London. Explain to Sir David that he, the best at solving crimes, was flummoxed and that the murder of Lord Rockberry would remain unsolved. Swindler's perfect record would no longer be perfect.

But leaving her here meant never having her in his life again, because it would be so much harder to lie about the crime with her at his side. It was even possible that the guilt would slowly nibble away at her, destroy what he had come to love. He could see it already having its way with her in such a short time. She was thinner than she'd been in London, her step heavier, as though she carried a great weight on her shoulders now. Her eyes were hollow, ringed in dark circles, dull. She was the woman he'd known in London and yet she wasn't.

He knew guilt's power. It had been his companion all these years. If only he hadn't lifted the damned watch. If only he'd tossed it aside instead of slipping it into his father's pocket. His father had always seemed larger than life, able to handle any situation. He found work when others couldn't, kept a roof over their head and food in their bellies. But there had never been money for extra items, only the essentials. The gold watch had looked so pretty.

Swindler shoved the dark thoughts back to the shadowy corner where they belonged. Thinking about them only served to distract him from his purpose. Besides, the water had cooled. It was time to concentrate on other things. He scrubbed off quickly. Leaving the tub, he toweled off before drawing on his trousers. He saw no need to put on anything more. Eleanor had surely returned to bed by now.

After tidying up the room, he took a lamp and walked through the house, making certain that no lamps had been left burning. Then he went up the stairs to his bedchamber.

The bed was turned down. He set the lamp on the bedside table. Stripping off his clothes, he crawled into bed, put out the flame in the lamp, and settled back. Emma's rose fragrance surrounded him. He tried not to think of her nestled in this bed.

He focused on the window, the draperies drawn back. Lightning flashed and he thought of the fireworks they'd watched, the kiss—

Every damned thing reminded him of Emma, of how much he'd enjoyed having her in his life. Every damned thing reminded him that she was no longer a part of the joy in his life—she was now a suspect. More than that, she was the one he had to arrest.

Eleanor may have done the deed, but Emma had played a part in Rockberry's demise. As much as he wanted to, he couldn't overlook it. And in not overlooking it, he couldn't ignore that she hadn't trusted him, had used him, had betrayed him.

It was so easy to forget all the wrongs when he was looking at her, studying her—when she was near enough to touch. It was also impossible to know how much of her true self she'd revealed to him in London. She'd duped him once. He didn't intend to fall into her trap again.

James awoke to dreary skies. The rain had stopped. The sun was striving to shine through the gray clouds that remained. The house was incredibly silent. Emma had been right. It was never this quiet in London.

Abruptly he sat up. It could also be so quiet because they'd left. Getting out of bed, he quickly dressed and hurried downstairs. He heard activity in the kitchen. When he got there, he saw only Eleanor kneading the bread dough. "Where is she?"

Eleanor peered over at him. "Good morning to you, too, sir."

"Where in the bloody hell is Emma?"

Wiping her hands on her apron, Eleanor edged past him. "Come with me."

She led him to a back door, opened it, and stepped outside. "Follow that well-worn path. It leads—"

"To the cove."

"Yes."

He strode along the edge of the dirt trail where the grass made the journey less muddy. Puddles abounded. At one point he considered removing his boots, then decided that giving them a good polish would at least occupy his hands later in the day.

The path eventually led downward and into an area where the waters created a still pool. A small fire was burning nearby. But what caught his attention were the slender bare arms slicing through the water.

Emma was beauty and grace. She rolled onto her back, kicking her feet. He didn't know how she managed to stay afloat. She wore little more than a chemise that clung to her body. He could see the outline of her taut nipples and the shadow between her thighs. He was well acquainted with the heaven her body offered. Although he knew he should look away, he couldn't. He remembered the taste, the texture, the sight of what was now barely hidden.

But what most astounded him was her face in repose. He didn't know if he'd ever seen her with absolutely no worries.

With a splash, she suddenly went upright and began paddling toward the shore. When near enough, she stood up. Holding his gaze demurely, she waded toward him until she eventually left the water. Snatching up a blanket that he'd not even noticed, she wrapped it around herself and sat beside the fire.

Only then did he realize that her lips had gone blue and that she was shivering uncontrollably.

"Good Lord, what have you done?" he demanded as he came around behind her and drew her up against his chest, rubbing her arms. "Are you trying to catch your death?"

"I've swum in the pool for years. Makes me hearty."

He continued to hold her until her teeth stopped chattering, then he simply folded her into his embrace. She leaned back into him.

"I didn't want to betray you," she whispered hoarsely.

Against his will, his arms tightened around her.

"A thousand times I wished that Father had sent me first and that I'd met you last summer when I was still filled with innocence and knew only happiness. There were times when I was with you that I could forget why Eleanor and I had come to London. Afterward I'd feel guilty for not focusing on retribution for Elisabeth. Ever since that afternoon when you approached me at Hyde Park, everything became so much more complicated. I didn't want to come to care for you, but you made that wish an impossibility."

He was acutely aware of her trembling, but knew it had little to do with the cold. She was weeping. He heard it in the rough edge of her voice.

"After that last night . . . in London . . . as you returned me to the lodgings, I'd prayed that Eleanor had not possessed the strength to go through with it. I was going to tell her to trust you. That I did. That I thought you would see justice done if you only knew the truth. But it was too late."

"Why didn't you come to me afterward?" he forced out through clenched teeth. It was torturous knowing how she suffered, hearing her speak of their time together—but she'd walked away from it. He couldn't overlook that. "Why not tell me the truth then? Why not trust me to protect you?"

She twisted around in his arms and touched his cheek. "You have so much pride. How could you not hate me for what I'd done? How could you not think that every word uttered, every touch, every kiss, were simply tools to seduce you into doing my bidding?"

"How could you have just walked away from what had developed between us?"

"Because I couldn't stand the thought of watching it shatter. I didn't want to see the disgust in your eyes when you realized what we'd done. And I was worried about Eleanor. She put on such a brave front, but I could see that she was devastated by what she'd accomplished."

He wanted to believe her, he wanted to forgive her. He wanted what they'd somehow managed to capture that last night, but he knew it was in the past.

"You're going to take us back to London, aren't you?" she asked.

"I have no choice."

She gave him a resolute nod. "I don't think the storm is completely over. We'll probably have a bit more rain."

"We'll go when I'm finished with the journal."

Drawing the blanket more securely around her, she worked her way out of his embrace. "I should go to the house now, change into some dry clothing."

"I'll stay and put out the fire."

She gave him a tremulous smile. "There's so much I want to tell you, but I'm not certain you'd trust the words. You might think I'm trying to sway you from your duty, but I'm not."

"Then don't say them."

He saw the hurt in her eyes, but at that moment he was struggling with his own demons, not certain that he could trust himself to do the right thing.

She rose gracefully and strolled out of the cove. He sat by the fire and stared out to sea. She was wrong. It was never completely quiet here. He could hear the thrashing against the cliffs, the water tumbling into the cove, splashing against the shore. But it was rhythmic and peaceful. Gave a man leave to think.

Yet all he could think was that no good options remained to him.

Chapter 17

Emma had been correct concerning the weather. The wind picked up in the late afternoon and the rain began to fall. They were enclosed in the house. Following dinner, the three of them retired to the front parlor, the ladies with their needlework and Swindler with the journal.

Although he was reading Elisabeth's words, he could clearly see Emma in each of them. Gathering seashells, feeding the seagulls. And he saw things that weren't written. He imagined her running barefoot to greet their father when he returned from town. He could see her chasing chickens and laughing on a swing.

"How did you come to work for Scotland Yard, Mr. Swindler?" Eleanor asked, never lifting her gaze from her needlework.

"I would report those who committed crimes in the rookeries, give the policemen descriptions so they could arrest the offenders."

Her fingers stilled as she lifted her gaze to his. "I see. So you've made it your life's work to see the proper people punished."

"I believe in justice, Miss Watkins."

Nodding, she returned to her embroidery.

"Exactly how did you do it?" he asked.

Her head came up so quickly that he heard her neck pop. "Do what?"

"Kill Rockberry."

Emma's eyes widened with alarm. "Don't force her to go through it again."

"If you don't want to hear, leave, but I have questions and I want answers."

Emma reached across and wrapped her hand around Eleanor's. "I'll not leave my sister to suffer alone."

Swindler's gut clenched with the knowledge that she'd gladly go to the gallows with her sister—and in doing so, she'd leave him alone. She was as courageous and reckless as he'd always believed. He turned his attention back to Eleanor. "You enjoyed a glass of wine with him."

"Yes. I caught him as he was going into the residence. He invited me in. Said I reminded him of Elisabeth, only more beautiful. No gentleman had ever told me I was beautiful before. To my everlasting shame, I began to succumb to his charms."

"But you didn't finish your wine."

"No. He jerked me out of the chair and tried to kiss me, all the while saying horrible untruths about Elisabeth. I had the dagger and I used it."

"Only one stab."

"Yes."

He took comfort in the fact that she wasn't gloating. He had a feeling she was caught between remorse that she'd taken a life and satisfaction that the man who'd trifled with her sister was no longer breathing.

"Did he die immediately?"

"Must you put her through this?" Emma demanded.

"It's all right, Emma," Eleanor said. "No. He writhed around for a bit, then went still. And I left."

"You should have taken the dagger with you."

"I thought of it later, but I just wanted to leave. And I certainly didn't want to touch him."

Something about that crime nagged at him, something that hadn't seemed right at the time. He was certain it would come to him.

"If you had it to do over—" he began.

"I'd do it again," she said succinctly. "Finish reading the journal, Mr. Swindler. Quite possibly you'll wish you'd had the opportunity to use a dagger on him."

He returned to his reading. Rather than returning to their needlework, the ladies went to prepare themselves for bed. Based on the sounds he heard coming down the hallway, he could only assume those preparations included bathing.

How could he concentrate on the words when his mind was suddenly filled with images of Emma soaking in the tub, drops of water rolling over her skin? Lord help him, he wanted to join her, wash her, dry her, hold her.

He fought to clear his mind of everything except the journal. Each page painted a portrait of a young girl growing into womanhood with dreams of love, family, happiness. There was an innocence in her descriptions, a joy for life, and excitement awaiting each day. Elisabeth Watkins had been purity. Sweetness.

She'd been very much like Emma.

Long after the ladies went to bed and the house had grown quiet except for the storm raging outside, Swindler indulged in another bath for himself. It wasn't unusual for him to bathe several times a week. He had a childhood in the rookeries to constantly wash off.

He thought of Eleanor's hands. Some things, no matter how often or how hard you scrubbed, were always there, just below the surface waiting to come forth.

Following the ritual he'd begun the night before, he grabbed a lamp and checked the house before climbing the stairs to the bedchamber.

He knew Emma was there the moment he opened the door, before he'd stepped fully inside and the lamp illuminated the room. He'd detected the presence of roses as though the petals were unfurling, not a lingering scent, but full and strong. His stomach tightened with the heady fragrance filling his nostrils.

Turning in its direction, he found her standing by the window, dressed in a night rail, her pale hair loose, inviting his fingers to comb through it. He imagined if there were no storm, she'd be limned by moonlight, but the wind and rain continued to thrash about.

"How long do these storms usually last?" he asked quietly.

"We can never predict the storms. Shut the door."

If he were a gentleman, he'd have shut it with himself on the other side. Instead, he pulled it closed, the snick of it blocking out the rest of the world reverberating through the room like a bullet fired from a pistol. With two steps he placed the lamp on the table beside the bed. With four more he'd joined her at the window and was cradling her cheek. "Emma."

"How do you know I'm not Eleanor?" she whispered.

"Because it's not Eleanor who holds my heart."

He heard her small gasp, saw her eyes widen as they filled with tears.

"Damn you, Emma, for not trusting me in London."

Anger and frustration drove him to pull her into his arms and slash his mouth across hers. Something stronger than affection, something he didn't want to truly acknowledge or give name to, forced him to gentle his plunder of her mouth. She'd taken possession of his heart slowly, with smiles and laughter and a touch of innocence such as he'd never experienced.

He'd known then that she was unlike any other woman of his acquaintance. She'd intrigued him. Even if he hadn't been ordered to follow her, he'd have followed her—to the ends of the earth if need be. He could claim all he wanted that he'd searched tirelessly for her in order to bring her to justice, but the truth was that he'd been obsessed with finding her because *he* was obsessed with *her*.

After she'd been in his apartment, it had suddenly become incredibly lonely without her presence there. After she'd become part of his days and nights, his life had hardly seemed worth living without her in it.

Greedily he trailed his mouth over her chin and along her neck until he reached the sweet shell of her ear. "Leave now unless you want to end up in my bed."

His voice was harsh, his breathing ragged, his body straining beyond endurance to claim her again, to fill her, to be surrounded by her.

"It's *my* bed," she said shakily, and he heard the same raw need in her voice that quivered through his.

Laughing, when he'd never expected to laugh again, released some of the tension in him as he dipped down and lifted her into his arms. "Then allow me to take you to *your* bed."

As she stroked her fingers over his bare shoulders, as his mouth returned to hers, as his long strides took her to the bed, Emma felt joy spiral through her when she'd never expected to feel joy again. She'd waited until Eleanor drifted off to sleep before slipping from the bed and coming to this room. She'd been waiting nervously for his arrival. A dozen times she considered returning to Eleanor's bed, but if her life was to be cut short or if it was to take her on a journey to the far side of the world where she'd never again be in James's company, then she wanted this time with him, and so she'd waited in anticipation.

And she'd not been disappointed when he walked through the door bare-chested and masculine, larger than life, bold and confident. He was everything she wasn't. Never doubting what he wanted. Never questioning his actions. She'd seen it in the graceful way he moved through the room, the heated awareness in his eyes as he'd neared.

Her heart had nearly burst with overwhelming gratitude when he rasped her name as though he understood how much she needed to hear her name on his lips at that precise moment. Every moment spent with him in London had been bittersweet, his whispering her sister's name painful to hear. Her deception adding to her misery. In London she'd been masquerading as Eleanor.

Here, for the first time, no shadows of deception eased between them. It was her name that he whispered. Now within her bedchamber, honesty reigned. He was hers and she was his, completely and absolutely. Regardless of what heartache tomorrow or the day following might bring, tonight would be as uncomplicated and as breathtaking as either of them could make it.

Without removing his mouth from hers, he lowered her feet to the patterned rug beside her bed. She thought she should step away, should remove her gown, but she seemed unable to stop running her hands over his bare chest, shoulders, and arms. His muscles quivered with anticipation. She did that to him, had power over him. She watched his face as his gaze followed the movements of his fingers as they quickly worked to release one button after another on her gown, the material parting of its own accord. Meanwhile, beneath her fingers, she felt his muscles growing taut, could feel as well as hear his breathing becoming more ragged.

His hands slid inside her gown, bracketing her ribs, his thumbs enticingly skimming the underside of her breasts. Stepping forward, he placed his open mouth on her throat where her pulse fluttered wildly. She relished the heat of his tongue swirling over her flesh as he nudged the material aside until he reached her breast and closed his mouth over it. Rising up on her toes, wrapping her arms around him, she pressed her lower body toward his while arching her back, lost in the sensations he managed to bring to the fore with seemingly so little effort.

He slowly moved his mouth across the valley between her breasts before giving the same attentions to the other. His low, throaty growl of satisfaction echoed between them, and she moaned in response, before straightening. He lifted his head and his eyes captured hers. With only the low flame in the lamp to provide light, the green was lost but not the intense desire glittering within their depths. She skimmed her hands down his chest, felt the muscles of his stomach quivering in anticipation as her fingers glided over them until she reached his trousers. His eyes darkened and the muscles in his face tensed. Ever so slowly, tormenting them both, she freed one button. She watched his eyes slam closed, the muscles of his throat work as he swallowed. When he opened his eyes, she could see the strain trying his patience.

"Emma," he rasped, "for God's sake. Move a bit more quickly. You're torturing me here."

"Say my name again."

"Emma."

She freed a button.

"Emma."

Another.

"Dear sweet Emma."

The last button released him and his torment. She wrapped her fingers around the velvety heat. With a low groan, he bracketed her face and brought his mouth back to hers, kissing her with a fierceness that matched the storm beating against the cottage. She was barely aware of them discarding what remained of their clothing before falling together onto the bed.

With their hands and mouths, they touched, explored, learned anew what they'd discovered that long ago night in London.

Swindler realized that she'd lost more weight than he'd thought, as he palmed her smaller breasts. As he held her close, he'd been able to feel every rib. He noted other changes: narrower hips, more bone in places where she should have more flesh. But nothing curbed his overwhelming desire for her. Her body delighted him because it was hers. But his favorite feature continued to be her eyes, the manner in which they roamed over him, initially with shyness, then gaining boldness as she grew more comfortable with their nakedness. He wondered if it would always be so between them. A few heartbeats of hesitation before they became lost in the pleasure they could bring each other.

No woman in his history could compare to her. No woman in his future could replace her. She was what he wanted now, this moment and the next, and the one that followed that, each one that led to the end of his life. He would make it happen, by God. He would keep her with him. He didn't know how. He would lie, he would cheat, he would steal. If need be, he would murder. He'd confessed that she held his heart. He'd yet to tell her that she possessed his soul.

He'd deceived himself when he began this journey believing that he sought justice. All along all he'd sought was her. Now that he'd found her again, it would kill him to give her up. He would find a way to save her if it was the last thing he ever did.

But for now all he wanted was to taste the sweetness of her mouth and flesh. All he wanted was to bring her unbridled pleasure. All he wanted was to possess her and journey with her into the realm of passion.

She moaned and sighed with every glide of his hand, every stroke of his tongue, every press of his lips. Hovering over her delicate form, he should have felt like a great oaf, but she had the ability to make him feel powerful without the usual accompanying intimidation, because as petite as she was, she possessed her own strength, her own determination. By God, she'd traveled to a strange city teeming with strangers in order to seek satisfaction for her sister's death, and asked help of no one other than a sister who shared the same purpose. She shared his belief in justice. On many levels she was his equal, in some ways she was his better, in no way was she less.

But here, beneath the sheets, was where they were the most well-matched. He fought off the distant fear that in spite of his best efforts, he would lose this, he would lose her. He joined his mouth to hers, kissing her deeply, hungrily, as though it were the first kiss, as though it were the last. Wedging himself between her thighs, he slid a hand beneath her and lifted her hips. With one long, sure stroke, he buried himself in her molten haven to the hilt.

A shudder of absolute pleasure rippled through

him as he released a low groan, tore his mouth from hers and buried his face in the curve of her shoulder. If he moved, he was likely to spill his seed before he'd seen to her ultimate enjoyment.

She tightened her body around him, and he moaned. "You are a witch."

"I love this, love the way it feels when we're bound like this."

Swallowing hard, he lifted his head and gazed down on her, saw the wonder in her eyes that after everything he could still want her. "Emma, how could I not?"

Emma felt the tears sting her eyes because he knew, *knew*, the doubts that plagued her, the questions that bombarded her. He answered them without her giving them voice, as though they were bound by something that went beyond flesh, beyond hearts. As though their souls belonged to each other.

As he began to rock against her, he spoke her name again. It contained a richness she hadn't noticed before. She relished the sound of her name coming from his lips. Her name. *Emma.*

It was her that he possessed, her that he touched, her that he stirred. His movements became more frantic and her body reacted in kind, meeting his thrusts, building the pressure toward release. Her skin, her muscles, tightened and curled.

Opening her eyes, she became lost in his. She ran her fingers through his hair, over his shoulders, down his back. She felt his corded muscles bunching and straining. Dew from his efforts to hold back pooled on his skin.

"Emma," he forced through clenched teeth as the pinnacle of pleasure rocked him, rocked her.

She emitted a tiny scream, before his mouth blanketed hers and absorbed the remainder of it. She trembled in the wake of the cataclysm, felt the tremors undulating through him.

Collapsing to the side, he rolled her flush against him, draping one of her legs over his hip. Still joined, they faced each other, breathing heavily, drenched in sweat. Reaching down, he brought the sheet and a blanket over them to ward off the chill, to create a cocoon of warmth, as their bodies basked in the lethargy.

Gently, holding her gaze, he palmed her cheek and stroked his thumb in a circle on her face. She strummed her fingers over his back. Slowly their breathing calmed, settled, no longer harsh, no longer blocking out the patter of the rain hitting the roof. Even as she grew drowsy, she had to face the truth.

It had been a mistake to come here, to think she could have him again and then blithely walk away to face whatever the future held.

"Don't think about tomorrow," he said quietly.

"How is that you always know what's on my mind?"

He didn't answer with words. He simply gave her a tender smile and pressed a kiss to her forehead before again positioning himself so he could see her more clearly.

"I told you about the watch I stole," he said.

She nodded, wanting to caution him that now was not the time for remorse, even as she wanted him to unburden his sorrows. As long as she was able, she would provide him with what strength she could.

"The irony is that I stole it because my father didn't have one. And it was his birthday."

She saw him blink back the tears. That the memory could bring this large, strong man to tears tore into her heart. "Oh, James."

He shook his head as though to shake off his morose musings. "I told you the story only so you'd understand how important justice is to me. It was a damned watch. It's value not worth my father's life. A year in prison perhaps, a few lashes of the whip, but not his life. And Rockberry's life is not worth yours. I'll not let you"—he touched his thumb to her lips—"or Eleanor be hanged."

"You can't control the courts."

"Don't underestimate my influence. I'm not

saying you won't have to account for your actions, but I swear I'll not see you hanged."

She fought to give him a reassuring smile. She wanted to believe him. She truly did. But he was not God. He was not king. He was not nobility. He was an inspector with Scotland Yard. The son of a man who'd been hanged for thievery, regardless of his innocence.

He was simply a man, even if he was the man she loved.

Chapter 18

When Emma awoke, her first thought was that she'd slept, amazingly a deep dreamless sleep. Her second was that she was alone in the bed, but not alone in the room. She sensed his presence before she located him sitting in a chair by the window, the lamp nearby providing him with sufficient light to read the journal in his lap. Although only his profile was visible to her, she could detect the deep furrow in his brow as he absorbed her sister's account of her life and time in London. With his elbow perched on the arm of the chair, providing support, he held his chin, his forefinger stroking just below his lower lip, a lip she had an urgent desire to nibble upon.

Beyond the window the dark of night still hovered. The storm was dying down, the rain a softer patter, the wind a quieter moan.

Emma studied James as he read. He'd drawn on his trousers. Pity that. She'd never considered herself a woman who would prefer a man in all his naked glory, but James was indeed a fine specimen. He made her feel tiny, yet strong. She had power over him. He desired her. She couldn't stop the small smile from forming. He could distinguish her from Eleanor. No one else had ever been able to tell the three sisters apart. She supposed it was odd to take such delight in his ability, but it made her feel special. Their entire life all three sisters had struggled to be seen as individuals. People thought they should wear the same clothes, should strive to be identical, but they each possessed their little quirks, their small differences, and in some cases large ones. Eleanor was headstrong, quick to anger, quick to act. Emma analyzed far too much. Elisabeth had been far too adventuresome. It was the reason their father had decided she would be the first to brave London. What a catastrophe that had been.

Yet it had put into place a series of events through which she'd met James. If not for the fact that it had cost Elisabeth her life, she might have been grateful. Guiltily, a small part of her was glad for James—but the price had been so dear.

As though suddenly aware of her thoughts, he set the journal aside, rose to his feet and strode toward the bed, shucking his trousers as he neared, revealing all of his masculine glory. The smile he bestowed upon her as he slid into bed beside her caused her heart to trip over itself.

"I thought you'd never wake up," he growled, before taking her in his arms and making her ever so thankful she had.

June 15, 1851

Tonight Cousin Gertrude escorted me to my first ball. I'm not quite certain how she is related to us, but I daresay Father could have given me as grand an introduction into society as she did. I don't wish to besmirch her efforts, but I swear she knows not a soul of any importance. How she enticed Lady Chesney into inviting us is beyond me. But invitations were extended and we accepted. I spent the first hour sitting with Cousin while gents eyed me from a distance—not quite sure what to make of me, I'm certain.

Finally, well into the second hour, our hostess introduced Mr. Samuel Bentley and he asked for the honor of a dance. He was not the sort to turn heads, but many heads did turn as he led me onto the dance floor. He was the fourth son of a viscount, desperate enough for funds to ask straightaway what sort of dowry my father was bestowing upon me. He laughed at the amount, then apologized for his rudeness. He assured me that I would have a time of it securing a husband.

I did not doubt his words as I spent another hour becoming further acquainted with my chair. To my shame,

I even cursed Father for sending me to London. I was ill prepared for flirtation or exuding confidence. I was the country lass stumbling about in a strange place of unencumbered sophistication and confidence.

I begged of Cousin to allow us to leave, but she wouldn't hear of it. I suspected she was enthralled with the gaiety, that it was as new to her as it was to me.

And then he approached. I'd never seen a man so handsome, a man so charming. The Marquess of Rockberry. He led me into a waltz, and the most boring night of my life suddenly became the most memorable—in the blink of an eye.

June 17, 1851

I can hardly properly hold my pen in order to write legibly. My fingers, my whole person, are trembling with such excitement. Lord Rockberry called on me today. He brought me a dozen roses and a tin of chocolates. Cousin was astounded by his generosity. She assures me he is one of the most respected lords in London and that he is in a position to select his wife without consideration of her dowry. I could not be happier nor have greater hope that I shall make a good match and be able to provide the means for my sisters to have their own Season and secure their own happiness.

June 21, 1851

Lord Rockberry again called on me. He took me for

*a ride in his open carriage. Cousin accompanied us.
Once we arrived at Regent Park, we disembarked so that
we might walk with a little privacy and speak without
Cousin hearing every word. Lord Rockberry is seeking a wife with an adventuresome spirit and believes I
might suit. He teasingly told me that he wishes to test
his theory. Without Cousin knowing we made plans
to meet at midnight tomorrow. I am breathless with
anticipation.*

July 1, 1851
*Lord Rockberry called. I told Cousin to inform him
that I've taken ill.*

July 5, 1851
Lord Rockberry called again. I am still abed.

July 10, 1851
*I have asked Cousin to make arrangements so I might
return home.*

July 15, 1851
I am home.

July 20, 1851
*I can see the concern in my sisters' eyes, especially
Emma's. She has always been the most sensitive. I have
failed my family. I do not know how much longer I can*

live with the shame of what transpired during that night of "adventure" with Lord Rockberry.

August 5, 1851
  I have no will to eat.

August 8, 1851
  I have no will to breathe.

August 20, 1851
  I walked to the edge of the cliffs today. How easy it would be to simply step into nothingness. But it would break their hearts and so I must continue on.

September 1, 1851
  The cliffs are calling to me again. I do not know how much longer I can resist the peace they offer. But I know I cannot depart this earth without writing of the "adventure," as Lord Rockberry so blithely referred to it. Perhaps in so doing, I will find the peace I seek.
  At midnight I slipped out of the residence with Cousin none the wiser. In the alleyway Lord Rockberry kissed me quickly and handed me up into his carriage. Excitement thrummed through me. He whispered words to make me feel beautiful, desired. He explained that he was a disciple of Eros, the god of sexual desire. He was a member of a secret society which initiates women into the art of love. He told me it involved a beautiful ritual

during which he would claim me as his. He seduced me with his words, his kisses. In the carriage he plied me with wine. I suspect now that it was laced with something that served to disorient me. I did not feel myself. And I certainly did not act myself.

We arrived at a residence. Inside, two ladies took me away and began to prepare me. They removed their clothes and mine. Beautiful silver filigree circled their necks. They draped the softest silk over me and explained what was required of me. I wanted to protest but my mouth seemed unable to form coherent words. My will was no longer my own.

They led me into a dark room where the only light came from flickering candles. Pillows were piled everywhere. There were other naked ladies wearing the same silver at their throats. Men in red cloaks wavered in and out of my vision as the two ladies escorted me to Lord Rockberry. I heard humming, a chant.

The ladies removed my silk. I stood before him exposed. I knew I should have covered myself in shame, but I was beyond caring. The world faded in and out. He bade me to kneel before him. When I did, he placed the silver around my neck and told me I was now a sister of carnality. He lay me upon a mound of pillows and took me.

There were cheers and laughter echoing around me even as I tried to push him away. The pain was indescribable, the intimacy barbaric. The room exploded into madness, chaos, as others—men and women—had their way with me. I remember so little except the agony and humiliation. I thought I'd awaken to discover it had all been a dream. But the nightmare was real. And even though I've returned home, I seem unable to escape it.

September 7, 1851
   Forgive me.

Chapter 19

When Swindler awoke, sun was spilling in through the window and he was alone. After he'd made love to her a third time, Emma slipped out of the room as he drifted off to sleep. She wanted to be sure she returned to Eleanor's bed before her sister awoke.

He rolled over onto his back, shoved his hands behind his head, grimacing when he bumped his healing wound, and stared at the ceiling. He'd finished reading the journal in the early hours. He'd heard rumors of the secret societies that engaged in depravity but had always heard that the members were willing participants in the orgies, so they'd been of no concern to him. It seemed Rockberry sought to bring a new, supposedly exciting element to the festivities. An innocent. A virgin to be sacrificed.

Swindler's blood boiled when he thought about what Rockberry had done, the people he'd harmed, the pain he'd wrought. *Damned, arrogant bastard.* If he wasn't already dead, he would have strangled Rockberry with his own hands.

Claybourne had killed a man for raping Frannie when she was twelve. Swindler had thought nothing as vile would ever touch him again. He'd been wrong.

He'd not known Elisabeth before he read her journal, but he mourned her passing now.

The storm outside had ceased, but within him a storm for further retribution was brewing. He got out of bed and walked to the window. His heart very nearly stilled at the sight of Emma standing at the edge of the cliff. He didn't know how he knew it was her. All he could see was her back and the cloak billowing out behind her. What little wind remained from the storm toyed with her hair.

Christ! Surely she wasn't contemplating joining Elisabeth at the bottom of the sea.

Snatching up his trousers and pulling them on, he selfishly thought she couldn't possibly be considering leaving him—not after what they'd shared last night, after he made her smile and laugh, after he brought her pleasure, after she brought him pleasure more intense than anything he'd ever experienced. Yes, she'd left him before, back in London, but now things were different. She'd left him because of her shame and secrets. She'd left him because she thought she had no choice if she wanted to escape the gallows. Now she knew differently.

He grabbed his shirt, pulling it over his head as he rushed out the door and down the stairs, nearly losing his balance and tumbling in the process. Taking a quick second to get his shirt situated, he carried on and burst through the door to the outside as though her life—and his—depended on it. He ignored the pain as his bare feet encountered tiny rocks and thorns. Afraid of startling her, of causing her to tumble over the edge, he didn't call out to her. When he was near enough to see that she wasn't teetering at the edge as he'd first feared, he slowed his gait and fought to regain his dignity. A bit difficult to do when his feet were bare and his shirt unbuttoned.

He was surprised that his feet pounding the earth in order that he could reach her quickly hadn't caused it to tremble and alert her to his presence. Or perhaps she simply wasn't yet ready to face him. Whatever the reason, as he came to stand beside her, she continued to stare out at the whitecapped sea as though it contained answers.

"Emma," he said quietly, wanting desperately to reach for her, to draw her farther back from the edge.

"Sometimes when I stand here I can hear her laughter."

"Elisabeth's?"

She nodded. "I yelled at her, you know."

"It's not a crime to yell."

She rolled her eyes toward the sky as though she sought salvation. "She wouldn't tell us what happened in London. We only knew she returned home with no marriage prospects. Father had no money with which to send Eleanor and I. Selfishly, selfishly, I wanted to go so desperately, to find a husband and have children, to be a wife and a mother. I screamed at Elisabeth, told her she'd been a disappointment to us all. I had the audacity to tell her that if Father had sent me, I would have snagged a husband who could ensure that my sisters had a Season and were well looked after. I wanted a Season so frightfully badly, so stupidly. I think my words may have caused her to kill herself."

"No, Emma." His arms were around her before he'd given it any thought. Turning her, he drew her into his body, pressed her face to his chest. "I read her journal. Nothing you said caused her death. Nothing you could have said would have stopped it. Rockberry is the sole blame here."

She tilted her head back to look at him, her delicate brow furrowed. "Had I been a better sist—"

He touched his finger to her lips before she could finish. "You mustn't think that way. Had I been a better son . . . you see? Nothing is to be gained." Although he had spent a good many years wondering how differently things might have been if he'd not taken the watch, if he *had* been a better son. Only now, while holding this woman close, trying to ease her pain, did a bit of his ease as well. Guilt and regret had taken the joy from his life. This woman returned it all to him. It broke his heart that she suffered, that she felt guilt and remorse.

"When I read Elisabeth's words, read what happened to her, at first I couldn't believe them," Emma said. "I thought surely they were a story she'd created or a rumor she'd heard about something happening in London. I wept when I finally faced the reality of them. How could someone in Lord Rockberry's position be as vile as all that? He trifled with her. Broke her heart, broke her spirit, and in the end broke her body."

"I've known people from all walks of life—from the beggar on the street corner to those who have dined in the presence of the queen. At all levels, I've seen people behave in ways that have turned my stomach. But at all levels, I've also seen people to be admired. Feagan was a thief, took me in, taught me to be a thief. I would have died for him. Claybourne, a lord with blood on his hands. I admire no man more than I admire him. Even Jack Dodger, scoundrel that he is, takes boys in off the street and gives them a job, keeps them out of trouble. Society is made up of good and bad, Emma. You cannot judge any portion of it based on a few."

She gave him a soft smile. "I think you would have liked Elisabeth."

"I know I would have." Grateful for her smile and the easing of sorrow in her eyes, he tweaked her nose. "But not more than I like you."

She released a bubble of laughter, and everything within him finally relaxed. "May we move away from the edge now?"

Her smile grew. "Do you not like the cliffs?"

"I don't like being so close to them, no."

"They're perfectly safe." Sadness suddenly contorted her features. "Unless you don't want them to be."

He couldn't ask her not to think about her sister, especially as there was unfinished business, but he suspected he could distract Emma for a time, especially as he'd already gone far too long without kissing her. Even as he took her mouth, even as she offered it, he was grateful that she wasn't the one who'd been charged with going to London last Season to secure a husband and a future for her sisters. The thought of Rockberry touching so much as a hair on her head caused Swindler's blood to scald. It seemed Emma wasn't the only one unable to stop thinking about her sister.

It was only when she eased her feet over his in

order to achieve a little more height that he realized she, too, was barefoot. How was it that something as simple and tiny as her bare soles could shoot sparks of desire through him? How was it that he could easily imagine laying her down on the cool grass, wrapping his fingers around her bare ankle and sliding his hand up her calf, over her knee, and along her thigh?

Only a few hours had passed since he'd taken her in his bed, yet at that moment he was as randy as a callow youth who had yet to experience his first woman. Pulling back from the kiss, he saw the yearning in her deep blue eyes and he realized, somewhat startled, that they matched the sea in the distance. She belonged here with her bare feet, her sea blue eyes, her gentleness. Even as his thoughts traveled that path, he remembered that she could be as fierce and as deadly as the storm. He'd underestimated her determination where justice was concerned once—he wouldn't do it again.

He slid his hand down her arm and laced his fingers through hers until their palms touched. He'd never considered how sensual it could be to hold a lady's hand intimately. If not for the weight of what remained before them, he might have felt carefree and lighthearted. Instead he wished they might have today forever and that tomorrow might never arrive.

She was the one who tugged on his hand and prompted them to begin walking back toward the house. He thought he could grow accustomed to this place, to having her near. Even with so innocent a musing, guilt and regret battled within him. London was where he belonged, fighting for the rights of the innocent.

"The roads will be muddy," she said quietly, as though she knew in which direction his mind wandered. "It would be best to delay our journey until they've dried."

"How long?"

She peered up at him, her lips forming a mischievous grin that made him want to lean down and kiss her again. "Twenty, thirty years."

The wind carried his laughter toward the road that would lead them to the village, and from there back to London. He sobered. "I wish it could be so, Emma."

"But you're a man of honor, a man of the law. It's one of the things I admire about you, that you believe in justice. But I don't see why Eleanor and I must both pay for one act. Spare her. Take me and leave her here. She already suffers greatly for what she did."

He stopped walking and touched her cheek. Was there anyone as courageous, as unselfish, as these two sisters, each willing to take the complete responsibility for Rockberry's death and to pay the ultimate price? He knew they weren't a threat to anyone else. Their actions had been motivated by grief and horror over what the marquess had done to their sister. Swindler had often released boys from gaol or failed to arrest them when their crimes were petty. But murder?

"Eleanor asked the same of me, to leave you behind. But it's not a simple matter, Emma. If there is only one of you, how do I explain my vouching for you? My word, my reputation, will come into question. My position with Scotland Yard will be in jeopardy."

"Then don't take either of us."

"I've never not been able to solve a crime."

"So it's your pride that drives you?"

Her words pounded into him. He'd never considered himself prideful. His work was altruistic. It brought him a sense of satisfaction to do for others what he'd been too terrified to do for his father— provide evidence that he wasn't the guilty party. "No, my efforts protect the innocent. I risk losing my ability to ensure it is the guilty who pay and not the innocent. I've spent my life striving to atone for my father's death. I can't turn my back on it or dishonor it now—no matter how much I wish matters were different."

With a small nod, she moved away from his

touch as easily as shadows retreated when touched by the sun. He sensed no anger in her. Disappointment, perhaps. Grudging acceptance of his decision.

They began walking again, but were no longer holding hands. He felt the absence of her touch like a huge, aching chasm in his chest. How could he make her understand that if he wasn't with Scotland Yard, he'd have no purpose in his life? As justified as he considered the death of Rockberry—the man was a beast—Swindler could see only two choices if he wanted to save her: let the murder go unsolved or allow only Eleanor to pay the price. And only Eleanor paying the price brought its own complications, as he'd already explained to Emma. He was also almost certain it would cost him Emma. She'd not forgive him for arresting her sister and not her. Truth be told, he could see Emma marching into police headquarters and claiming she'd done the deed. The sisters would work together to confuse the courts—or they'd accept their punishment.

After reading Elisabeth's journal, something else had begun nagging at Swindler. Business remained undone. Finishing it might bring salvation for both ladies, but the dangers couldn't be overlooked.

"In her journal, Elisabeth mentioned silver filigree that Rockberry placed around her neck."

Emma peered over at him, and in her eyes he saw that she didn't want to discuss the particulars of what had transpired between her sister and Rockberry. But in the jut of her chin, he recognized her determination not to retreat from what could well turn into unpleasant discourse. "Yes."

"Do you know if she kept it? Have you seen it?"

She flushed. How easily she was embarrassed, even after the incredible intimacy they'd shared. He wondered if Elisabeth had been as quick to blush. Had Rockberry taken delight in it? Had he even noticed the smallest things about her, or had he seen her as only a sacrifice to his brutal masculinity?

"Eleanor and I discovered it among her things after . . . afterward."

After her death. Once they'd read the journal, he didn't think they would treasure the piece. "What became of it?"

They'd neared the house. Emma stopped to face him as though she wished this conversation to end outside, so Eleanor would not have to endure so painful a topic. He couldn't fail to notice how protective the sisters were of each other. "We took it with us to London and had it delivered to Lord Rockberry, along with a message."

"The words of the message?" he prodded.

Again she blushed, her face turning a darker red than he'd ever seen it. "She's dead. Soon you shall be as well."

"A bit melodramatic, but no doubt effective. That's the reason when he went to Scotland Yard that he could sound so confident that you meant to kill him."

"Did he show the missive to Scotland Yard?"

"Not to my knowledge—although it's quite possible he did. My superior was quite adamant that I keep watch over you, determine your purpose and sway you from it."

"So your interest in me was all a deception."

Her voice carried no doubts. She'd not offered a question, but had made a statement. Her eyes dared him to denounce the truth, but he was as weary of lies between them as she was. Even as he thought it, he realized her coming to his arms last night could have been deception as well, an attempt to engage his heart so he would leave without either sister. He wanted to trust her motives, but the pain of her initial betrayal was still a hollow ache. He wondered if they'd ever completely trust each other—and if they didn't, how could she believe that he'd truly given her his heart?

"In the beginning, yes," he said. "My plan was

to gain your favor, entice you into telling me your reasons for following Rockberry." He wanted to touch her but didn't dare. She suddenly appeared as fragile as a piece of hand-blown glass. "But I quickly fell under your spell."

"So you think I bewitched you?"

"I'm beginning to understand that just as I was playing you, so you were playing me. We were both involved in separate, but equally as elaborate, swindles. I wanted to entice you into revealing your purpose; you wanted to seduce me into providing you with an alibi."

"And last night?"

"It's my hope that we were completely honest with each other. But I also recognize that we've both become quite skilled at duplicity, and it's possible neither of us would recognize honesty if it bit us on the arse."

She averted her gaze from his and stared out at the cliffs, at the sea. "The one time I've always been honest with you is when I've lain with you."

Gently, he molded his hand around her chin and turned her head so he could see the deep blue of her eyes. "The only time I haven't been honest with you was my reason for pursuing you."

She gave him a tremulous smile. "We have a very rocky foundation beneath us."

"But it is a foundation, Emma. Only we can determine what we want to build on top of it now."

"Don't be so fanciful, James. We can't build anything. We're at cross purposes. I've committed a crime. And you solve crimes."

Damnation! How could he make her understand? They were going back and forth, covering ground that had already been plowed.

"Emma, not everything I do is within the law."

"But you're an inspector."

"And sometimes I look the other way. I can't on this matter because he's a blasted lord, but I can assure you that if your sentence is not just, I will see you released from gaol. I will see that you have another life, but first, I would like very much to try to see that you return to this one."

"You said you have influence."

"I have a duke and an earl in my pocket."

"Claybourne and Greystone."

He nodded. "And Jack Dodger could purchase all of London if he wanted. They have power, Emma. I'm not above asking them to wield it."

"And what of you, James Swindler?"

"My power is not as visible as theirs, but I have it. I've earned it. Now back to the silver. Do you remember exactly what it looked like?"

She nodded. "I believe so, yes. It very much resembled a choker, but strands of silver flowed from it. It was really quite lovely. Ironic that it symbolized something so ugly."

"Can you help me draw it?"

She looked taken aback. "Whatever for?"

"Because swindles are my strong suit, and I believe one more is needed to put this matter to rest."

Chapter 20

The main part was a web of tiny strands that fit snugly around a lady's neck," Emma said, sitting at the table in the kitchen and watching as James sketched what she described. She loved the way he looked when he concentrated. Whether it was at the paper or her, he gave each his full attention. She knew her actions in London had put him in an awkward position regarding his feelings for her and his responsibilities toward his duties. He cared about justice. He cared about her.

"And on either side of the part that rested at the hollow of a woman's throat, several knotted strands dangled down," Eleanor explained. "Their length increased as they moved toward the center until the one in the middle was long enough to dangle between—" Clearing her throat, she looked at Emma.

"I think I have the gist of what it dangled between," James said quietly, and Emma smiled at the sight of his cheeks turning red. He didn't often show discomfort—at least not with her. It was interesting to see this aspect of him, and to know that he did feel different toward Eleanor than he felt toward Emma. He was not as comfortable with her sister. "What else?"

"Reminded me of a collar more than a choker," Eleanor said. "And the clasp was very difficult to maneuver. I should think one would need help getting it on and off."

"We didn't try it on," Emma said. "We didn't even want to touch it once we realized what it was."

"So beautiful," Eleanor whispered, "for something so hideous. How could he do that to her?"

James stopped drawing and studied Eleanor. Emma was fascinated watching him, as though she could actually see his mind working. "Did he say anything to you that night in his library?"

She could have kissed him for the wording he used, for not throwing at Eleanor that she'd killed him. Emma hadn't caught Eleanor scrubbing her hands once today. With a little more time, perhaps her hands would heal.

Tears swam in Eleanor's eyes and spilled over onto her cheeks. "He taunted me. Told me Elisabeth enjoyed it, wanted it, *begged* for it. I've never hated, despised, loathed anyone so much in my entire life. I wanted him to at least show remorse before he died." She looked as though she might be ill. "He gloated."

She began frantically rubbing her hands. Emma laid hers over them. "It's all right, Eleanor. He can't gloat any longer."

"He was so horrid." She turned her attention back to the sketch. "That's a very good likeness of the necklace, don't you think, Emma?"

"Yes."

"It's not really a necklace," James said. "It's as you indicated—a collar. I've seen one just like this before. On a woman we found murdered in Whitechapel."

"Do you think she was part of the debauchery?" Emma asked.

He gave a brusque nod. "Based on discreet inquiries I've made, I believe there are secret societies that engage in rituals such as your sister described. I always assumed they were composed of eager players, and so I had no interest in pursuing them. But the one into which your sister was initiated seems to have taken matters into a darker direction."

"Would they have eventually killed Elisabeth?"

"If they thought she was a threat to their discovery."

"Is it possible"—Emma wasn't certain she even wanted to think what she was thinking—"that they came here and killed her?"

James leaned back in the chair. "Possible, but unlikely. Because of what she wrote in her journal the night she died, I suspect"—she could see him struggling with the words—"she sought peace however she could find it."

At that moment she thought she couldn't have loved him more for not giving voice to what her sister had truly done: taken her own life, sinned against God. The family had told the clergy and the villagers that Elisabeth fell to her death. An accident. Even among themselves they'd been unable to face, to accept, what had truly happened.

"So. Where do we go from here, Inspector Swindler?" Eleanor asked. It was the first time either of them had addressed him as such, thus recognizing the authority he had over them. Emma's stomach quivered with the implications. She found it difficult to draw in a breath, but she didn't look away, waiting for his decision, his judgment.

"Rockberry harmed your sister but he wasn't alone in doing it."

Emma and Eleanor exchanged glances. "He was the one responsible," Eleanor said.

"The others must still be held accountable."

"We don't know who they are," Emma said. "Elisabeth only mentioned Rockberry. I don't think she knew who the others were."

"I didn't even think to ask Rockberry for names,"

Eleanor said, and Emma heard her disappointment in herself.

"He wouldn't have provided them," James said, exonerating her.

"Then how do we find out who they are?" Emma asked.

"Do you remember that first night in Cremorne Garden, the woman Rockberry spoke with?"

Eleanor nodded.

"She was wearing something that might have been this," he said, tapping the paper. "It's possible the assignations begin there. If I can retrieve the collar from the new Lord Rockberry, and can find a woman willing to wear it through the gardens, it's possible she'll be approached—"

"I'll do it," Emma and Eleanor said at the same time before he could finish explaining.

"Don't be ridiculous," Eleanor said. "I'm the older, it falls to me."

"No, you took the risk in killing him. Now it's my turn to do more."

"I won't allow it."

"I won't allow you not to allow it."

"Emma—"

"Eleanor—"

"Ladies!" James said, coming to his feet. "I need someone with a bit more experience with the rougher parts of London, someone who can take care of herself."

"They'll know all the ladies who have been initiated into their society," Emma said. "You need someone they recognize. We told only Rockberry that Elisabeth was dead. It's possible he didn't tell anyone else. And even if he did, if they see someone who looks like her, they're likely to think he was misinformed or lying. It has to be one of us."

He shook his head. "It was a bad idea. We should just let it go."

"We can't, because you have the right of it," Emma said. "Something needs to be done. We were obsessed with Rockberry. We went no further than that and we should have. In memory of our dear sister. To bring her soul peace. We must finish what we've begun."

Wearing her night rail, Emma sat at the vanity in Eleanor's room and brushed her hair. They'd left matters regarding what needed to be done when they returned to London unfinished, although James had said he'd contemplate the situation and how best to handle it. She loved him for not wanting to put either her or Eleanor in harm's way, but she'd seen in his eyes that he knew her argument had merit.

"You don't have to wait until I fall asleep to go to him," Eleanor said from where she sat on the bed, leaning her back into the mound of pillows. "I just hope you know what you're doing. If you get with babe, I suppose you can at least plead the belly. They don't hang women who are with child. Or so I've heard."

Emma rose from the bench, hurried over to Eleanor, sat on the edge of the bed and took her hands. "We won't hang, Eleanor. He's promised me that."

"Who made him king?"

"I think he has some influence. We must trust him."

Eleanor squeezed her hands. "And you must trust me. I should be the one to play the part of Elisabeth if we go through with this ruse."

"Eleanor—"

"Emma—"

They were at another impasse, just as they'd been in the kitchen, unable to get beyond saying each other's names. But Emma knew she had James's ear. She would see to it that Eleanor wasn't the one who was placed in harm's way. "Let's just see what happens when we return to London, shall we?"

Eleanor gave the slightest of nods.

"Very good," Emma said succinctly. She would find a way to protect Eleanor whether she wanted to be protected or not. Her sister had done the lion's share when it came to acquiring retribution, now it was Emma's turn. Releasing her hold on Eleanor, she folded her hands in her lap and studied them, knowing her cheeks were burnishing red. "Will you at least roll over and pretend you're asleep?"

Thankfully, Eleanor did as she requested. Emma knew it was hypocritical, but she was self-conscious going to James with her sister openly knowing. What she and James shared was intended for two people who were married to each other. That would never come to pass for them. In spite of her brave words to Eleanor, and James's promises, Emma knew it was very likely that the gallows did await her. With that thought, she was determined to make the most of what little time she might have.

She slipped out of Eleanor's bedchamber and into her own. She wondered if her heart would always dance around wildly whenever she set eyes on James after a brief separation. Within the shadowy room, he stood at the window. But with the quiet click of the door, he was crossing over to her. She met him near the bed, offering her mouth up to him. But he didn't take the gift. Instead, he combed his fingers into her hair and held her, studied her as though something weighed heavily on his mind. With all they'd discovered, all they planned, she shouldn't have been surprised, but she'd hoped that for these few hours they could pretend nothing existed beyond the door, beyond them.

"That night at my lodging, when I wanted everything off you except the pearls," he said, "did it remind you of your sister's encounter? Did it taint your enjoyment of the night?"

Feeling relief that it was something inconsequential furrowing his brow, she released the breath she'd been holding. "No. Absolutely not. They were a treasured gift, not a symbol of subservience. Nothing, nothing about that night, was anything at all like what I'm certain my sister endured."

"Good."

She was aware of his hands shifting and something weighty, smooth, and cool settling against her skin. With a small exclamation, she touched the pearls that circled her neck and smiled. "How did you manage . . . I didn't see you holding them."

"I might not have been the most skilled with my hands, but I picked up a trick here and there."

She couldn't believe the daring response that entered her head. She almost kept it to herself, but this was James, a man who knew her every secret as well as those of her flesh. "I think you have very skillful hands."

He gave her a slow, sensuous smile, his eyes heated with desire. "Let's put your belief to the test, shall we?"

Before she'd released her next breath, her gown was floating to the floor and his trousers were quickly discarded. Then they were flesh against flesh, and mouths eagerly exploring the familiar, still discovering new treasures.

Their lovemaking was bittersweet, as though they both knew that once they left for London in the morning, all of this would remain behind. They would be back in the world of propriety. More important, they'd need to focus their endeavors on the plan more than each other.

He took his time, touching her with a slow reverence, as though he intended to memorize every line and curve for the nights ahead when she'd not be in his arms. She skimmed her fingers over him with a heightened awareness so she'd have the ability to recall the firmness of his muscles, the taut smoothness of his skin, the coarseness of his hair.

When pleasure was beyond bearing and passion reigned with aching need, they came together in a conflagration of sensations that carried them to greater heights. Her name was a growl upon his lips, and his was a cry upon hers.

Afterward, lying exhausted and replete in each other's arms, she couldn't stop the tears. Neither could his whispered murmuring of assurance prevent the arrival of the dawn.

Chapter 21

E mma had not expected their first stop after they arrived in London to be the residence of the Duke and Duchess of Greystone. She, Eleanor, and James stood in the entrance hallway, with her and Eleanor's small trunk behind them, waiting while the butler announced them.

"It seems we should have at least attempted to find lodgings first," Eleanor mumbled.

Emma suspected Eleanor was a bit cross because from the moment they'd departed from their home, James had left no doubt that he was the one in charge of their little expedition. It seemed to Emma that the farther from the cottage they traveled, the more he distanced himself from her. She knew he did it because hard choices needed to be made, but it didn't make the loneliness any easier to bear.

"Jim!"

Emma glanced toward the hallway and saw the duchess hurrying toward them. Emma had been terrified that she'd give away that she had not met the duchess until the night of the ball. It was Eleanor who'd spoken with her in the parlor at the lodgings. Afterward, Eleanor described her in excruciating detail, but even without so fine a description, Emma would have known the duchess by the softness that appeared in James's eyes when he greeted her. The same gladness that he showed now as the duchess patted his shoulder, before walking past him to study her and Eleanor.

"I see you found there were two after all," she said. "They're almost indistinguishable. Imagine what Feagan could have done with them."

"You don't have to talk about us as though we're not here," Eleanor said.

"And which one would you be?" the duchess asked.

When Eleanor took on her mulish expression and remained silent, Emma said, "She's Eleanor. I'm Emma."

The duchess scrutinized Emma as though searching for something upon which her life depended. Then she smiled. "You're the one who attended my ball, the one who struck Jim's fancy. But it was Eleanor I met in the parlor."

"No one can tell us apart," Eleanor snapped.

"Except Mr. Swindler," Emma reminded her quietly.

"I was raised to read the subtle nuances in people," the duchess said. "How else was I to determine who best to fleece?" She turned her attention to James. "So what do you require?"

"A place for them to stay," he said.

Based on the certainty in his voice that he knew he'd not be denied, Emma thought he and the duchess might as well be related by blood.

"Here, should suffice for that purpose. What else?" the duchess asked.

After settling into her room, Emma crossed the wide expanse of hallway to the bedchamber Eleanor had been given. It was much the same as hers, with a large four-poster canopied bed, a dresser, a bureau, a vanity, and a small sitting area near the window. Extending from the window itself was a seat covered in pillows. Eleanor was sitting there, gazing out into the garden.

"What have we gotten ourselves into, Emma?" she asked without turning around.

Emma sat beside her. "Into the thick of things I'd say."

"I thought the duchess had only recently married the duke. If that's the case, who is the boy?"

Looking out, Emma saw the duke and a young boy standing in front of easels, pallets in their hands as they each painted a section of flowers in the garden. "James mentioned that she'd taken in one of her orphans. Peter, I think he said his name was."

"I always wanted children."

"You may have them yet."

"Yes, I'm certain a gentleman would be delighted to take to wife a woman who has no qualms about plunging a dagger into a man's heart." Eleanor began rubbing her hands, and Emma stilled her actions by placing hers over them.

"A man would be most fortunate to have you."

Her sister gave her a small smile. "I don't regret what I did, Emma. It's simply that it's a bit more difficult to live with than I'd anticipated."

"What *we* did, Eleanor. You must never forget that we did it together."

Eleanor nodded reluctantly and gazed back out the window. "The duke is a handsome fellow."

"And to think he married a thief."

"What of you, Emma? Will you marry a thief?"

"In a heartbeat," she whispered. "But I seriously doubt he'll ask."

* * *

Midnight.
Greystone's.

—J. S.

The missive was sent to five, but only four answered.

"Graves sends his regrets, but he's attending to the queen," Claybourne said. "She seems to think she has some ailment that only he can cure. If we can't do this without him, we're to send word, and he'll do what he can."

William Graves was another of Feagan's brood. A former grave robber who was quickly becoming one of London's most noted physicians.

The others in the duke's library included Claybourne's wife, Catherine, Jack Dodger, Frannie, Greystone, Emma, and Eleanor. Swindler hadn't considered when he sent word that he would find himself surrounded by men of incredible wealth and power. His own was not lacking, but he didn't flaunt it. Two of them possessed the one thing he didn't: a title.

He wondered if Emma would be content with a man who would never ascend into the aristocracy. Was she even now looking at Greystone and Claybourne and thinking that they were the type of men she deserved to wed?

"I'm assuming you called us here for a reason," Claybourne said. "Can we get to it?"

"Yeah, right," Swindler said, clasping his hands together and leaning forward. He'd purposely arranged the seating so he sat opposite Emma and

Eleanor. He wanted a clear view of their faces in order to judge their reactions and determine what they were thinking, in the event they decided honesty wasn't the way to go. "As I'm sure you're well aware, Lord Rockberry recently left this world. Emma and Eleanor were responsible for his demise."

Aware of Eleanor stiffening beside her, bracing for what accusations or unkind sentiments might come, Emma felt her own chest tighten. It was the first time the truth of their actions had been shared with anyone. She'd expected that moment to carry with it shame and humiliation. Instead she didn't know what to make of it because of the way James had spoken, the inflection in his voice, as though he'd been revealing something as common as them sewing a button on a shirt.

"I take it he deserved it," Claybourne said, giving the impression that he was the patriarch of this unusual clan.

As Eleanor squeezed her hand unmercifully, a shiver of dread raced through Emma. She despised having to endure this moment when they heard all the sordid—

James gave a brusque nod.

Claybourne nodded in turn. "Right, then. What's your plan? Provide them with new names, set them up somewhere?"

"Wait," Eleanor said, loosening her hold on Emma. "That's all you require? A nod? What sort of people are you?"

"The finest you'll ever meet," James said. "I wouldn't have called them here otherwise."

But more weighed on Emma's mind than the trust they so easily granted James. "You mean to send us away?"

"It's possible that may be our only recourse to ensure your lovely neck isn't stretched," James said, "but before we work on the particulars of how best to handle your disappearance, we need to attend to other matters." He glanced around, to find everyone's attention still riveted on him. "My plans at the moment involve finishing what the ladies began. Rockberry didn't act alone. We need to discover who the others were and bring them to justice."

"I suppose you've thought through the particulars," Jack Dodger said.

"Within reason, as far into the future as I can see—which isn't far." Without revealing any of the sordid details involving her sister's encounter with Rockberry, James explained about the society that had lured her in. He then removed a sheet of paper from his jacket pocket, unfolded it, and passed it to Claybourne. "Rockberry placed that around

Elisabeth's neck in a ritual that welcomed her into servitude."

"It's a very intricate piece," the Duchess of Greystone said, looking at the drawing. "And quite lovely. Where is it now?"

"Hopefully in Rockberry's residence. I intend to go searching for it tomorrow night."

That was news to Emma. "Within his residence? Are you mad?"

James bestowed upon her a very somber but determined expression. "If we're to have you or Eleanor pretend to be Elisabeth returned to town for another taste of pleasure, we need to find the necklace. While the marquess's home is large, people tend to hide things in rather conspicuous places. Ten minutes, fifteen at the most, and I should have it in hand." He gave his attention to Mr. Dodger. "Thought perhaps you could invite the new Lord Rockberry to a private game of chance at your club tomorrow around midnight."

Mr. Dodger shrugged. "If Claybourne and Greystone are up to it."

Both men were, and particulars were worked out as they discussed how best to keep the new marquess occupied while James searched his residence. Emma didn't like it. If he were caught—

"What of his servants?" she asked. "You don't

think they'll notice you traipsing through the house?"

"Most will be abed. I'll be most discreet."

Although she still didn't like it, she quickly realized that she and Eleanor were here as a courtesy. The others were making the plans. They were so comfortable with each other working out what needed to be done that it occurred to her this was not the first time they'd plotted together to bring some plan to fruition. If she'd been honest with James from the beginning, it was quite possible that he could have instructed her and Eleanor on the best method for getting rid of Rockberry without getting caught. They'd thought they were so clever, but had relied on games they played as children. She wondered if there'd ever come a time when they weren't ruled by naiveté.

When the final details were worked out, Mr. Dodger, Lord Claybourne, and his wife took their leave. The only question that remained was which sister would be placed in harm's way.

"It has to be me," Emma said as she walked through the garden, her arm entwined around James's. He'd asked for a few minutes alone with her, after which he, too, would take his leave.

The gas lamps cast a faint glow over the path they walked. Roses, hyacinths, and other blossoms scented the air around them. Another time, Emma thought it would have been a relaxing, calming diversion before retiring to bed, but her nerves were far too jangled as the silence built between them. "James?"

"The situation may turn deadly. Eleanor, at least, has killed. She might not hesitate to do what she must."

"She might think twice about it. As you're well aware, the guilt gnaws at her. And I'm not too shabby in a dangerous—"

Before she'd finished making her case, he snatched her up against him and began plundering her mouth as though it were the last opportunity that he'd ever have to taste her. They'd had few moments alone on the journey here. Perhaps that was the reason she welcomed his advance and clung to him almost with desperation. She didn't want to consider that it was because their time together was quickly coming to a close.

After this little ruse to get to the others, she and Eleanor would still be held accountable for their role in the death of Rockberry. Whatever her punishment—death, transportation, or years in a women's prison—James wouldn't be there with her. He would remain in London, solving crimes, and eventually marrying. She didn't want to think about another woman lying in his arms, but neither did she want to contemplate the lonely years ahead of him if he remained a bachelor. Or the lonely empty years she would face without his hands gliding over her back as they did now, his kiss stirring her passions.

She wished they could retire to his lodgings, lock the door, and never leave. She wanted to awaken in his bed surrounded by the musky fragrance of their lovemaking. She wanted to feel the heat of his body lying heavily over hers.

He dragged his hot, moist lips along her cheek before nibbling on her ear. "Don't ask me to risk losing you," he said in a tortured voice that caused her heart to ache and rejoice. She was truly precious to him. But as much as he meant to her, she couldn't be so selfish as to willingly put her sister in harm's way again. It was her turn to take the risk.

"Don't ask me to risk losing another sister."

He grew so still, the tension in his body a silent thrumming. When he released her, she felt as though something of monumental importance had shifted between them.

"You'd give up everything we might have so easily?" he asked.

"There's nothing easy about this, but you must know that what we have is only temporary. As wonderful as it is, James, it will be taken from us whether we wish it or not."

Even in the shadowy garden, the intensity of his stare was unnerving.

"You should retire now," he said flatly. "Sleep well. You'll need your wits about you when it happens."

"You've decided, then—it'll be me?" She didn't know if the small tremor in her voice was fear or excitement.

He didn't reply. He simply walked away, disappearing into the darkness.

When Swindler had sent his missive to his childhood mates, he'd sent one other.

London Bridge
Four o'clock

He wasn't surprised that Sir David had arrived before him, on the banks of the Thames beneath London Bridge. They'd met there many a night when Swindler was engaged in activities that required he not be identified with Scotland Yard. As usual, Sir David was smoking his pipe.

"So Swindler, you've returned to London. Why the secret meeting? Am I to assume you don't have Rockberry's murderer in hand?"

"It's become rather complicated."

"Fell for her, did you?"

It was difficult to admit, even to himself, that he'd fallen madly in love with Emma—especially difficult when Emma insisted on protecting her sister at the expense of a future with him. He knew he was being selfish, but dammit, his entire adult life he'd sacrificed his own happiness for others. Just once, he wanted to put his own needs first.

He explained everything to Sir David, sparing no details. Emma wasn't there to be embarrassed by the truth or the sordid tale.

"Good God!" Sir David said when Swindler was finished. "Are you certain?"

"Yes, sir. The lady explained it all in her journal, then took her life. She had no reason to lie at that point."

"And you think other nobles might be involved?"

"It's possible. We'll know more once we've set the trap. I'd like Scotland Yard involved—"

"No," Sir David responded tartly before Swindler had finished outlining what he had in mind. "Not until we know who falls into your net."

"Will you be falling into it, sir?"

The pipe fell from Sir David's mouth as he spun around to face Swindler, the first time he'd looked at him directly since the meeting began. "I beg your pardon? Have you gone mad?"

"At the risk of appearing arrogant, I'm your best

man. Yet you charged me with the simple task of following a lady through London. It was a waste of my talents."

"On the contrary, Swindler, look what you've uncovered."

"If you suspected this all along, why not tell me?"

Sir David reached down, picked up his pipe, and studied it. "Damnation. Can't put that back in my mouth, now can I?" He tossed it into the river. "You're not the only one who's given orders, Swindler. Let's just say that mine come from high up, very, very high up. We suspected Rockberry might be engaged in something unsavory when he first came to us. Why he didn't just see to the matter himself is beyond me. Arrogant bastard expected us to see to it for him. Which I suppose, all in all, based upon your findings, was to the lady's benefit in the end. Be that as it may, there have been rumors of this society. Nasty stuff that. Especially as Queen Victoria and her husband have a very strict moral code. People need to behave with a good deal more decorum." He cleared his throat. "Forgive my rant. Carry on with your plans. When you know who all is involved, get word to me. Then we'll decide how the matter is to be handled with the least amount of scandal and embarrassment."

"Yes, sir." Swindler turned to go.

"Swindler?"

Swindler gazed back over his shoulder. "Yes, sir?"

"Take extreme care with this matter. Not a whisper of it is to make the rounds. Keep everything discreet, man. There could be a knighthood in it for you."

"Your orders came from *that* high up?"

Sir David simply stared at the river.

Chapter 22

The marquess has accepted our invitation for a private game at Dodger's at midnight. Enjoy your freedom.

—C

According to the note from Claybourne, the new Marquess of Rockberry might be mourning the death of his brother, but not enough to give up all his pleasures and vices. Swindler had heard the younger possessed a weakness for games of chance. And no man with such a weakness would pass up an opportunity to pit his skills against Claybourne, Greystone, and Dodger. The men were legendary in their conquests of the gaming tables—when they indulged. Since taking wives, all three were rarely seen at the tables. Who

could blame them when their wives were the love-
liest ladies London had to offer?

With the exception of Emma, of course, who
wasn't really of London. Still, James thought her
by far the most appealing. It amused him now to
think that he'd once thought no one would surpass
Frannie for his affections. Yet Emma had managed
to do exactly that.

Swindler waited behind the hedgerows at the
marquess's London residence until he saw the
man's carriage rattle by at half past eleven. Then he
waited another half hour for the servants to settle
in after their master's departure before making
his way to the servants' entrance. Kneeling, he removed a small candle from his pocket, lit the wick,
studied the lock, and within seconds was inside
the kitchen.

An incriminating item such as the choker would
be in one of two places: the library or the master bedchamber. Swindler decided to start with the library,
remembering its location from his previous visit,
when he'd come to inspect the scene of the crime.

Using the small light from his candle, disturbing nothing, barely breathing, he cautiously crept
along the corridors, like a silent wraith. No servants
crossed his path. He hadn't expected any to be
about. When the master was away, sleep beckoned.

Opening the library door, he stepped through

and closed it behind him. Holding the candle aloft, he made his way around the numerous small sitting areas to the large desk at the far side of the room. He noted that the carpet was a different pattern than when he'd last been in the room. No surprise there. Blood seldom made an attractive decorative accent.

After setting the candle on the desk, he began opening drawers, searching for latches that would release hidden compartments. The former marquess wouldn't want his secrets easily discovered. But that was not unusual for the aristocracy. Hence the reason Feagan had trained them regarding the mysteries of a desk.

"Looking for something, Inspector?"

Swindler jerked his head up to see the new Lord Rockberry stepping out of a dark corner. Thinking himself quite alone, he hadn't bothered to check the areas to the side or behind him. The new marquess didn't carry the stench that his brother had, so Swindler hadn't noticed his scent. Unfortunate, that. He was trying to devise a logical explanation for his presence when Rockberry held up his hand. Silver dangled from it.

"This perhaps."

Swindler realized he was definitely losing his edge. He'd become so obsessed with ensuring Emma's freedom that he was becoming careless when it was critical that he be his most diligent. Closing the drawer he'd just opened, he held out his hands in acquiescence. "How did you know to expect me?"

"An invitation from the infamous Lord Clay-bourne for a private game with the notorious Dodger himself, not to mention a duke of the highest caliber? Me? A new marquess who has yet to fully embrace his title? Besides, I know that you all have ties to each other and the gutter." He shrugged. "I'm young but I'm not a fool. I sus-pected someone wanted me out of my residence for a reason."

"So you sent an empty carriage."

"I did indeed. I must say I thought it very clever on my part." He took a step nearer. "I know I didn't lie about what I saw that night when my brother was murdered, which means that you lied about the woman being with you."

"I didn't lie."

"Which must mean that you were with her and helped to kill him. Perhaps you plunged in the dagger. Jolly good for you. Pour yourself a drink, man. It's well deserved. As I've recently discov-ered, my brother was as vile as they came. I won't take the blame for a murder I didn't commit, but I'll do what I can to get you and the lady out of the country."

"I didn't lie about my lady not being here that night. And I can prove it."

"Twins!" Rockberry exclaimed, looking and sounding astounded.

"Triplets," Eleanor said tartly, "until your brother destroyed our sister."

Swindler had brought Rockberry to Greystone's, knowing the ladies would be awake, waiting to see if he'd met with success in finding the silver. The gentlemen, too, were in the library, suspecting trouble and having returned when Rockberry failed to show for their private game.

In appearance, Rockberry favored his brother very little. He was slender, but not as tall. His facial features were not marred by arrogance. He looked back at Swindler. "I found his journal. He wrote of his shameful exploits in minute detail. Why he would keep an accounting regarding his abhorrent behavior is beyond me." He turned back to the ladies. "To which of you do I owe an apology for Cremorne Gardens?"

"That would be me," Eleanor said, with her usual biting tone.

"He told me you were a prostitute who refused to let him be. He told my friends and I to have our fun with you."

"And you thought forcing me would be fun?"

To the marquess's credit, he blushed and took great interest in the shine on his shoes. "Perhaps I'm not so different from my brother after all. A cad when it suits me."

"You're very different," Swindler said as he crossed over to a table, poured whiskey into a tumbler, then handed it to Rockberry. "Do you still have the journal?"

Rockberry appeared surprised by the question. "No, I took great pleasure in burning it. Is there a way to keep this situation from making its way to the *Times*?"

"Sit down," Swindler said. While his order was to the marquess, everyone else followed suit. He wished he'd been nearer to Emma so he could have joined her on the small couch. Instead, she now sat beside Eleanor, holding her hand. He wanted to be the one to comfort her. He'd been angry with her when she insisted he put her in harm's way rather than her sister. Now he just wanted to hold her.

Leaning forward, with his elbows on his thighs, Swindler asked of Rockberry, "Did your brother reveal where the meetings took place?"

"No. My sense was that it was always somewhere different. The night was the same, however. Wednesday. The ladies—if you can call them that—were to go to Cremorne Gardens, wearing their silver. Each would be approached by a gentleman who would lead them to a carriage. I take it the gentlemen knew the location, but the ladies did not. I suppose the fewer who knew, the better."

"Did the journal offer any names?"

Rockberry took a sip of whiskey. "No. My brother was far more interested in describing the rituals and the orgy than the particulars of how it was all arranged. I do know they periodically initiated women into the society and those women were not always willing. They used blackmail, coercion, fear, and shame to keep the women from speaking out about them. He also wrote about . . . " His voice trailed off and he shook his head.

"What did he write, my lord?" Swindler prodded.

Rockberry finished off the whiskey, holding the glass in a white-knuckled grasp.

"My lord?"

Rockberry again took to studying his shoes. "He . . . he killed someone. Got too rough with her. I couldn't stomach to read the particulars. They made me ill." He gazed up at Swindler. "What do you intend to do with this information?"

"We intend to find the others. And if Wednesday is the night they meet, then that shall be tomorrow."

"I'm willing to help in any way I can."

"Allow us to borrow the silver."

"You can have the deuced thing. So what's your plan?"

Swindler supposed he couldn't blame the man for his interest. He explained how they intended to set a trap.

Eleanor was acutely aware of Emma stiffening beside her when Mr. Swindler announced that it would be Eleanor who walked through Cremorne Gardens the following night. It was only fair. After all, she was the older of the two, even if only by moments. If he hadn't selected her, she'd have had to give Emma a sleeping draught. She wasn't going to allow her younger sister to be placed in harm's way. Especially as Emma had a gentleman very much interested in her. It was quite possible that Mr. Swindler would see to it that Emma did not have to pay for what happened to the former Rockberry.

After details were explained, while people were taking their leave, Eleanor slipped out the door and into the garden. She wasn't nearly as comfortable or trusting around these people as Emma. She simply wanted the entire matter to be done with.

"Miss Watkins?"

She'd only just reached the hyacinths when her name was called. Strengthening her resolve, she turned slowly, shoulders back, chin held high, to face Rockberry. "My lord."

"You're the one who ended . . . my brother's ability to breathe."

"It could have been my sister." She didn't know why she'd said that. Until that moment she'd been proud of her actions, but then, until that moment she'd not faced someone who might have cared about the blackguard. She had never considered that he possessed family or friends. All she'd seen was that he was a man who'd taken from her someone she loved.

"No. Your eyes contain a heavier sorrow than hers." His voice was soothing, compassionate, and for some reason it irritated her.

"You misread me, my lord. I'm not sorry for what I did. Your brother forced my sister into submission. When he was done with her, he allowed others to have their way with her as though she were no better than a scrap of meat to be tossed to the dogs. My only regret is that he died so quickly."

A heavy silence built between them, as though he didn't know how to respond to the accusation.

"Shall we?" he asked finally, indicating the cobblestone path.

She was grateful to begin walking again, and he fell into step beside her.

"You act valiantly to pretend you don't care, but I don't think murder is in your nature," he said quietly.

"You know nothing at all about my nature, my lord."

"Dear God, I think you could have sliced my brother to death with your tongue."

"How dare you!" she spat, turning on him, her arms flailing, her fists pounding into his shoulders. "You have no idea what he did!"

Grabbing her wrists, he pressed them to his chest. In spite of her own agitation, she could feel the rapid thudding of his heart.

"I know exactly what he did, and probably in considerably more detail than you. My brother did not want for particulars in his writing."

All the fight left her. She hated that others knew exactly what fate had befallen her sister. "Thank you for burning the journal."

"It was not as though it was difficult. It can't compare with the dangers you'll face tomorrow night."

"I can't bear the thought of anyone else enduring what Elisabeth did."

"I didn't think you were as heartless as you pretended."

She didn't realize that he'd released his grip on her wrists until his hand was at the back of her head, leading her into the curve of his shoulder. As hard as she tried, she couldn't stop the tears from falling, large hot drops that scalded her cheeks. "I'm sorry if you loved him," she said.

"I didn't. Not after I read . . . how could anyone?
I'm glad he's dead, Miss Watkins. I'm only sorry
that you had to be the one to see to the matter."

His voice was strangled, as though he'd had to
push the words out, and she wondered if he, too,
was crying.

"I shall take solace in those sentiments, my lord,
when my sentence is handed down."

He drew back, and in the low lamplights of the
garden, she could see the dampness of sorrow glis-
tening on his cheeks, even as he glided his thumbs
over her face to capture her tears. "Don't be so
quick to see yourself hanged, Miss Watson. Many
murders go unsolved. I suspect this shall be one
of them."

Emma had not spoken a single word when James
announced that it would be Eleanor who would
be used in the ruse. She possessed far too much
dignity to engage in a fit of screaming in front of
people she barely knew, especially when so many
of those people were nobility.

As she prepared herself for bed, however, she
was restless. James had left with little more than
a good-night. As much as she wanted to talk with
him, she was certain she couldn't sway him from
his decision. She'd used her wiles on him once. The

delicate balance of their relationship would topple over if she sought to seduce him into giving her what she wanted.

Still, she couldn't deny the disappointment that he'd care so little for her wants as to disregard them completely.

The light rap on her door surprised her. Probably Eleanor, unable to sleep, or wanting to discuss how she thought tomorrow night might go. Or maybe Eleanor wanted her opinion of the new Lord Rockberry. Emma had not missed how the two of them watched each other, or how much her sister had blushed after returning from a stroll through the garden with him. He didn't resemble his brother overly much, but she couldn't quite overlook the fact that he'd meant Eleanor ill that first night at Cremorne Gardens. She didn't like that her sister could so easily excuse the offense.

Her breath backed up in her lungs when she opened her door and saw James.

"I know you're angry at me, but—"

"I will only be angry at you if you don't bring her back safely."

"I promise you I'll do all in my power—"

"And if your power isn't enough?"

"Please trust me, Emma. I grew up doing these sorts of things, arranging swindles and ruses. Even after I went to live with Luke's grandfather,

I'd often slip out to help Feagan with one thing or another."

"I do trust you, but I just . . . I can't lose her, James."

He nodded, as though it was all he could provide, a silent acknowledgment of what she asked of him.

"And I don't want to lose you either, I don't want anything to happen to you," she said.

"That, too, I'll do all in my power to prevent."

They stood there for a moment. She heard the chiming of the clock down the hallway. Two gongs.

"I thought everyone had gone to bed," she finally said.

He gave her his familiar grin. "They have."

She gave him a look of chastisement. "I don't suppose they gave you a key to this residence."

"No, but then I've never needed one." He touched her cheek. "I know what I'm asking of you and your sister, Emma. I would like very much to hold you tonight."

With a demure smile, she invited him into her bedchamber and her bed.

It was long minutes later as she lay replete in his arms that she said, "Last night, there was talk of sending us away. I had the impression it was something you'd done before."

Lazily, he stroked her arm. "On occasion we've helped deserving people start a new life, sometimes getting them out of prison before they've served their time."

She rose up on her elbow to look down on him. His hair was mussed, his face in need of a shave. He smelled musky from their lovemaking. She quite simply wanted him again. "Before, you've mentioned your influence."

He shrugged. "I have access to records, documents, gaols, and prisons. If I think someone has been sentenced unfairly, if I think intervention is justified, I might remove them from prison or replace them with someone who is deserving of the crime. Pentonville Prison is lovely for that, as the prisoners are not allowed to speak and they must wear hoods over their heads anytime they leave their cells. And of course, transportation always provides possibilities for switching one person with another."

"Do you make a habit of this?"

"Hardly. But when the circumstances are right . . . Frannie has a skilled hand. She can forge any document or signature. I daresay, she could make me a duke and even the queen wouldn't be able to detect that it wasn't her signature on the document. Dodger often hides people in his gambling establishment or gives them a job. Cleaned up, dressed properly, with a new name in an area of London where no one knows them . . . they're safe. Graves, who you've yet to meet, was a grave robber in his youth. If we ever need a body, he's our man. Claybourne provides whatever financing is needed and is the one who usually serves as a go-between. He's very good at straddling the upper levels of society as well as the lower. When we work together, we can give someone the opportunity to start over."

"That's what they thought you wanted to do for Eleanor and me."

He trailed his fingers along her face, eventually taking some strands of her hair and twisting it around his finger. "It's still a possibility. My hope is that by taking care of the others in this society, your earlier transgression might be overlooked."

She laid her head on the center of his chest. "And if it's not?"

"We'll go to America."

She jerked her head up. "You'll go with us?"

"I know what it is to have you in my life. I know what it is to have you walk out of it. I will do whatever I must to see that you don't walk out of it again."

Tears burned her eyes. "Tomorrow, let it be me instead of Eleanor."

"I can't." When she made a motion to move away from him, he stilled her actions by threading his fingers through her hair and holding her in place. "She's suffering, Emma. I know you can see it. She needs to be the one who goes to Cremorne Gardens."

She couldn't deny the wisdom in his words, but she didn't like it. She eased off him and rolled over onto her side. His arm came around her, holding her close, her back to his front.

"Trust me, Emma. Please trust me."

"I do," she whispered. But while her heart meant the words, her mind continued to worry.

As she studied her reflection in the cheval glass the following evening, Eleanor couldn't deny there was a measure of anticipation thrumming through her that very much matched what she'd felt the night she confronted Rockberry. A bit of danger, a bit of risk, a bit of uncertainty. Regardless of how she tried to anticipate every scenario, it was always possible something would arise she'd not foreseen.

"You should have some weapon," Emma said, standing nearby, scrutinizing every aspect of the red gown that the duchess had loaned Eleanor.

"Mr. Swindler said he'd provide me with one when I get into the carriage." She studied her sister's furrowed brow, the taut line of her mouth. "Please don't worry, Emma."

"I should at least go, to be there in case I'm needed."

Turning from the mirror, Eleanor hugged Emma. "I'd be worried silly if you were anywhere near the gardens. I'm certain Mr. Swindler would as well. At least this way he'll be focused on the task at hand."

"You could call him James, you know." It wasn't often that Emma sounded petulant.

"He's your beau, Emma, not mine."

Eleanor walked to the vanity. It was time. She took a deep breath. "Will you place the silver around my neck?"

Emma crossed over cautiously, as though she dreaded looking once again at what Rockberry had given their sister. "How can something so pretty be so evil?" she asked.

"I don't know," Eleanor said.

Both sisters simply stared at the intricate, delicately designed jewelry for several minutes, neither picking it up, neither beginning the process of what needed to be done.

"If it wasn't so pretty, it really would resemble a collar, something to indicate subservience," Emma said.

"I hate it," Eleanor said.

"Then don't wear it."

"I won't be approached if I don't. Come on, let's just get this over with."

With a brusque nod, Emma lifted the necklace and very carefully placed it around her sister's neck. Eleanor was surprised by how weighty it felt, in spite of how delicate it looked. Emma fiddled with the clasp for a few minutes, and finally Eleanor heard it *click* into place.

"There, all done."

"I thought you'd try to trick me and put it around your neck," Eleanor said.

"I almost did. But I didn't see the point. James would simply remove it and do it properly."

"I think he cares for you very much, Emma."

Emma nodded and reached for her, but not before Eleanor saw the tears in her eyes. "Please be ever so careful," she whispered. "I won't be able to stand it if I lose another sister."

"Not to worry. I don't plan any heroics."

But as she marched from the room, Eleanor knew that matters didn't always go as planned.

Chapter 23

Emma plucked at her needlework. She didn't know why she bothered. She'd never had a skillful hand when it came to using needle and thread. Well, except for once when she'd stitched up the gash in James's head.

Sitting in the parlor, she could hear the *tick, tick, tick* of the clock on the mantel. It was likely to make her go insane. They'd been gone for two hours now. How long would it take? Was Eleanor all right? Was James? How much danger were they in? She stood up, then immediately sat back down.

"The waiting is always the most difficult," the duchess said quietly. "I remember whenever Feagan would take a couple of the lads out for a burglary or a swindle, time seemed to move so slowly before they ever returned safely."

Emma appreciated that the duchess was trying to distract her from her own painful musings, but they were running rampant. "I'm afraid I'm not very good company."

"You don't have to entertain me, Emma. I know you're worried about your sister and Jim, but Jim knows what he's doing. And the lads will keep watch over your sister."

Emma almost smiled at the duchess's reference to the lads. She'd come to realize that it was how she referred to any of the men who'd been part of Feagan's den of thieves. James. Claybourne. Jack Dodger.

"You're very close to them all."

The duchess smiled in fond memory. "They're the brothers of my heart, if not my blood."

"They're very fortunate."

"On the contrary, I'm the one who is fortunate. Now, tell me. Have you a place in your heart for Jim?"

With a deep sigh, Emma shook her head. "I'm so angry at him right now that I'm not sure. I know I should be flattered that he'd not risk me running about Cremorne Gardens, but if I lose another sister . . . I might very well lose my mind."

"You must trust him."

"I do, I just worry that he may have misread things."

"He is the very best at what he does."

"But he is not invincible. *I* fooled him."

"I suspect because his heart was involved." The duchess looked past her to the doorway. "Yes, Wedgeworth?"

"Lord Rockberry has come to call," the butler announced.

"Please show him in, then."

With her stomach quivering, Emma rose to her feet, along with the duchess.

Lord Rockberry strode in, his brow furrowed, his eyes showing concern. He bowed slightly. "Your Grace, Miss Watkins. Has there been any news?"

Offering him an encouraging smile, Emma shook her head. "Not yet."

"I didn't mean to intrude on your evening, I just . . . I could hardly sit still at home."

"You're more than welcome to wait here with us," the duchess said. "Surely we'll have word soon."

"Thank you. I appreciate your kindness."

The duchess indicated a chair.

Rockberry suddenly seemed nonplussed. "Now that I'm here, I'm not certain I can sit still for more than five minutes. I think a turn about the garden would serve me better. Miss Watkins, would you be so kind as to join me? I was quite taken with your sister. I would very much like to speak with you about her."

She smiled warmly. "I would so enjoy talking about Eleanor."

"Would you excuse us, Duchess?" Rockberry asked.

"Certainly. Here, Emma, you may borrow my wrap."

Emma was grateful for the shawl as she drew it over her shoulders once she and Rockberry stepped outside.

"It's almost midnight," she said quietly as they reached the hyacinths. "I would think the plan would be well under way by now."

"Yes, I quite agree. Midnight seems to be the magical hour. I'm anticipating hearing the outcome of tonight's adventure."

Adventure. A tingle of unease skittered up Emma's spine. She thought about turning back, then silently chastised herself for being silly, so she continued on. "You said you wished to talk about Eleanor."

"No."

She peered over at him. His gaze was locked on her. If Eleanor had not sung his praises, told her how he'd wept knowing what his brother had done, Emma might have been frightened. Instead, she was certain it was worry over Eleanor that had her seeing danger in the shadows of his face. "But in the parlor, you said you wished to talk to me about my sister."

"Yes. But not Eleanor. Elisabeth. I was quite taken with her, and I'm wondering if you'll be as satisfying."

Before she could react, he had his hand covering her mouth, while his arm held her against him. She could sense his determination. Then suddenly two more men were grabbing her, lifting her, carting her toward the alleyway. In spite of her valiant struggles, she couldn't break free of their hold and her muffled screams mocked her.

No one would hear her. No one would save her. She had little doubt she was about to suffer the same fate as Elisabeth.

Growing weary, Eleanor headed toward the entrance to the pleasure gardens. It was long past midnight. No one had approached her. No one had called her Elisabeth. No one had commented on the silver filigree. She felt as though she'd failed a good many people, but she wasn't certain what more she could do.

The gentleman to whom she'd been introduced on the way to Cremorne, the one who followed her as she took her leisurely strolls along one path and then the other, came to stand beside her. He smelled of rich pipe tobacco.

"Do you think Mr. Swindler had the right of it?" Eleanor asked.

"I'm afraid so, yes," Sir David said.

"It seems I'm as poor a judge of a man's character as my older sister was."

"Don't be too hard on yourself. Men like Rockberry—both the previous marquess and the present one—learn to hide what they are."

It didn't make her feel any better knowing that Emma could be in danger.

"Perhaps we had the wrong night," she said.

"Perhaps. But I doubt it."

"I wouldn't be opposed to your providing a bit of hope."

"I'm sorry. I fear I've always been more a realist than a dreamer." He made a signal, and a half dozen men stepped out of the shadows. They, too, had been following her as discreetly as Sir David. They reported to him, were part of a special unit of detectives that he oversaw. "You men are free to leave. I'm going to see Miss Watkins home."

As the men silently left the gardens, Sir David placed his hand on her elbow and began guiding her toward a waiting hansom.

"May I ask you a question, Miss Watkins?"

"Certainly, sir."

"The night you confronted Rockberry, do you know for certain that he was dead when you left?"

She staggered to a stop and looked up at him. He wasn't nearly as tall or broad as Mr. Swindler, but he had a commanding presence. She couldn't even begin to guess his age. At certain angles he appeared to be quite up in years, and at other angles he gave the impression of being a much younger man. "I . . . well, yes, I . . . I thought so. I jabbed him, and he fell to the carpet. He writhed for a bit, then stilled. Didn't move. Made no sound. There was so much blood that I felt certain he was dead."

"You only stabbed him once, then."

"Yes. Straight in the heart."

"Mmm. Interesting, that."

"Why? What makes it so?"

" 'Straight' into the heart." He made a jabbing motion. "Like that? No twisting of the dagger, no turning it, no moving it out a little and pushing it back in at a different angle, a better angle?"

"No. Why ever would I do all that?"

"To kill him, Miss Watkins."

"I don't understand, Sir David. I stabbed him."

"Indeed you did, but I'm beginning to suspect that someone else came in and finished him off."

Eleanor stared at him. "I'm not a murderess?"

"I don't believe so, Miss Watkins."

"Oh."

He handed her up into the hansom and settled in beside her. "You sound disappointed."

"I wished to avenge my sister. And afterward, oh God, it was not as easy to live with as I thought it would be." A sob of unmitigated relief broke free, and tears burned her eyes. "Oh, I'm terribly sorry."

Sir David put his arms around her and drew her into the comfort of his chest. "It's quite all right, Miss Watkins. No harm done here."

For the second night in a row she found herself in a man's embrace, but this one was very different from the one last night. It was exceedingly comforting. Sir David was a man of outer as well as inner strength. She could tell it in the way he held her, as though he would protect her at all costs. Or was she simply being fanciful again? Wanting so desperately to discover what Emma had with James Swindler?

"Do you think it's honestly possible that I didn't kill him?" she asked hesitantly.

"Would you like it to be possible?"

Not daring to look at him, squeezing her eyes shut tightly against the truth, she nodded.

"Then I suspect we shall discover, Miss Watkins, that it was not you who delivered the killing blow."

"It's a great relief. Thank you, Sir David."

"My pleasure, Miss Watkins."

Swindler was damned tempted to leap from the carriage in which he was traveling and run to the carriage they were following. He'd hoped he was wrong about Rockberry. But something about the man had bothered him, put his senses on heightened alert. That he had properly judged the man should have brought him some satisfaction. Instead all he wanted was to make the man rue the day he was born.

When he'd seen Rockberry and his blackguard associates taking Emma, only Claybourne and Dodger holding on to him and reminding him that something larger was at stake had kept him from revealing his presence. At the last moment he'd almost switched the sisters' roles, but he'd known Rockberry was expecting Emma to be in residence.

After leaving Emma last night, Swindler had met with Sir David and explained his plans and his suspicions. Sir David had volunteered to keep watch over Eleanor at the gardens while Swindler, Claybourne, Dodger, and Greystone were watching over Emma.

Or that was the plan. At that precise moment all they were doing was following discreetly behind Rockberry's carriage.

"Relax, man, my driver has him in sight," Greystone assured him. "Ever since the night I almost lost Frannie, I've hired men who have the skills to protect her. He knows what he's about. He'll see that tonight ends with no harm coming to Miss Watkins."

"I can't believe the man is fool enough to do this," Dodger said.

"Arrogant bastard," Claybourne said. "He's just inherited the title. He considers himself untouchable. His brother was."

Swindler wrapped his hand around the gun in his jacket pocket. "If I don't kill him tonight I shall see him hanged. And if he's hurt Emma . . . "

He could hardly stand the thought without feeling a bit of madness consuming him.

"They won't harm her until they've performed the ritual," Dodger said.

"And that's supposed to make me feel better?" Swindler asked.

"No, that's to emphasize that you don't need to kill him as soon as you see him. We don't need to be brash and careless."

"You're one to talk. If it was your wife—"

"He'd already be dead. But unlike you, I don't

give a bloody damn about any justice except my own. You've always wanted to save the world."

Not any longer. All he wanted was to save Emma.

Emma's head lolled back against the carriage seat. She *thought* she was still in the carriage. It was so hard to be certain. Everything was blurred. She was aware of a rocking motion. She supposed she could be on a train by now.

She remembered them forcing her into the carriage and climbing in after her. She remembered them holding her down, pinching her nose until she had to open her mouth to breathe, and when she did, they'd poured some sweet wine down her throat. At least she thought it was wine. But it made her grow dizzy so quickly, made her lethargic, made it so difficult to concentrate.

"I don't understand." Her words were slurred and came from a far distance. "You can't think you'll get away with this."

"It's all about the thrill, my dear," Rockberry said. "The excitement that we might get caught. And if we do"—he shrugged—"we have power and influence. Someone might slap our hand, but no one cares about the daughter of a viscount whose title died with him."

"James cares."

He snorted. "The son of a thief? Do you really think his word will carry any weight? Especially after I explain that during our stroll through Greystone's garden, *you* suggested we slip away for something a little more intimate. That you wanted to experience a night with the society. That you begged me . . . "

She tried to shake her head but it sat so heavy on her shoulders. "James will know you're lying."

"But what of my peers? I'm a lord now. I'll be tried by my peers. And that, too, my dear, is part of the fun, the pleasure, the excitement. Fooling people into believing me." He released a harsh laugh. "Like your sister, Eleanor. I do believe she expected me to drop down on bended knee last night. And Elisabeth. When my brother brought her to us, it added a new element to our fun. She tried to fight, as I'm sure you will as well. But in the end . . . " He drew in a deep breath that sounded like satisfaction.

She wanted to claw out his eyes, tear away his mouth so he couldn't continue saying these ugly things. "James will kill you."

"Mmm. Yes. He might try, but right now he's still following Eleanor through Cremorne Gardens. Did he really think we'd rendezvous there and go elsewhere? No. We always meet at the same place on the outskirts of London, where no one will bother us. And your Inspector Swindler will never find us."

"You misjudge how good he is."

Sitting beside her, he removed the pins from her hair. She wanted to move away from him, but her body wouldn't listen to her commands.

"No, my dear, *you* misjudge how skilled he is."

He buried his face in her hair and sniffed, while the other two gents sitting across from them chuckled. She could see their smiles like some sort of obscene painting. She hated it, despised them.

"I don't know why my brother went to Scotland Yard when he discovered you following him. Or was it Eleanor? Doesn't matter. I think his conscience was beginning to eat at him. Stupid clod."

It occurred to Emma, in the back of her mind where she was struggling to stay clear-headed, that he was telling her too much. As though it didn't matter what she knew. Did he think she'd forget?

Then she remembered that his brother had killed a woman. Or so he'd claimed. Perhaps it was the man holding her who'd done the deed. Perhaps he meant to see her dead as well.

Somehow, she found the strength to break away and reach for the door, but they grabbed her, wrestled her to the floor, pinched her nose—

As she choked on the too sweet liquid they were pouring into her again, she snatched at her memories of James. If she was going to die, she wanted her last thought to be of him.

As they traveled into a less populated area, Swindler was aware of the carriage slowing, the driver increasing the distance between the two vehicles. Where the bloody hell were they going?

The carriage suddenly came to a stop. Swindler didn't wait for the footman to open the door. He did it himself, leaped to the ground and glanced around at a good deal of nothingness. The others joined him.

"They passed through a gate a short distance back, Your Grace," the driver said as he climbed down and joined the footman who'd already disembarked and was relighting the lantern they'd extinguished in hopes of not being noticed as they followed Rockberry.

"Let's go, then," Swindler said.

Claybourne grabbed his arm, stopping his forward movement. "Do we have a plan?"

"Get Emma out alive and I don't care who the hell dies in the bloody process." Breaking free of the hold, Swindler began running toward the gate.

"I do hope he's not including us in the 'who the hell dies' arena," he heard Greystone mutter.

"I wouldn't be so sure if I were you," Dodger

responded. "I do believe the man's in love."

Love didn't seem a strong enough word for what Swindler felt for Emma. He only knew that if she was harmed, he'd never forgive himself, and if she died, his entire life would be meaningless.

It was a lovely residence. Too lovely for what Emma knew occurred here.

One of the swells had carried her from the carriage, because her legs had been as substantial as jam. Rockberry had yelled that they'd given her too much. Whatever it was, she feared he was correct. As she sat on a chair in the entrance hallway, her stomach was roiling and she thought at any moment she might be ill.

"Come along, dear," she heard a soft feminine voice say.

Where had the lady standing before her come from? Another was with her, helping her to her feet and assisting her up the stairs. The blond introduced herself as Helena. The dark-haired woman was Aphrodite.

In a bedchamber upstairs, they began removing her clothes. She tried to resist, to shove them away, but her limbs had no sturdiness to them. Someone was brushing her hair. Why were they doing this?

She tried not to imagine how Elisabeth had felt,

how frightened she'd been. Or had she thought she was being prepared to become Rockberry's bride? Oh, she despised these people. No matter how much wine they gave her, they could not drown out that single bit of knowledge, that hammering conviction. These people had hurt Elisabeth. Now they meant to harm her. She would fight them.

If only she could think clearly. If only she could regain control of her limbs. She wanted only to curl up and go to sleep, but the ladies wouldn't let her be.

Emma thought of James. Would he ever look at her the same if Rockberry touched her? Would he be consumed with guilt because he'd left her unguarded? He suffered enough because of his father. She didn't want to add to his burdens.

When the ladies—*what were their names again?*—had her prepared to their satisfaction, they draped the softest of silk around her. It felt so wonderful, wrapped her in a cloud. She almost forgot what it heralded. Then they began to escort her somewhere. She was vaguely aware of hallways and passages, candle flames flickering. She wanted to remember what everything looked like so she could describe it to James later. Maybe he could find it. But nothing seemed to stick in her mind. Whenever she saw something new, whatever she'd seen before disappeared from memory.

They were no longer walking, simply swaying. She realized she was in a large, cavernous room. Pillows were everywhere. Here more candles provided a soft light. Some might have even considered it romantic. She could hear chanting. Men in red robes, Satan's followers, stood in a circle around her. Hoods kept their faces in shadows. She had little doubt they were the wicked, the beasts who had taken advantage of Elisabeth—and now had plans to harm her.

She was vaguely aware of the silk slithering down her body. She wanted to pull it back up from its place on the floor but it was so far away. And her limbs seemed incapable of following commands, as though they were somehow detached from her thoughts.

"Kneel," Rockberry ordered.

She focused on his voice, focused on his face. He was one of the men who'd hurt Elisabeth, had destroyed her. She fought back the lethargy. "No."

"Kneel. Down."

"No."

He laughed harshly. "Your unwillingness will not prevent what is to come. Kneel."

"Rot in hell."

She could see the anger contorting his features, knew things would probably go much worse for her, but she was beyond caring. She'd not willingly follow him into hell. She'd not even follow him into heaven. She refused to become his slave, his concubine. Whatever he offered, she wanted nothing to do with it.

He snapped his fingers and she felt strong hands pushing her down until her knees thudded painfully against the floor.

"Daughter of Eros—"

She saw him holding up the silver filigree collar.

"Bride of Eros—"

The silver touched her neck, just as it had touched Elisabeth's. Cold against her flesh, causing chills to race through her. It was so pretty but so heavy, a symbol of subservience, an indication of ownership. She didn't know where she found the strength, but she gathered whatever remnants remained and slammed her balled fist up between his spread legs—

With an agonizing shriek, Rockberry buckled and dropped to his knees before her. She was vaguely aware of her fingernails clawing rivulets in his face, his screams, hands grabbing her—

And then the chaos that Elisabeth had written about truly erupted.

Chapter 24

Swindler burst into the room as though he were leading the horsemen of the apocalypse. He'd had a time of it picking the lock at the gate. Their efforts to find Emma had been delayed as they dealt with the drivers and groomsmen of Rockberry's carriage as well as two others. The front door had not been locked, the people inside obviously feeling safe and secure in their little world. Swindler and his group had dealt with one butler. No other servants were about. These disciples of whatever the bloody hell they were had no doubt determined that the fewer witnesses to their depravity, the better. But finding the correct room in this monstrosity of a residence had taken more time than Swindler would have liked. It had been the echoing chant that finally led them in the right direction, and then the high-pitched shrieks that confirmed they'd found where they needed to be.

They'd fired shots over heads—more to distract

and intimidate rather than harm. Six men wearing red cloaks, and two ladies—scrambling for their wraps—had dropped to their bellies like the snakes they were and covered their heads. One man was already writhing on the floor, fighting off the hellion who was intent on causing him serious bodily harm. Swindler, knowing it was Emma, was tempted to leave her to it, let her have her satisfaction, her triumph, but he needed to reassure himself that no harm had come to her. God, but she was glorious in her fury.

Grabbing the silk pooled on the floor, wishing he had something better for her, he draped it over her and gently tried to tug her off Rockberry. But she fought him, lost in the madness of whatever potion they'd given her, whatever horrors they'd inflicted on her. Wrapping his arms tightly around her, holding her as still as he could, he pulled her away and onto his lap.

When Rockberry made a motion to lunge for her, Claybourne planted his booted foot on the man's chest and directed his pistol at his head. "I wouldn't if I were you. You should know by my reputation that I have no problem killing lords. I've no objection to adding you to my list."

Rockberry sank back down, his small excuse for manhood as shriveled as his soul.

Swindler rocked Emma while tears coursed

down her cheeks and tremors cascaded through her. "It's all right, sweetheart. You're safe now."

"He's worse than his brother," she sobbed.

"I know." He hated to ask but he had to know. He buried his face in her hair, near her ear, and whispered, "Did he . . . did he hurt you?"

Shaking her head, she relaxed against him. "Frightened me more than anything. How could they?"

"They are warped, perverted. I can't explain it." He glanced over his shoulder to see Greystone's driver and footman tying the hands of the men and ladies.

His gaze averted out of respect for Emma's modesty, Greystone knelt before Swindler. "Christ, we've got three lords here. And one of those ladies is the daughter of a duke."

Swindler nodded, not surprised by that discovery. Idle people searching for something to fill their lives. People of influence thinking that they couldn't be touched. "We'll take them to the back door of Scotland Yard. Sir David will decide how best to handle this matter. Bundle them up into their carriages. Warn their drivers that if they don't cooperate they'll answer to Scotland Yard."

"Right." Greystone cast a quick glance at Swindler before looking away. "How's Emma?"

"Shaken, but brave."

"She was a lioness, your Emma."

His Emma. God, he hoped that was true, but he had no idea if she'd forgive him for what had happened tonight.

Emma would have been content to wear nothing except the silk. She simply wanted to get out of this hideous place as quickly as possible. But James insisted that they had time to find her clothes and get her properly dressed while Greystone's driver went to fetch their coach.

Now they were alone inside it, his friends having decided to divide themselves among the other carriages and ensure that the blighters crammed inside them were properly delivered to Scotland Yard.

Leaning against James, Emma was exhausted from the draught and the ordeal. His arm was around her, his hand stroking her arm, so comforting. "However did you find me? How did you know where to look?"

He stiffened beside her, as though preparing himself for a blow. "We never left Greystone's."

She shook her head. "But, Eleanor . . . "

"She went to Cremorne Gardens, but Sir David and several men from Scotland Yard accompanied her. I can't explain it, Emma. I just felt as though we were missing something. Rockberry was so forthcoming with information, and in spite of the horrors his brother had committed, the new Rockberry almost seemed to relish telling us what a monster his brother had been." Shifting around, he cradled her chin and turned her face up until he could gaze into her eyes. "Forgive me, Emma, but I couldn't tell you what I suspected. I knew that they'd give you some draught like they did Elisabeth, and it might cause you to say things that would have alerted them to the fact that we were in pursuit."

Reaching up, she touched his beloved face. "Do you think there will ever come a day when we'll be completely honest with each other, when we'll hold no secrets from each other?"

"From this day forward, I swear to you."

Nodding, she buried her head in the nook of his shoulder. And could only hope that his words were true.

She didn't recall drifting off to sleep. She hadn't wanted to, actually. She'd wanted to enjoy what little time remained to be in his arms. But she awoke to his lips pressed against her temple as he nudged her awake.

"Emma, we've arrived."

With a sigh she struggled to open her eyes. It was the draught, she supposed, continuing to make her lethargic. Then she came fully awake with the realization that she would learn the truth of Eleanor's fate. But the alertness quickly disappeared, and if not for James's arm around her back, guiding her up the steps, she wasn't certain she could have avoided lying down to sleep once again.

The butler opened the door. James only barely led her into the parlor when Eleanor popped up from the sofa—who was the man sitting beside her?—rushed across the room and hugged her as though her life depended on her doing so.

"Oh, Emma, dear Emma, you're all right! Did he harm you?" She leaned back, studying Emma's face, touching her cheek, her hair, as though needing to reassure herself that her sister was alive and as well as could be expected under the circumstances. "What did they do to you?"

Emma forced herself to smile, to try again to shake off the lethargy. "Nothing."

Eleanor's gaze shot to James.

"They gave her a draught or something to make her more easily bendable to their will, only to discover she's not easily manipulated," he said. "She's not fully recovered."

"Oh, then you must sit down," Eleanor ordered her sister.

"Yes, I'd like that. I'm frightfully unsteady."

Eleanor guided her to a chair. It felt wonderful and cozy to Emma as it enveloped her body.

"Emma," Eleanor said, kneeling in front of her, touching her hair again. "Are you truly all right?"

She nodded.

"She fought him off," James said, his voice echoing with pride. "She was quite remarkable."

"She always has been." Eleanor squeezed her hands.

"What of Sterling?" the duchess asked, and only then did Emma realize that she was in the room also.

"He's fine, Frannie. He's escorted the blighters to gaol. He should be home shortly," James told her.

"Oh, thank God."

"Then I suppose I should be off to see to them," a deep voice said.

Eleanor smiled, looked up, then refocused her attention on Emma. "This is Sir David. He was with me in the gardens."

A very distinguished-looking gentleman with dark hair and eyes, he bowed slightly. "Miss Watkins, it's a pleasure to make your acquaintance. I'm sorry you had to go through so much tonight, but we appreciate your help in bringing these blackguards to justice."

"You're welcome." The words seemed silly once she'd said them. Everything she'd done was further retribution for Elisabeth. Her mind, however, was slow in thinking, and she didn't know what else she could have said.

"Emma," Eleanor said with a tinge of excitement laced in her voice, "Sir David doesn't believe I killed Lord Rockberry."

"That's good." The fewer people—

"No, no. He truly doesn't believe I did it! He said it appears that Rockberry was alive when I left and someone came along afterward and dug the dagger further in."

"Oh, my God! You didn't murder him?"

"Exactly. His brother most likely is the culprit. It all makes sense, doesn't it?"

Even though Emma was still groggy, she heard the desperation in Eleanor's voice that it could be as Sir David described, that she could be innocent of killing the man. Emma nodded. "Oh, yes, it makes perfect sense."

Leaning in, Eleanor hugged her tightly. "Oh, Emma, everything might turn out all right after all."

Looking over Eleanor's shoulder to the two men standing there with unreadable faces, Emma thought perhaps her sister was right.

"Miss Watkins, I must be off," Sir David said. "I hope you will favor me by allowing me to call on you tomorrow afternoon, to make certain you've recovered from the ordeal of this night."

Eleanor twisted around and looked up at him. "Oh, yes, sir. I would be most pleased to have you call."

"Very good, then. Swindler, I'll be waiting for you outside. Five minutes, man. We need to see to getting everything in order with these miscreants."

"I'll escort you out, Sir David," Eleanor said, coming to her feet.

James took her place, kneeling in front of Emma. "Will you be all right?"

She thought she nodded. She wondered how much longer before she had full use of her faculties again. "I'm just so very weary." She touched his face. He turned his face into her palm and placed a kiss at its center.

"I wish I didn't have to leave you," he said.

She wished he didn't either, but she knew the choice was not his. She also realized that she needed to reassure him. "I want them punished. I want them to pay for what they did."

"I'll see to it, I promise you."

"I know you will."

She heard a door opening, followed by rapid footsteps. Then Frannie was dashing across the room.

"Sterling!"

Emma looked over to see the duchess wrapping her arms around the duke, holding him close, while he buried his face in the curve of her neck. James glanced back over his shoulder at the reunited couple, just as the duke began leading his wife out of the room.

"Are they seeking privacy?" Emma whispered.

"Perhaps they're giving it to us," James responded, his voice low. He gently cradled her chin, leaned in and placed the softest of kisses on one corner of her mouth and then the other, as though she were somehow more fragile than she'd ever been, when in an odd sort of way, she felt stronger.

Before he could pull back completely, she pressed her lips to his, kissing him deeply, making certain that he understood that she didn't consider any of tonight's horrors his fault and that she believed him—there would be no more deceptions or secrets between them.

Frannie insisted that Swindler and Sir David take Greystone's carriage to complete their night's work. As the carriage moved at a steady clip through the streets, Swindler studied Sir David's silhouette as the man sat across from him.

"Do you really believe that Eleanor didn't kill Rockberry?"

With a sigh, Sir David turned his head to gaze out the window. "She's a slight of a woman, Swindler. I don't believe she'd have had the strength to plunge the dagger deeply enough."

Swindler thought of Emma bringing the new Lord Rockberry to his knees. "Revenge for a sister you dearly love is a powerful motivator. Could give you strength that you might not normally have."

"Sorry, Swindler. Can't see it. I think it more likely that she stabbed him, the shock of it caused unconsciousness, then his brother came in for his nightly brandy and decided he wouldn't mind having the title after all. Finished what Miss Watkins began. You're my best man. I'm surprised you didn't draw the same conclusion. Think about it."

Swindler felt Sir David's gaze fall heavily on him. "The new Rockberry is cut from the same cloth as his brother."

"There you are," Sir David said.

"A knife to the chest is not something from which one easily recovers. Even if his brother had not come in and finished the deed, it's quite possible Rockberry would have died of the wound eventually. And if she caught his lung—"

"Perhaps, perhaps not. Hard to say."

"Just to be clear, sir, you intend to charge the new Lord Rockberry with the murder of the previous Lord Rockberry?"

"Depends, Swindler. Does my best man believe it happened as I described?"

Swindler remembered studying the gaping wound, remembered Eleanor saying that she'd jabbed Rockberry and stepped back. Sir David's scenario was possible. And if it hadn't happened that way—he couldn't see giving either Rockberry the power to ruin another sister's life. "Yes, sir. I concur that it could have happened just that way."

"Jolly good. I shall write up my report, and we shall so testify if called before the House of Lords."

"Yes, sir."

"Now that we have that nasty business out of the way, tell me everything you know about Miss Eleanor Watkins—the real Eleanor."

With a low chuckle, Swindler proceeded to do exactly that.

They treated Emma as though she was a princess. Eleanor and the duchess bathed her and washed her hair. They toweled her dry and braided her hair. They helped her slip into her softest night rail. When Emma crawled into bed, Eleanor clambered in with her and they held each other tightly, just as they had when they were young girls, and as on the night after they discovered Elisabeth at the bottom of the cliffs.

They stopped sharing the same room shortly after their father died and Eleanor had moved into his bedchamber. But tonight they needed to be together. Still, there was an emptiness to the bed.

"I miss her so much," Eleanor said, as though reading Emma's mind.

"Eleanor, I . . . " She let her voice trail off.

"What, dear sister?"

"I felt as though she was with me tonight. In that horrible room. That she was there, urging me on, giving me the strength to attack Rockberry. If so, then perhaps she forgives me for yelling at her."

"Oh, Emma." Eleanor squeezed her tightly. "She knows you didn't mean it."

"I hope so. I'd give anything to have her back."

"I know. I would, too."

They lay in silence for several minutes, each lost in their own reflections of Elisabeth. Her sweet nature, her adventuresome spirit.

After a long while Emma said, "Eleanor, tell me about Sir David."

Eleanor's laughter circled around them. "Isn't he absolutely wonderful?"

"How did it all come about?"

"Mr. Swindler—"

"You can call him James."

"All right. James led me to the carriage, handed me up, and there was this man sitting there in the shadows. Sir David. James's superior. James told me that Sir David would see to matters at the gardens. I was so nervous. But Sir David calmed me with quiet words and reassurances. He had such faith in me.

"He explained that he had other men at Cremorne to keep an eye out. I was simply to walk around until someone approached me. No one ever did. I can't imagine what Rockberry was thinking to abduct you from here. He must have known that they would know it was him. He took no pains at all to disguise what he was about."

Emma fought to remember what she'd heard in the carriage. "It was part of the game, I think. To be so bold, so arrogant. And then to find a way to get away with it. He thought no one could touch him."

"I wonder what they're going to do about him."

"And the others," Emma whispered. "They all need to pay. I know James and his friends have the means to see someone punished who deserves it, by making him trade places with someone who doesn't. We should have trusted him from the beginning, Eleanor."

"But we trust him now. That should count for something."

They lay in silence for several minutes before Eleanor said, "The duchess has offered to introduce us into society."

"All I want, Eleanor, is to return home."

Chapter 25

Sir David's office was again shadowed. Standing before his desk, Swindler was acutely aware of the presence in the corner, although this time the scent wafting toward him was decidedly feminine.

"We've identified the men you picked up two nights ago," Sir David said. "The ladies have been released to their fathers, but the gentlemen—although I'm offended to refer to them as such—must be dealt with. Rockberry will be tried by his peers for the murder of his brother. The other five we would prefer to simply transport, but as two are lords, matters must be handled with a bit more delicacy. They must disappear, but we wish no harm to come to them in the process.

"I'm well aware, Swindler, that you have the skills to make undesirables disappear, and that you often remove from prison those who have been condemned to live within its walls. We would like it to appear as though the lords have died so their heirs may take the reins. Are you up to the task?"

Swindler gave a brusque nod. Sometimes it was better not to voice words.

"There will be a knighthood in it for you, Swindler," Sir David said.

Swindler turned to the corner, knelt, and bowed his head. "I require no knighthood to faithfully serve her majesty. I would request that Misses Emma and Eleanor Watkins be granted pardon for any crimes that might be brought against them now or in the future in relation to this incident."

"So it shall be," the soft feminine voice said.

Swindler did not look up as the swishing of skirts heralded the queen's departure.

"Didn't trust me to see to matters, Swindler?" Sir David asked.

"No offense, sir, but I learned long ago to never let an opportunity pass for gaining what I wanted."

"No offense taken, Swindler. Now, what's your plan for dealing with the lords?"

"They make a lovely couple, don't you think?" Emma asked.

She and Swindler were strolling in Hyde Park, following only a short distance behind Eleanor and Sir David. During the past week, Emma had begun to gain weight, and she'd lost the dark circles beneath her eyes. She looked calm, content, almost happy.

"Sir David is a good man," Swindler said. He hadn't quite gotten accustomed to the idea that Sir David had an interest in Eleanor, yet it appeared his superior was quite smitten.

"He told Eleanor that we wouldn't be arrested."

"There's no reason. As we see it, and will testify, Rockberry murdered his brother. The fact that Eleanor stabbed him first is incidental." He could feel her gaze on him, but he stared ahead, not wanting her to see anything in his eyes that might indicate compromises had been made.

"I suppose then that we can return to the cottage at any time."

The thought caused a profound emptiness to sweep through him. During the past week, he'd visited with her every afternoon and had dined with her twice at Frannie's. He couldn't deny that their reasons for being with each other in the beginning had not been pure—they'd both been guilty of deception. But neither could he deny that he cared deeply for Emma. That in spite of his reason for pursuing her, her reason for allowing herself to be caught, something very precious existed between them.

"I'm certain that Frannie would be pleased to give both you and Eleanor a Season if you wish it," he said, part of him hoping she'd accept so she would be in London longer and he might have the opportunity to see her again; part of him hoping she had no desire to be courted.

"I don't wish to have a Season," she said quietly. "I don't think any ball could ever compare to the last one I attended."

He stopped walking. So did she. She was looking at him now, her blue eyes locked onto his.

"I will never be a man of wealth and means, Emma. I make a respectable income. Claybourne and Dodger both offered me the opportunity to go into business ventures with them, but the risk was too high. I could have ended up with nothing. They are wealthy beyond imagining and I have enough to keep me content."

"I don't care about money," she said.

"It is quite possible that I will be knighted. It has been mentioned, but—"

"I don't give a fig about rank."

Good God, the woman was impossible to please. What did she want? What could he offer her?

"Emma—"

She stepped nearer to him. "You once told me I owned your heart."

"You do."

"Are you going to allow me to leave, then? To return to my cottage by the sea?"

"I want you to be happy."

"Then ask me to marry you."

It was a beautiful day in the spring in the village near the small cottage by the sea. They said that the sky had never been as blue, the breeze as gentle. Everyone who lived in the village or nearby, sat in the church, quivering with excitement and anticipation. Their small community had never had such a gathering of prominent persons.

The Duke and Duchess of Greystone, the Earl and Countess of Claybourne. In addition, there was a man who held no title, but everyone knew by the way Jack Dodger dressed and held himself that he was a man of immense wealth. At his side was a lady who was obviously nobility. It was rumored that the last newcomer, Dr. William Graves, was a personal physician to the queen herself.

All the whisperings about the illustrious guests settled into silence when the brides strolled side by side down the aisle. No father accompanied them, no ladies waited on them. The sisters were as they'd been throughout their lives: the truest of friends. But where they'd once needed no more than each other, now they needed—wanted—the two men who waited for them at the altar.

While Eleanor took her place beside Sir David, Emma smiled warmly and took the arm that Sir

James offered her. She could scarcely believe that this wonderful gentleman was going to marry her.

As the vicar began talking about love, she barely listened because there was nothing he could say that she didn't already know, nothing he could describe that was more wonderful than what she saw reflected in James's eyes.

Within the green depths was the truest of adoration and pride. This man wanted her as his wife forever. And she wanted him as her husband. She never wanted to look away from him, never wanted to be without him. He stood so tall and handsome, so confident and sure. A boy with regrets who had grown into a man determined to atone for childish mistakes, a man who accepted her as she was, flaws and all.

Against his waistcoat, she could see the gold chain attached to the watch that he'd tucked into his pocket. It had been her wedding gift to him. On the back she'd had inscribed, NO GREATER LOVE.

"To honor your father," she'd told him. "Because of his sacrifice, I have you."

Tears had welled in James's eyes. He'd not spoken—she thought because his throat had tightened with emotion. But he had closed his strong fingers around it. And now he wore it for the first time—as she became his wife.

Emma listened as Eleanor and Sir David exchanged vows. She and Eleanor would be living in London, in residences not too far from each other. Emma wasn't certain how James and Sir David had managed it, but she was beginning to realize that there was nothing James couldn't accomplish if he thought it was the way things should be.

Then it was their turn—hers and James's—to profess their love, to make their promises. For better or worse. For richer, for poorer. In sickness and in health. She would have it no other way. She would stand by this man until she drew her last breath, knowing that he would always stand beside her as well.

As the vicar pronounced them man and wife, the sun coming in through the stained-glass windows seemed to shine a little brighter, and Emma imagined it was Elisabeth smiling down on them.

Eleanor and Sir David left for London shortly after the ceremony ended, leaving the cottage for Emma and James. Now, after having locked up, he stood in the doorway of the bedchamber and watched as she, sitting on the edge of the window, glided her brush through her hair.

"Did you know I was watching that night when you brushed your hair in the window at your lodgings?" he asked.

With a mischievous smile, she peered over

at him. "I thought I could sense you there, but I wasn't certain. Eleanor said for our plan to work that I needed to seduce you. I didn't know where to begin."

He'd discarded his jacket, waistcoat, and neck-cloth earlier. He strode over to her and took the brush from her hand. "I fell for you so quickly and so hard I made it far too easy for you to seduce me. I stood outside your window like a besotted lad and imagined doing this." He dragged the brush through her hair, relishing the silkiness of the strands going through his fingers. He would have a lifetime of this.

"I sat in that window and imagined you doing it as well."

"I love your hair," he said. "I love your eyes. I love everything about you."

Rising from the window, she wrapped her arms around his neck. "I love everything about you as well. And I've missed you terribly these past few months."

She and Eleanor had returned to their home to begin preparing for their wedding, and although Swindler had come to visit and they'd come to London on occasion, Swindler had not been able to secure a moment alone with Emma for anything more intimate than a kiss.

Tossing the brush aside, he took her in his arms

and lowered his mouth to hers. All the restraint he'd been exhibiting stormed through him, reminding him of that first night he'd been here when the wind howled and the rain had pounded. Passion poured from her into him, heating his desire. He wondered if it would always be like this—powerful and strong. Her rose scent wafted around him. Her bare feet crept onto his. So much about her was familiar, so much was endearing.

Ending the kiss, he gazed deeply into her eyes, saw them heavy-lidded and smoldering. Her lips were damp and swollen. While her gown covered her body, it could not hide that her nipples had hardened. Bending down, through the cloth, he took one in his mouth, biting down gently. She moaned softly, arching back, digging her fingers into his shoulders.

It had been too long, too too long. He wanted her now with a ferocity that was almost overwhelming. At the same time, he wanted to savor each moment. She was his wife, his love. Tonight should be special for her, for them. Tonight was the first night of their married life.

Easing past her, he opened the window slightly to allow in the cool spring breeze. The curtains billowed slightly.

Lifting her into his arms, he carried her— laughing and joyous—to the bed and laid her down upon it. While he quickly divested himself of his remaining clothing, she eased provocatively out of her gown. She released a small scream as he leaped onto the bed and tucked her beneath him, absorbing the softness of her skin melding with his.

"I've missed this, missed you," he growled as he began to explore her with his hands and mouth, once again learning all the subtle nuances of her body, glorying in the curves and softness that made her so unique, made her special to him.

Emma ran her hands over him, savoring the firmness of his corded muscles, the length of his limbs. She skimmed her fingers over his marred back and wondered if her eyes would always sting when she encountered the reminder of how cruel his childhood had been.

"What was your father's name?" she suddenly asked.

He lifted his head from the valley between her breasts where he'd been giving her his undivided attention. Holding her gaze, he said, "Geoffrey Harrison."

She combed her fingers into his dark hair. It was shorter than usual, trimmed for the occasion. "We'll name our first son after him."

He grinned at her. "I'd like that."

"Perhaps it'll happen tonight. I want to give you children."

Winking at her, he returned his mouth to her breast, eliciting pleasure with the wicked things he did. As often as they'd been together in the beginning, she thought there should have been nothing new to learn, and yet each time they came together, the familiarity brought something new with it. A heightened awareness, more daring touches.

Swindler used his hands, fingers, and mouth to explore every inch of Emma as though rediscovering old territory and finding that it had changed slightly, but he was just as pleased with the new landscape as he'd been with the old. She'd added back some of the weight she'd lost after she first left London. Her hips were a little more round, her breasts a little fuller. He took his time, watching as he gently reshaped her breasts, before dipping his head down, his mouth lingering to taste, taunt, and tease.

From this moment on, every night, he would have this remarkable woman in his bed. He would go to sleep surrounded by her sweet scent, and she would drift off with his arms around her.

He would watch her body change as their children came into the world. He would relish everything about her, just as he relished it now.

As her sighs and moans grew louder, as she writhed beneath him, turning into him, opening herself to him, he plunged into the velvety heat that welcomed him and closed around him.

Stilling, with a deep groan of satisfaction, he absorbed the full impact of his penetration. He framed her face with his large hands and kissed her. "I love you, Emma."

Emma thought she would never tire of his saying those words, of his melding his body to hers. He kissed her chin, her cheek, her neck. Then ever so slowly, tormenting them both, he began to move against her.

Her body rocked in rhythm with his, the pleasure ebbing and flowing, building until the maelstrom couldn't be held back. She cried out his name while he ground out hers through clenched teeth, and they rode the crest of fulfillment together.

Afterward, they lay in each other's arms, allowing their saturated, replete bodies to bask in the glory of what they'd just shared. Tucked up against him, their limbs intertwined, she drifted off to sleep, content.

Swindler awoke sometime later, lethargic and sated. Marriage, he decided, was going to be very wonderful indeed.

Opening his eyes, he saw the silhouette of Emma standing in front of the window, a blanket draped around her, as the sea breeze blew into the room.

Getting out of bed, he went to her, wrapped his

arms around her and pressed his lips to the top of her head. "Come back to bed, Emma."

She leaned into him, her head finding its familiar place in the nook of his shoulder. "I was just thanking Elisabeth for you."

Dipping his head down, he kissed the nape of her neck. "Were you?"

"She was supposed to ensure that Eleanor and I found husbands. In an ironic, twisting way, she did exactly that."

Turning in his arms, she tilted her face up to him. He was grateful to see only a smile—and no tears—on her face. He wanted from this day forward to fill her life with nothing except joy.

"I shall miss this place," she said softly.

Tomorrow they would close it up and begin their journey to London.

"We'll return occasionally," he assured her. "I rather like the way it smells out here."

In the moonlight, he saw the smallest shadow of doubt cross over her face.

"What is it, Emma?"

"Do you think if it had been Eleanor that afternoon at Hyde Park that you'd have fallen in love with her?"

"No. Never. You began to claim my heart the first time you smiled at me."

Epilogue

From the Journal of Sir James Swindler

Lord Rockberry had misjudged his peers. They, however, did not misjudge him. He did not face the gallows with the dignity that my father had, confirming my belief that it was not a title that was the measure of a man.

As for the others in the dark society who were involved that night, the daughter of the duke married a titled gentleman who took the other lady as his lover—although there were rumors that the two ladies were fond of each other. The remaining men lived their lives on the far side of the world, even though evidence seemed to indicate the two other lords had died from mysterious circumstances. William Graves, physician to the queen and to the poor, was handy at providing corpses beyond recognition. Two men destined for a pauper's grave now lie at rest in the finest of settings.

When I was younger, a darkness hovered inside me. A combination of guilt, remorse, and a determination to make myself worthy of my father's sacrifice. They were heavy burdens to bear, but bear them I did, in gratitude for every breath I drew. I often think of him standing tall and broad upon the gallows, the slight curve of his mouth, his final wink. *We fooled them, lad. We fooled them all.*

Indeed we did.

I'm not certain I quite understood how he could have gone so willingly—until I was blessed with children of my own. I was humbled by the trust my flaxen-haired daughters placed in me when, mere moments after their arrival, they each wrapped their small hands around my fingers, a touch that reached far into my heart. Twin daughters. Ah, the pranks they play. They are outdone only by their brother, who came into the world two years later and brought with him his grandfather's smile.

I do wish my father could have met my Emma. I cannot help but think he would have appreciated her as much as I do. She shines a light into the darkness of my life. She and my children.

As I sit in the small cottage by the sea writing in my journal, I can hear them laughing near the cliffs. Soon I will join them.

I have loved my Emma dearly these many years, and I shall continue to do so until the day I die. She is the light of my life, the one who took the darkness away, the one who completes me.

Emma is the one who gave the lost and lonely orphan who lived inside me a true home at last.

Unforgettable, enthralling love stories, sparkling with passion and adventure from Romance's bestselling authors

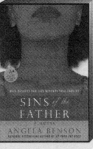

At Avon Books, we know your passion for romance—once you finish one of our novels, you find yourself wanting more.

May we tempt you with . . .

- **Excerpts** from our upcoming releases.

- Entertaining **extras**, including authors' personal photo albums and book lists.

- Behind-the-scenes **scoop** on your favorite characters and series.

- **Sweepstakes** for the chance to win free books, romantic getaways, and other fun prizes.

- Writing **tips** from our authors and editors.

- **Blog** with our authors and find out why they love to write romance.

- **Exclusive content** that's not contained within the pages of our novels.

Join us at
www.avonbooks.com

An Imprint of HarperCollins*Publishers*
www.avonromance.com

FTH 0708